"You're angry," Bethany murmured.

"Bethany, you're one of the strongest, most stubborn people I know. What good would arguing have done? All this time I've kept out of the way, giving you space and privacy at every turn. Everything you said would make you happy, I agreed. Now I want more."

"More?" Her voice cracked. "Why are you doing this?"

"Last night you said you'd give me whatever I wanted," he reminded her.

"And look how that ended," she muttered. "I keep hurting you, Matt."

"Not intentionally," he said. He kissed the soft, delicate skin where her neck and shoulder merged. Her body seemed to sigh in response. "I want you. Trust that." He turned her slowly within the circle of his arms. Her gaze was fixed on his chest and he tipped up her chin, the moonlight painting her face in a lovely glow. "Trust me."

As soon as his lips touched hers he knew. Nothing had changed...

* * *

If you're on Twitter, tell us what you think of Harlequin Romantic Suspense! #harlequinromsuspense

Dear Reader,

Allow me to introduce the Rileys. Rooted in love and bound by honor and heritage, this close-knit family maintains the highest expectations of what military service entails both at home and abroad.

During my husband's thirty years of military service there were moments that left me wondering what I'd married into. The laughter we shared over silly things—like whether POV meant point of view (as it does for authors) or personally owned vehicle (as it does for the army)—was offset by the tears and stress of deployment separations and other challenges.

We made good friends along the way and came out of the experience stronger as a couple and as a family. It takes determination and no small amount of courage to do what needs to be done, especially when doing so isn't much fun.

As the eldest of the five Riley children, Major Matt Riley followed his father's footsteps from West Point into a career as a US Army officer. Through it all, he has done everything in his power to uphold the standards of the army as well as the strong values he was raised on.

Having a child out of wedlock—and keeping both the mother and child a secret for fourteen years—will definitely change the family dynamics...

Live the adventure!

Regan

A SOLDIER'S HONOR

Regan Black

ISBN-13: 978-1-335-66183-8

A Soldier's Honor

This edition published by arrangement with Harlequin Books S.A.

For questions and comments about the quality of this book, please contact us at CustomerService@Harlequin.com.

Printed in U.S.A.

Regan Black, a *USA TODAY* bestselling author, writes award-winning, action-packed novels featuring kick-butt heroines and the sexy heroes who fall in love with them. Raised in the Midwest and California, she and her family, along with their adopted greyhound, two arrogant cats and a quirky finch, reside in the South Carolina Lowcountry, where the rich blend of legend, romance and history fuels her imagination.

Books by Regan Black

Harlequin Romantic Suspense

The Riley Code

A Soldier's Honor

Escape Club Heroes

Safe in His Sight
A Stranger She Can Trust
Protecting Her Secret Son
Braving the Heat

The Coltons of Shadow Creek

Killer Colton Christmas
"Special Agent Cowboy"

The Coltons of Red Ridge

Colton P.I. Protector

Visit the Author Profile page at Harlequin.com for more titles.

This book is dedicated to military families everywhere. Thank you for courageously serving through love, care and support of the men and women in our armed forces.

Chapter 1

Bethany Trent pulled into her driveway and checked the clock on the dashboard. Her son, Caleb, still had thirty minutes of soccer practice. She'd arranged for him to have a ride home so she could swing by the grocery store and get a head start on dinner. Overhead, tall white clouds puffed slowly across the rich blue of the October sky, and she paused to appreciate the view as she unloaded the car. This was her favorite time of year, with the heat of summer gone and winter still weeks away.

If she hustled, she could get chocolate chip cookies—his favorite—into the oven before he made it home. Motherhood had taught her that teenage boys were easier to manage and more prone to chatter over food, particularly when their mouths were full. She figured the two of them had earned hazard pay for surviving his angst-ridden year of thirteen, and she was grateful that the sharpest of those edges had smoothed out over the past year.

As was the habit of children, change was inevitable. With Caleb, the changes and growth spurts often happened before she was ready. With his fifteenth birthday just over a month away, he'd started pushing back and, in some instances, shutting her out. His grades were still good, and he hung out with the same friends, but something had shifted. A girl, maybe? She didn't know because so far she hadn't found the key to open him up.

While putting away the groceries and gathering the ingredients for the cookies, she let her mind wander through the various approaches. She understood the logic and timing as Caleb asserted his independence. She'd been a teenager herself and recalled that internal tug-of-war between wanting to be autonomous within the steady framework and safety net of her wonderful parents.

She set out the butter to soften, preheated the oven and stirred dry ingredients. Cookies would never make up for the fact that Caleb was still one parental unit short. The pang of guilt she hadn't felt in years prickled under her skin. As a single mom, she'd counted herself blessed with Caleb from day one. He was an amazing kid, who was growing toward a remarkable adulthood. He was a wonderful teenager, who had never met his father.

Beating the butter and sugar, and then adding the eggs, she coached herself a bit. It wasn't as if she'd hidden everything from him, only the name. Through the years, when he'd ask, she'd assured Caleb his father was an upstanding man, who was committed to his Military career. She'd told him over and over that his father cared and provided for him; he just had to do it from a distance.

Caleb had never demanded to learn his father's identity. He'd never thrown a fit, insisted on a meeting or raged at her about the situation. All things she'd heard other mothers cope with, usually in the case of divorce. Yes, she had an amazing kid.

Still, as she finished mixing the cookie dough, the scent of chocolate wafting up as she stirred in the chocolate chips, she worried. If having a father-in-absentia *was* the source of his recent withdrawal and curt moments, what would be the best next step?

She cut short the litany of "what-if" scenarios that crowded her mind. Caleb had given her no signals of the precise trouble weighing on him. Jumping to conclusions wouldn't help either one of them. Please let it be girl trouble, she thought.

Well, the cookies were her strategy for today, and with luck, they would soften him up. Dropping the dough on baking sheets, she reminded herself she'd been strong enough for everything else, from giving birth to teething to sitting through the *Alien* movies while he recuperated from wrist surgery. She slid the first dozen cookies into the oven and set the timer. Telling Caleb the whole truth about his father was likely to expose her to a world of hurt, but she'd do it.

She'd do anything to ensure her son continued to feel safe, valued and loved. Maybe rather than aching over the past, explaining the circumstances and their choices would grant her a sense of relief and closure. And maybe pigs would sprout wings and put on an aerial display in that pretty afternoon sky.

The oven timer went off at the same moment the security system chimed and announced that the front door was open. She'd count that perfect timing as a good sign.

"I'm home," Caleb called out as the door closed with a thud.

"Kitchen," she replied, pulling the finished cookies from the oven and sliding the next baking sheet inside.

She turned as he walked in, his backpack slung over one shoulder, cleats dangling by their laces. There were grass stains on his knees, the side of his shorts and one shoulder of his T-shirt. The ripeness of his practice gear almost overpowered the aroma of freshly baked cookies. With his hair mussed and damp with sweat, he took a deep breath and a smile bloomed across his face. The one dimple, inherited from his father, creased his cheek. Here was her heart, her whole world. Today, her normal influx of love and pride was overshadowed by the lingering remorse that she'd kept Caleb to herself all these years.

No. She would not presume to know the trouble. She'd wait for him to confide in her. And she would answer his questions honestly and completely—if he asked. The answer to "why" had been rattling around in her head since the beginning: leaving his father out of the equation had been the best decision for everyone at the time. At twenty, they'd both been too young, with too much on the line to try to build a life together. It would have been a disaster.

Every year around this time, she debated broaching the topic first and asking Caleb if he wanted to extend an invitation for his father to become involved in his life. Every year, she managed to pull back before she blurted out the words and changed everything.

The idea of sharing her son wasn't the problem. It was the potential for a disastrous fallout that scared her. Opening herself to those old emotions made her feel vulnerable in ways she'd never learned to overcome. She and Caleb were a family of two, a team where the dynamics were clear. For years, she'd chosen to give Caleb that familiar stability over the unsettling unknowns of a father on a high-profile Military career path.

After dropping the mail on the counter for her, he kept going toward the laundry room, where he dumped his cleats and backpack and stripped off his sweaty socks and shin guards. "How much longer on the cookies?" he asked.

She checked the oven timer. "Give this first dozen another minute before I take them off the cookie sheet. Then they're fair game." She plucked a spatula from the utensil carousel on the counter. "Did you have a good day?"

"Pretty much." He shrugged and eyed the bowl of raw cookie dough.

"Don't." Bethany laughed. "I saved you the beater. It's in the fridge."

"Sweet!" He lunged for the refrigerator and pulled out the treat.

She pounced on his good mood and stole a hug before he could protest or dodge. Leaning away, she fanned her face. "Whew! Finish that and go grab a shower. You stink."

"You always say that's the smell of hard work," he joked around a mouthful of cookie dough. He hooked a finger around the beater, dragging another chunk of dough into his mouth.

"It is when the smell isn't a foggy stench in the kitchen. Go." She wrinkled her nose. "I'll try not to eat all the cookies before you get back."

He dropped the beater into the sink with a clatter and dashed off, his feet pounding on the stair treads.

Hopefully the promise of hot cookies would encourage him to keep the shower brief.

She flipped through the mail, part of her mind sifting through dinner choices to go with the cookies. The timer went off and she swapped out cookie sheets again. Returning to the mail, she'd decided on spaghetti for the speed and ease, as well as the sheer volume, when her hands landed on an envelope with an official government agency seal in the return address corner.

Seriously? Alone, she let loose an aggravated groan. As a contracts officer for the federal government, she'd heard about the breach of Military personnel records. Last week, it was all anyone could talk about at the office. Since she and most of her coworkers had security clearances at one level or another, they were aware their information had likely been compromised, as well.

This must be the formal confirmation that her information had been part of the breach. Good thing she'd taken precautions against personal identity theft years ago. Resigned, she opened the envelope and unfolded the single sheet of paper. Not an official notice at all, despite the proper agency letterhead. The two handwritten lines in the center of the page offered up a message far more sinister.

Your bank records don't match your income.
Your secret will soon be common knowledge.

Blood rushed through her head, making her feel hot and cold simultaneously. She slumped to a counter stool, the single paper fluttering in her unsteady hands as she tried to bring her racing thoughts into logical order. She only had one secret and Caleb deserved to hear it from her, not some sneaky outsider with a gift for breaking through firewalls.

Addressing a threat like this was outside the scope of any standard identity-theft service. Clearly someone had discovered the banking discrepancy, courtesy of the support Caleb's father sent her each month, but who would bother to look for something so benign in the first place?

She reached for her phone and snatched her hand back. Through the years, he'd practically *begged* her to call. Anytime, and for any need, his early letters and voice mails had vowed he'd be there for her and Caleb.

Did the two lines on the letterhead *really* warrant this phone call? Better to ask her attorney to reach out to him through the security office, except that wasn't her primary concern.

Keeping her hands busy with the last of the baked cookies and then the dishes, she forced herself to think before calling anyone. First and foremost were Caleb's rights and feelings. The people in charge of her clearance status already knew what the author of the note threatened to expose. Although the extra money might appear questionable to an outsider at first glance, an inquiry would quickly prove that everything was above board.

As a single mom with a daily routine leaning dangerously close to boring, she was hardly scandalous headline material. Good grief, her last promising date had been at least six months ago. None of the contracts currently on her desk were particularly sensitive. No one with any authority would care about her financial life or the private support agreement.

Why would anyone put in the effort to try to frighten her this way?

She dried the mixing bowl and measuring cups, stacked the cooling cookie sheets for Caleb to finish when they were done with dinner, the question stewing. Personally, her concerns revolved around how the news would impact Caleb and their extended family. Temper was a given, she'd known that deep in her heart for years. Her son would likely hate her for keeping the truth from him this long. Once he had the facts, she would be facing the very real possibility that Caleb would think the grass looked greener on his father's side of the fence. And he was old enough now to speak for himself if his father—or his father's family—pushed for custody rights.

Bethany scrubbed at her cheeks, wiping away a tear as it slid down her cheek. She would not let her mind run so far ahead and tumble off that particular cliff. She would think, assess and be logical about the next steps.

Officially, she supposed it was possible that this threat posed a real problem for Caleb's father, putting a dent in that stellar career he had going. Yes, she would have to make the call.

Hearing the water shut off upstairs, she sighed.

It was time to tell Caleb everything about his dad and that side of his family. She couldn't let him hear it from anyone else. Better if she and his father could do that together.

As she heard him moving around upstairs, she thought maybe the phone call to Caleb's father would be a cakewalk compared to the challenge of hanging on to her son's trust in the aftermath.

It was just past eleven when Major Matthew Riley and his boss, Major General James Knudson, walked out of the sports bar to meet the general's driver waiting in the parking area. Shortly after setting up shop in the Pentagon, the general decided that the Monday-night football game would be a good weekly morale builder for his staff.

Arranging the event was Matt's first official task as the general's adjutant. It fell to him to locate a bar willing to accommodate their group and convince the staff members they'd enjoy it. Several weeks into the season, the effort seemed to be working. No one grumbled about the outing and a few spouses had started showing up as well, with the general's encouragement, since no professional talk was allowed.

From all walks of life, everyone in the office had a different home team and creative methods of disparaging that team's rivals. The inevitable jokes and teasing had given them common ground and sparked lively conversation and debate. It was the first of many excellent lessons in management and leadership Matt was filing away for the days when he assumed command of an Army battalion.

"I always feel a little guilty when I root against the local team," the general said. Barrel-chested, with a long, confident stride, he stood a couple inches taller than Matt, who was six-one. His gaze continuously scanned his surroundings, proof that lessons learned in combat didn't fade easily.

"Isn't the phrase 'When in Rome'?" The night had turned crisp while they'd been inside the bar, and Matt turned up his collar against the chilly breeze, and then tucked his hands into his pockets.

"It is," Knudson replied. "You know, the Army has sent me all over the world, and I'm still the little kid from the West Coast who wants to stand up and do a wacky touchdown dance when my team comes through."

"Wouldn't mind seeing that," Matt joked.

Knudson gave him an assessing glance. "You'd plaster that all over the internet."

"No, sir," Matt said, earnestly. "I'd only send it out as an internal memo."

The general's booming laughter carried through the clear night as they approached his car. "Need a lift home?" His driver hopped out of the front seat and opened the door for him.

"No, thank you, sir." Matt pulled out his cell phone. "The app says my ride is only a few minutes out." His one complaint with his Washington, DC, assignment was leaving his treasured, newly restored 1967 Camaro in a parking garage six days out of seven and letting someone else do most of the driving.

"Tired of my company already?"

Squealing tires interrupted Matt's reply and headlights momentarily blinded him as a car barreled toward them, narrowly missing parked cars. Matt and the general came to alert and the driver moved into a protective position.

Matt shoved the general into his car through the open rear door, cutting off Knudson's bellowed protest. "Stay low!" He barked the order at his superior officer and closed the door.

Huddled behind the protection of the car with the driver, Matt told him to call the police.

"On it," the driver replied.

"Good." Matt reached for his sidearm before he remembered they weren't armed and this wasn't a war zone. He didn't have enough information to decide if that was good or bad news. The car had screamed past them, but was turning up the next closest aisle. Matt popped up long enough to confirm an escape route and hopefully get a license plate number.

An object hurtled through the air, forcing him to duck. He swore. The police would need more than the make and model of the dark sedan to track down this idiot. Black or dark blue cars with four doors were far too prevalent in this area. The erratic driver might as well be invisible.

A loud crack sounded when the object the driver had thrown hit the windshield of the general's car before bouncing to the pavement near Matt. "What the hell?"

Tires screeched again and Matt peeked over the top of the trunk just enough to glimpse the sedan speeding away, taking the most direct route to the main street that looped around the hub of restaurants and stores. Thankfully sirens were close.

"Should I stay or go?" the driver asked.

"I'd feel better if you waited for an escort back to the general's house."

With a nod, the driver scrambled into the car and started the engine. He must have told the general the threat was over, because the back door flew open, nearly clipping Matt's knees. Knudson lunged from the car. "What was that, Riley?"

"I'm not sure, sir." He held out the object that had been thrown.

It was a baseball with a note scrawled on the side.

You will pay.

The ball wasn't new. Grubby and battered, with several stitches popped, it looked as if it had been through as many campaigns as the general. Matt wasn't an investigator, but he didn't think this would give the authorities much to go on.

Emergency lights spilled over the pavement, glaring off the nearby cars while Matt, General Knudson and the general's driver relayed every detail they could recall about the incident to the responding officers from both the Alexandria, Virginia Police Department and the Metropolitan Police from Washington, DC, who turned out after hearing who had been attacked.

The team from Alexandria sealed the baseball into an evidence bag and labeled it. Based on their grim expressions, it seemed they weren't confident an old baseball thrown by an unseen assailant in a nondescript car was much to work with either.

"Drunk driver maybe?" One officer wondered aloud.

"Doubtful," Matt said. "He didn't clip a single car as he raced up and down the lanes. His reaction time on the corners was spot-on."

The officer took detailed notes and gathered both work and personal contact information for each of them before letting them go. Matt exchanged business cards with the officers as well. Watching the general's car drive off, he was pleased to see two metro police cars providing an escort.

Checking the app on his cell phone, he saw the ride he'd called for had waited five minutes at the pick-up point and left. On a sigh, Matt paid the nominal fee for missing his ride and walked back to the bar to call a cab, his mind recycling the incident and reviewing it from every angle.

The attack in the parking lot seemed like an over-the-top effort to break a windshield when such a bland, three-word message could have been sent anonymously by mail, phone, email or even as a text message. The ball could have been thrown with more accuracy and equal impact by someone standing a few yards away. The baseball had to be significant. He'd mention it to Knudson tomorrow.

When the cab dropped him at his building, he was weary and more than a little grateful the Tuesday briefings were always scheduled an hour later in deference to their Monday-night schedule. Accommodating Knudson's request, he sent a text message that he'd arrived safely.

He took the elevator up to his floor and walked into his dark condo, facing another wave of what might have been. The sensation struck him whenever he took on a new stateside assignment. Though he'd been here almost three months, the persistent melancholy lingered. Working a more nine-to-five role in a vibrant city full of parks, museums and monuments only emphasized what he was missing most: family to unwind with at the end of the day.

It was easier to forget what he didn't have—what he'd chosen not to pursue—when he lived and worked on Army bases or when he was deployed. Not that he didn't encounter plenty of families on Military installations; it was just more obvious in civilian surroundings.

A Military brat and proud of it, Matt felt more at ease within the necessary structure of an Army post. He flipped through the mail he'd dropped on his counter when he'd come home after work to change for the game, and then he tore open the envelope with the formal letter about the recent cyber-security attack on Military personnel records and swore. He'd known it was coming, but in his mind the successful breach remained a black mark against the world's finest Military.

After opening the envelope, he read the precise statement on the first page. The dispassionate phrases were laced with legalese carefully worded to avoid any true claim of responsibility or liability, while promising to track down the culprits.

"Good luck with that," Matt murmured.

The second page offered instructions on how to register with the selected identity-protection monitoring service.

He laughed. Were people really supposed to trust a recently hacked department to make the right choice on protective measures? The idea seemed counterintuitive to him. Matt wasn't sure it made much difference these days. Personal information, from social security numbers to credit cards, seemed to be at risk every day, and clearly this incident proved no system was foolproof.

That didn't make it any easier for Matt to accept. The men and women in uniform should be able to expect that their service records and their personal details, as well as the details of their dependents, were protected.

The only personal risk he could foresee with the breach was that someone other than his attorney and the security-clearance investigators might learn there was a woman out there raising his child. A child he'd never seen. He sent her money each month, had done so from the very beginning, not that she'd shown much enthusiasm for even that minimal involvement from him.

For some ridiculous reason, Bethany's mile-wide streak of independence put a bright spot in his weary mood. He'd always admired her independence until she used it as both a reason and an excuse to keep him from his son.

He couldn't see the son he'd never met or publicly acknowledged as being of much interest to whoever breached the personnel information office. Anyone bidding on the data would be eager to cash in on the fast, easy targets of credit cards and social security numbers to recycle and resell.

Matt tucked the letter into the folder with the other bills and business he would deal with tomorrow. Pushing a hand over his short hair, he walked back to the bedroom, too tired to appreciate his sparkling nighttime view of the marina nestled along the Washington Channel.

He made mental notes along the way. He'd call his lawyer first thing in the morning, just in case someone followed the money he sent to Bethany each month. Broadcasting the information wouldn't be much risk for blackmail or any other unsavory action, but it was better to be prepared. His arrangement with Bethany was legal and only the people who needed to know, knew. If the news got out, it might be uncomfortable for both of them for a time, but it wouldn't be devastating.

Unless the information wound up on one of those notorious leaks pages and his mother heard about it there before he had a chance to tell her. Matt swore.

His first call should be to his mom. She didn't deserve to hear she had a grandchild from a hacker leak. That was the kind of error that could get him benched for the next few Riley-family flag football scrimmages. Again, not the end of the world, but not something his siblings would let him live down.

He unbuttoned his shirt and tossed it into the laundry hamper, and then toed off his shoes. He flopped back on the bed and just stared at the ceiling for a few minutes. It was too late to call his mom tonight and he should probably give Bethany a warning call first, in case his mother insisted on learning more about the grandson Matt had kept hidden from her.

Briefly, he entertained the idea of riding it out. Wait and hope to maintain the status quo or come clean and hurt the people he loved most? The odds were in his favor that news of their son wouldn't come out at all.

Too bad he couldn't be sure if that was denial, logic or wishful thinking.

Troubled and restless, Matt went back to the kitchen and poured a glass of cold water. As he leaned back on the counter, he drank it down and set the glass aside. He should call his dad and tell him about Bethany and Caleb. His dad's wisdom and calm insight had been the underpinning throughout his life. Maybe his dad would dredge up a little pity for his oldest son and help him break the news to Matt's mom and help him find the words to explain that she couldn't contact the kid.

Now *that* was wishful thinking.

General Benjamin Riley, US Army, retired, believed choices and actions had consequences, good and bad. When Ben found the love of his life, Patricia, he'd married her, and together they'd raised their five children into adulthood with that core principle as a cornerstone of character. Life as the family of a career officer had been more than strict rules and high expectations. There had been plenty of love, laughter, bickering and tears to round things out.

Despite that vast, wonderful, messy experience to

draw from, he'd never been able to convince Bethany to give them a chance to grow as a family. That was the piece of this puzzle that would disappoint his father.

When he stopped to think about it, the security breach was less daunting than the Riley family consequences of keeping such a big secret for the better part of fifteen years. Recently his mother had been dropping hints as subtle as carpet bombs about the potential delights of becoming a grandmother. She would be furious when she discovered he'd been holding out on her.

After loading his empty glass into the dishwasher, he headed back to bed. He supposed it was too much to hope that one of his four siblings was ready to confess a character flaw as significant as a child floating around in the periphery of their lives.

He was being an idiot, he decided, waffling and overthinking the ramifications. The situation—the secret—would have to change in light of the security breach. Since Bethany had sent the first picture and their son's birth stats to the JAG office almost fifteen years ago, he'd known this day would come. It was really a miracle it had taken this long.

This had to come out, and better if they got ahead of it. First they needed to give Caleb the full, big picture of his family tree. He pressed his hands to his eyes as the first step kept shifting on him. Figuring this out was like walking across loose sand. One footprint changed both the previous and subsequent steps. Regardless, Caleb came first. After that, he and Bethany could figure out how he and his parents could be woven into Caleb's life.

He rolled his shoulders, trying to sort out what was relief and what was more stress. Countless times through the years, Matt had been tempted to unload this burden on one of his siblings or a good friend. Somehow he'd always managed to keep his mouth shut. According to Bethany's updates, Caleb was pretty awesome and growing more so every year. The way things stood, Matt couldn't share school pictures or sports heroics with anyone other than the JAG office.

No, his family and friends wouldn't be happy he'd lied by omission, but they would come around. "They will come around." Matt stated the affirmation to the empty condo.

He had his phone in hand and had started to dial before he remembered what time it was and dropped it back on the nightstand. Bethany had been a night owl once. Most likely a career and a kid had revised those habits. He missed that quirk and so much more. The bone-deep longing for her and his son seemed to be the one wound time couldn't heal.

He stripped off his jeans and socks and tossed them into the hamper and crawled into bed. As he set his alarm for the morning, his cell phone vibrated and rang with an incoming call. Matt gawked at Bethany's smiling face filling the display. He'd pulled the picture from a post on social media. Maybe she was still a night owl after all. "Hello?"

"We have a problem." The abrupt statement aside, Bethany's voice was like silk brushing over his skin. He wanted to wallow in it.

"Yeah, the security breach is inconvenient," he began, pulling himself together. "But it's not the end of the world. The odds are a million-to-one they'll connect the two of us. We have some time to develop a strategy."

"It's already happened," she said, her voice flat.

"What?" He couldn't have heard her correctly. "What do you mean?"

"I received a creepy, handwritten threat today on official letterhead."

Those two things didn't mesh. "I'm not following," Matt said.

Her soft sigh came over the phone, reminding him of the stolen moments they'd shared when they were younger. Moments that eventually became a wedge between them when she wound up pregnant.

How many times had he dreamed about convincing her to marry him? He hadn't expected it to be a smooth road, but he'd been willing to navigate every pothole and speed bump with her. With her soft breath in his ear, he could imagine them in this bed right now, together, doing something far more fun than talking about a security breach.

"Matt? Are you there?"

"Yeah." He sat up and pinched the bridge of his nose. *Focus on the reality.* "What kind of creepy threat?"

"Instead of the letter I expected about the security breach, this is handwritten. Two lines. The gist is someone has done the math and decided I'm banking more than I make. The threat is that my secret will become common knowledge."

"On the agency letterhead?" That was as strange as sending a threat via baseball. "Weird."

"Yes," she agreed.

He could tell she expected him to say something more profound. "Legally, you're good."

"I know that," she said. "I'm not worried about the job or the clearance—I'm worried about Caleb." She paused and he could so easily picture her teeth nipping into her full bottom lip. "I'm worried about your mom."

"That makes two of us," he admitted.

"You've never told her?" Bethany asked.

Was she joking? "If I had, you would've known."

"True enough," she said.

His parents had a reputation for their unflagging emphasis on maintaining family and balance within the Military framework. "I got my breach letter today, too. Mine was standard issue," he added. "I figured I'd make time to speak to my parents tomorrow. *After* I spoke with you. I didn't feel right saying anything until we talked."

"Thanks."

"I would've called sooner, except I just got home about an hour ago and thought you'd be happier if I called in the morning."

"Oh." The single syllable stretched out. "I couldn't sleep and just wanted to make a plan," she said briskly. "I'd like to tell Caleb before you tell anyone else."

Was she asking for his permission or advice on breaking this news to their son? "Of course. How is he doing?" The last real-time conversation they'd had about Caleb was over three years ago, when he'd broken his wrist during a soccer game. Otherwise, she kept things vague, only sending Matt his school picture and occasional noteworthy updates about his grades or sporting successes.

Those small glimpses of Caleb had never been enough for him, yet he respected her wishes, her rules, because she'd given up everything to protect his place at West Point and, subsequently, his Army career. Time and again, he capitulated to the limits she set, because anything else made him feel grasping and whiny.

"He's great," she was saying. "I just don't want him hearing this from anyone else. I'm not entirely sure how he'll react," she added.

"Has something changed?" The worry in her words felt like a knife twisting in his gut. This was only the second time he'd heard anything less than full confidence out of her. The first was when she'd been debating how best to be a mom and fulfill her career goals. "What's going on with him?"

"Nothing," she said a little too quickly. "Nothing's changed. It's still soccer and school, school and soccer. He's a teenager, that's all."

Matt opened his mouth to push her, to make demands, but bit back the hard words. Instead he changed the subject. "Is he driving yet?" The query was a transparent attempt to learn if there was anything of him in his son.

"He's studying for his learner's permit. We'll take care of that next week, while he's on fall break."

Matt remembered how excited he'd been for that same day as a kid. "Has he had any experience behind the wheel?" he asked, wondering if Caleb would have any interest or appreciation for the restored Camaro. Assuming they met.

"My dad has let him drive the four-wheeler on camping trips, and he's let him drive the tractor on their property. I'm told he's still pretty rough on the manual transmission, but he's improving."

"That's good. It takes time," he said. "You have enough set aside to buy him a car? I can send more money—"

"When that time comes, we'll talk about it," she said in a stern voice that bore a striking resemblance to Patricia Riley's mom voice. "It's still a good year or more away."

He'd always believed the two women would get along well. They'd met once during a family day at West Point and seemed to hit it off, though his mom hadn't known how vital Bethany was to him at the time. If she hadn't forced him to keep Caleb a secret… well, now Matt had no idea what his mom might say or do when they met again.

And they *would* meet. Once Patricia learned about Caleb, she would be adamant about welcoming him into the Riley clan.

"Look, Matt, I called to make you aware of the creep-factor in this note," she said. "I'll report it to the security team at my office tomorrow."

"Good."

"Matt, I'd like you to be here."

"At your office?" He held the phone back from his face as if that would clear up his confusion. "Huh?"

"When I tell Caleb, I would like you to be here with me. Us."

His hand tightened around the phone. "You mean it?"

"Yes. I think it will help him understand if we're telling him together. Help him feel valued and that we've always wanted what was best for him."

He was going to meet his son. His heart hammered against his ribs. "Sure." He had to find some real words. After all these years of wishing and wondering, he'd get to look his kid in the eyes, maybe even hug him or shake his hand. "Tell me when and where," he managed at last. Too many emotions were warring for dominance. “I’ll be there.”

“Here, please. He’ll be home from practice around six and we could eat at seven.”

Matt was already doing the mental juggling over the drive time from Washington to her place in New Jersey, calculating how early he might need to leave work. He’d speak to General Knudson first thing in the morning, but there was no way he was missing that invitation.

“Once Caleb knows, you’ll be okay with me telling my parents?” he asked.

“I have to be, don’t I?”

He would have preferred the catalyst for meeting his son wasn’t her feeling cornered by some vague threat in a letter. Bethany didn’t have enemies, not like General Knudson or even his dad had. In careers as long and storied as theirs, enemies of several varieties began to stack up, from disgruntled soldiers to politicians, both local and abroad. He sighed. He could hear the conflict and misery in her voice. As much as he hated to give her a pass on this, he felt obligated.

“I can’t think of any reason anyone would target the three of us,” he said. “If you’d like to ride it out, we can. Whoever sent that threat will know soon enough there’s nothing to be gained. If you want to wait a bit before we have these conversations, I *will* respect that.”

“No.” Her voice was calm and steady, if not delighted by the prospect of tomorrow’s family dinner. “I’ve put this off long enough. I won’t risk him learning about this from another source.”

“All right.” Once more, he gave her full control, let her dictate how this played out. “I’ll be there at seven.”

"Thanks, Matt."

"Thanks for the invitation." She could have handled this mess alone and told Matt after it was done. She'd made it clear through the years that she could manage this parenting gig on her own.

He thought he heard a sniffle, but when she spoke, her voice was steady, if quiet. "I know this will change everything," she began. "I only ask that it doesn't change everything immediately. Caleb will need time to process this."

"I understand." She was warning him away from any abrupt changes over their custody agreement. "I've only ever wanted you and Caleb to be safe and happy."

"Thanks for that," she said, ending the call.

Matt held the phone to his chest. When he closed his eyes and thought of her, he still saw the athletic young woman he'd met when they were new cadets at West Point. Her big brown eyes had been full of nerves and excitement and eagerness for the challenges ahead. Like every cadet before him, he'd entered West Point with nothing more than his career on his mind.

Bethany had changed that. Success took on more meaning than simple pride in doing a job well for the sake of reaching his goals. She made him want to set and accomplish goals for the good of the team. Meeting her had made him a better person and student from that first day forward, though it hadn't yet made him good enough for her to keep.

Matt reached up and turned out the light, but he couldn't sleep. His mind flipped back and forth between the baseball lobbed at General Knudson and the creepy letter sent to Bethany. For both of them to get direct threats in the same twenty-four hour period made him question the motive behind the breach of the personnel records and who was buying the information.

Who would gain from exerting that kind of pressure? And how many other Military personnel and families were suddenly feeling exposed and vulnerable tonight?

He read the reports as they came in with cautious optimism and rising confidence. His first warnings had been successfully delivered. Shots over the bow, so to speak, and now he waited to watch their response.

He imagined them scrambling, racing about in circles and jumping at shadows. They would chase the leads he gave them all the way to inevitable dead ends, only to start over on another path of his choosing. Having the world's best Army dancing to his tune was an excellent feeling.

His plans were finally coming together. Years in the making, he found a delicious irony in using the security breach to his advantage. His team had been handpicked and painstakingly groomed to the tasks ahead. He'd deliberately given them a cause they could understand and support as he moved both key players and pawns into place for his ultimate revenge.

His charisma was a skill his superiors had consistently undervalued. The pompous fools had been unwilling to blur their clear vision and mission parameters to improve the overall morale in a way that would practically guarantee success on any field of battle.

Their loss.

The skills they didn't value, he would now use to wreak havoc at both the individual and institutional levels. This was going to be phenomenal fun, as well as a just reward for everything they'd taken from him.

He swiveled his chair away from his desk until he could gaze out at the gathering night through the floor-to-ceiling window. At this end of the compound, there wasn't another person for miles. Not another soul from here to the horizon. He'd earned the solitude, worked alongside the others to carve this quiet, impenetrable place out of the desert.

Now it was merely a matter of time before his first target came out into the open.

Once he had Matt Riley centered in the crosshairs, the first shot in this war would be fired, with brutal, irrevocable accuracy.

Chapter 2

Nervous energy plagued Bethany all through the night. First she couldn't sleep, and when she'd finally dozed off, her dreams had quickly turned to nightmares. Centered on change and loss and the unknown, it was easy to figure out the trigger. In the last one, she'd been listening to Caleb tell a judge all the reasons he didn't want to live with her anymore. The judge had been giving his ruling that Caleb should spend the next fifteen years with his dad, denying her all visitation and contact, when her alarm had interrupted.

Eyes gritty, a knot of dread in her stomach, she dragged herself out of bed and tried to remember dreams and nightmares weren't real as she showered and dressed for work. Matt wanted what was best for Caleb, and he was too honorable to play dirty and steal her son with the aid of family court.

Downstairs, she sipped tea while Caleb scarfed down his breakfast. No matter what she did, she couldn't quell the notion that this was their last normal day as a family of two. Tonight, when he met his father, he would look at her differently, judge her through the lens of his teenage values and find her lacking. They were close, but suddenly she wasn't sure their relationship could survive the turmoil ahead.

"You okay, Mom?"

"Sure." She waved off his concern with a smile. "Didn't sleep well—that's all." That was an understatement bordering on a lie. Clearly every conversation today would be guilt-inducing no matter how unrelated it might be to the revelations in store for Caleb tonight.

Without the usual reminder, he cleared his place and rinsed his dishes before loading them into the dishwasher. She found it refreshing and counted it as the first happy spot in her gloomy morning.

She double-checked her purse while he shrugged into his backpack. "How does Greek chicken sound for dinner?"

He paused and aimed a speculative look at her. "That's company food."

"Not always," she said. "I'm just in the mood. It doesn't sound good?"

"It's fine." He picked up his soccer bag. "Coach said practice ends with an endurance run. I might be a little late getting home."

She glanced toward the calendar over the kitchen desk. "When did he add that?"

"There's the bus," Caleb said.

"Here." She dashed over and gave him a quick hug. "Have a great day. Love you."

"Love you, too," Caleb said on his way out the door.

She watched him jog to meet the bus rumbling toward the stop on the corner, one hand pressed to her queasy stomach. She didn't want Caleb home late. That would mean time alone in the same room with Matt, a situation she'd successfully avoided since she'd told him the pregnancy test had come back positive.

She could call the coach and ask him to give Caleb a pass on the run, but that would also mean picking him up and dodging her astute son's inevitable questions. The better option would be calling Matt and pushing dinner back by half an hour. Feeling good about that decision, she headed out to the office.

Her discussion with her supervisor went almost as smoothly as she'd expected. She showed him the letter, a little surprised by how seriously he handled the implied threat and her explanation that the source of the discrepancy was the child support she received from a closed agreement. He called security and they joined her in his office so she could relate the incident again and give them the doctored letter and envelope for further analysis.

She didn't think they'd get much from it, but she agreed it was best to try. It was midmorning when she was finally able to get to her desk, only to find the department assistant had left two messages on her desk that were both from Caleb's school. Bethany pulled her cell phone from her purse and found two more voicemail messages from the school, as well. She listened to them quickly and they all amounted to brief requests to return the call as soon as possible.

Worried now, she dialed the school and waited for someone in the office to pick up. "This is Bethany Trent," she said when the school's secretary answered. "I received—"

"Yes, Ms. Trent. The principal asked me to put you right through. Hold just a moment."

In place of hold music, a chipper voice recited the upcoming school events. Bethany tapped a pencil against a notepad on her desk until, at last, the line clicked and Principal Andrea Ingle's voice greeted her.

"Bethany?"

"Yes." She'd met Andrea long before Caleb became a student in her school, back when they'd first moved into the neighborhood. She counted the principal as one of her closest friends. "Has something happened?"

Andrea mumbled an oath. "I take it Caleb isn't home with you?"

Her skin chilled and her heart kicked hard in her chest. "No. I'm at work. I saw him get on the bus." She heard the desperate note in her voice and stopped to take a breath.

"Right, okay. We do have him checking in at homeroom, but he didn't make it to Spanish class this morning."

Bethany glanced at the clock over her desk that Caleb had made during an art project in second grade. Spanish class had started almost two hours ago, while she'd been in her supervisor's office.

"Per your instructions, we've been trying to reach you while doing all we can to find him. I've spoken with the school resource officer. We haven't yet called in the police."

"Thank you, Andrea." She forced herself to keep breathing. Panic wouldn't help anyone find Caleb. "He's not in the building?"

"No. I think he left on his own after his homeroom teacher took attendance."

He was safe. He had to be. And when they found him, she'd wring his neck and ground him for the rest of his life. "Is there a camera or anything to verify that?"

"Unfortunately, all I have is a hunch. There are only cameras at the main doors and he didn't use either of those. We've walked the building and grounds twice. Do you want me to call the police?"

Her heart dropped at the suggestion. "Not yet. I have an app installed on his phone. Let me check that first. Are his friends in class?"

"Yes," Andrea said. "I thought of that too and I've spoken with each of them. They don't know where Matt is or why he might have left. Keep us posted and let us know how we can help."

"I will," Bethany promised. She replaced the handset in the cradle on her desk phone and immediately brought up the app on her cell phone. Her hands trembled as the app showed Caleb's phone was somewhere near Philly.

She called him immediately, but he didn't pick up. She sent a text, and as she waited for a reply, she struggled to find a logical explanation for his behavior. Had Caleb overheard her conversation with Matt last night? Had he been in more trouble or more upset than she'd thought?

She wasn't buying into those scenarios. He'd been himself over spaghetti last night and in a good mood this morning. She groaned, reviewing his behavior in her mind. He'd been planning this.

Still waiting for a reply from Caleb on her cell phone, she used the office phone to call his soccer coach. Dread and fear were an icky congealed mess in her stomach when the coach said there was no practice at all tonight. Caleb had been lying about being home late.

She sat back. Anger and hurt quickly burned away her initial worry. What was he up to?

The standard school policy when a child was absent was an automated call after 6:00 p.m. Because of her unique situation with Caleb, she'd had a standing request at every school that she be notified immediately if anyone other than her or her parents asked about Caleb or tried to pick him up from school.

She wasn't so paranoid that she thought Matt would try something as outrageous as taking him right out of school; she just needed the extra layer of confidence and support. Fortunately school administrators had been cooperative and, until today, her precautions hadn't been necessary. Thank goodness she'd never shared that particular safety detail with her son.

Whatever Caleb was up to, she had to assume he thought he'd have an entire day to himself. Why did he have to do this today? And why run off to Philadelphia?

Her head pounded from lack of sleep and a resurgence of worry. Matt was coming today. Lovely that Caleb would pull this kind of stunt on the day she wanted to introduce him to his father.

On a hunch, she checked his bank account. She'd opened a checking account for him and started teaching him about personal finance as soon as he'd started mowing lawns in the neighborhood for extra cash. Reviewing his recent activity, she gaped at the screen. Despite the evidence in front of her, she resisted the truth.

Once more, she picked up her desk phone, this time dialing the Pentagon's switchboard. "Major Matthew

Riley, please. He's currently the adjutant for General Knudson."

It took some time for the call to reach Matt, but when he picked up the call, she wasted no time. "Dinner's off."

"Bethany?"

"Yes. It's me." Her heart was pounding and everything in her was urging her to leap into action, to chase down her son. "I'm sorry to be so abrupt. I think Caleb is on his way to see you."

"What? Did you tell him already?"

"No." They'd come up with a plan, and she intended to honor it. "He's skipped school, Matt. First time ever." She forced herself to slow down and relay the facts. "I'm looking at his bank account. He purchased a train ticket to DC two days ago. He's not answering my calls or texts. The app I have is showing that he's close to Philly."

"You have a tracking app on his phone?"

The censure only sparked another flash of temper. "Pardon me," she snapped. "How many busy and bright teenagers have *you* raised?"

"None," he admitted. "Though I recall volunteering for the task plenty of times."

She took a deep breath. "That was rude. Sorry," she repeated, this time meaning it. "I'm just worried."

"And mad."

Was that anger in his voice, as well? "Yes, and mad," she admitted.

"You think he skipped school and put himself on a train to Washington in order to find or meet me."

"That's as much logic as I can make of his actions," she said. "He's not skipping with any of his friends."

"All right. If he's in Philly now, it won't be long before he reaches Union Station. I'll get down there and find him."

"Thank you." Relief coursed through her at his confidence.

"I'll have him call right away. I'll bring him back home, and we can all have dinner as planned."

"Oh." She couldn't come up with a reason why they shouldn't go ahead with dinner. "You don't have to do that." Caleb had purchased a round-trip ticket.

"Would you rather come to DC and have dinner at my place?" he queried.

"No." She heard the reply came out more like a question.

"Well, I'm not dumping him back on the train."

"Matt, you really don't have to—"

"Bethany, I was planning to drive up anyway. This is exactly what I *want* to do. Caleb and I will be there by seven."

"Okay." What option did she have? She couldn't get to DC ahead of Caleb. Rushing after him, having this conversation on Matt's turf, wasn't her idea of a good time, either. "Let me know when he arrives, okay?"

"I promise."

"One more thing." She closed her eyes against a sudden rush of tears. "Let him know he's grounded."

Matt tried to disguise his bark of laughter as a cough. She wasn't fooled. "That's not funny."

"It is," he said. "My first parenting milestone is discipline."

His humor in the situation lifted the burden, eased the sadness a little. "I wanted us to tell him together."

"I know. I'll do what I can to save the hard questions for you."

"Again, not funny." So why did she want to laugh? She plucked up a pen and started doodling on her pad of sticky notes.

"Any idea how he found me?" Matt asked. "Or why he came looking today of all days?"

"None. Hopefully he'll confide in you." It seemed an odd thing to sincerely wish for under the circumstances. Clearly they'd entered new and uncharted territory. "I'll text you his cell number. Thanks for your help," she said. "I know this is an inconvenience."

"Don't say that."

His voice, low and kind, rumbled across her senses. She blamed the resulting shiver on stress. "I need to notify the school that we think we've found him. I don't want them to worry any more than I have been."

"All right."

And yet, long minutes after the call ended, she still sat there, paralyzed by fear of how the evening would go and how her relationship with Caleb would change. She was his mother, not his friend, but they'd been an unbreakable team since day one. Honest with each other, candid and clear, she'd made every effort to give him a stable life, while assuring him that his father was a good man, doing good work in the Army.

On top of that nonnegotiable stability, she'd given Caleb roots and tradition with her side of the family, let him know he was loved and valued. She'd created opportunities to explore various interests, while fostering an appreciation for history that matched hers and Matt's.

That had been her one calculated effort once she'd

accepted that this day would come whether she wanted it to or not. Matt had respected every limit she'd set in her quest to raise Caleb alone. The two of them deserved to have some common ground from the first introduction.

Strange that until now, when she could only guess at Caleb's reactions, her choices had never felt quite so selfish or self-serving. She'd been so confident that giving Matt room to have a Military career unencumbered by a whoops baby was the right thing for everyone.

Now she felt as if she'd done them all a grave disservice.

Matt gathered his thoughts before striding to the general's office. He supposed this conversation would be good practice for telling his parents about Caleb. It was rather surreal that he'd be having that conversation tonight.

He knocked lightly on the open door. "Do you have a minute, sir?"

"Come in," Knudson said. His normally jovial smile was slower to show up today. "Have you heard something from the police?"

"No, sir. This is a different matter. Personal." He closed the door and came forward to stand next to the guest chairs.

"And serious," Knudson observed. "Have a seat."

"Thank you." Better to just get it out there as efficiently as possible. "I have a son." *Wow.* He was finally getting to share this with someone. A surge of pride shot through him as the general's eyebrows lifted. "He's fourteen, almost fifteen," Matt added, thinking aloud. "His mother has been raising him alone. She insisted on complete privacy on the issue, although I've contributed financial child support since the start."

"Well, that's the responsible move, son."

"Thank you, sir."

"I can assume there's a legal arrangement?"

"Yes, sir," Matt confirmed. "And it's been noted properly all the way through my security clearance investigations."

"All right." Knudson bobbed his chin. "Why has it become an issue today?"

Matt kept his shoulders back when he wanted to slouch with relief. "It seems he's learned about me. He didn't find out from his mother."

"The security breach?"

"Possibly, though I don't see how a fourteen-year-old would have access to my personnel records, even if he knew to look for them. His mother just called to let me know he skipped school and appears to be on a train scheduled to arrive at Union Station in about forty minutes."

The general gave a short bark of laughter. "Sounds like he's a chip off the old block after all."

"Possibly," Matt allowed, trying not to smile. "I suppose my mother would know that answer." Assuming his mother had known he had a son.

"Always admired your mother," Knudson said. "Ben and Patricia are dear, dear friends." He studied Matt long enough that it was a struggle not to fidget. "I take it I'm the first person you've told?"

"Yes, sir. Outside of the JAG office and the security clearance investigators," Matt replied.

Knudson's gaze grew serious. "If I could offer a piece of advice?"

"Please, sir."

"You'll want to soften up that delivery some and show more remorse about keeping the secret—whatever the reasons—when you tell your mom."

"Thank you, sir." Matt intended to do all of that and more.

He'd been trying to be as efficient as possible with Knudson, in the interest of time. He already had a shopping cart loaded with her favorite wine and chocolates waiting online. All he had to do was complete the purchase and request rush delivery. He'd also made a mental note to bring flowers with him whenever he saw her in person, for now until the end of time.

"Take the rest of the day off," Knudson said. "But if you bring him for a tour, I'd like to meet him."

Matt made appropriate assurances and escaped the office, arranging for a ride to Union Station. By the time he arrived, the train Caleb was likely on was only a few minutes out. Matt breathed a sigh of relief. If he hadn't been here in time, Bethany would have cause to skin them both.

It wasn't easy trying to spot one teenage boy as passengers flooded from the trains and into the terminal. He'd only ever seen Caleb in school or soccer-team pictures. Bethany was commendably stingy about posting more candid photos of him online. Understandable, but it meant he had to look at how people moved in groups rather than for the individual face. Even at midday, the terminal was busy enough that he almost missed a young man of the right height and age passing by alone, his face down as he fiddled with his cell phone.

Matt fell in behind him and dialed Caleb's number. The kid who was a few paces in front of him stepped out of the flow of foot traffic and swiped the screen to answer. “Hello?”

Matt heard it through the phone a half second after he watched Caleb’s mouth form the word. “Hi, Caleb,” Matt answered. The kid looked so much like his mother, it was uncanny. He had her big brown eyes, under straight eyebrows. His dark blond hair, cut in a modern, subtle Mohawk, was streaked by the sun from his time on the soccer field. Matt had seen the resemblance in the pictures. In real life, the similarities were startling. *What now?*

Caleb’s gaze darted around the terminal before landing on Matt. The hand holding the phone seemed to melt as he stared.

Matt couldn’t move. His heart had lost its rhythm and his breath stalled. He’d felt stronger on his first jump from an airplane to graduate Airborne School. This was his son. *His son.* Those two words comprised the entire sum of his thoughts, and time seemed to slow to a crawl.

And he was a father, damn it. Gathering himself, he took a firm step forward, catching himself before he yanked Caleb into a bear hug. One more step and he closed the distance, sticking out his hand. “Matt Riley. Pleased to meet you.”

Eyes wide, the kid met his handshake, and words seemed to fail him.

Matt understood the magnitude of the moment and sympathized. He was still on the verge of losing it himself. “You are Caleb, right?” The boy nodded. “Good.” Matt tried to smile. “Your mom, Bethany Trent, called and told me you might be here.”

At the mention of his mom, Caleb blanched. "She already knows I'm here?"

Matt nodded. "She says you've dodged her calls and texts."

"No." He hunched his shoulders, as if he could slouch into the shelter of his backpack. "Technically my phone is supposed to be off during school hours."

Technically. Matt remembered how poorly that excuse worked on his mother. "Do you know who I am?"

Caleb nodded, swallowing hard.

"Good. Call your mom. Let her know you're safe."

Matt waited, laying a hand on his son's shoulder when he saw him sending a text. "*Call.* Use the speaker."

"Yes, sir." Caleb swiped to a different screen and held the phone so Matt could see the display, as well.

When Bethany answered, her relief was obvious but it didn't take long for that relief to give way to blistering anger. "I'm glad you're safe," she said. "Matt and I have decided he will bring you home and we'll discuss this together."

"Mom, I just—"

"Tonight, Caleb." She cut him off. "There will be consequences. Behave for Matt. I love you."

"Yes, ma'am. Love you, too." He pocketed the phone and stared up at Matt.

"I'm supposed to tell you you're grounded."

"A given," Caleb said with a shrug. "I thought I'd have a few hours at least before she had a chance to say that. The truancy calls don't go out until the evening."

Matt didn't know anything about truancy calls. His thoughts were tied up with the realization that it wouldn't be too long before he was looking his son in the eye. He'd missed out, been held back, from so much.

"So," he began, worried about making the wrong move here. "This wasn't a school-sanctioned field trip. Did you have a plan?"

Caleb's narrow shoulders slumped. "Sort of."

"You were going to navigate Washington, DC, on your own?"

"To find you and meet you? Yeah." He bumped one heel against the toe of his other foot. "I really thought we'd have some time to talk before she realized I wasn't where I was supposed to be."

What had motivated him to take this kind of chance now? "How did you even know to come looking for me?" Matt asked.

Caleb turned away, hefted his backpack. "Mom told me you—"

"Try again."

Caleb's head snapped up. "What?"

His mother would have corrected him, but Matt wasn't going to mark this first hour of parenting with discipline and lessons in manners. "I know your mom's never told you my name." Matt watched a glint of battle fire in Caleb's eyes and braced for an argument, but he subsided with another shrug. "She invited me to dinner tonight so we could tell you together."

"I knew it," he muttered. "Greek chicken is always for company."

Matt wasn't sure he followed that topic change, chalked it up to the communication deficit. It had been a long time since he'd dealt with kids this age.

"Come on, let's walk." He resisted the urge to put his arm around the kid's shoulders.

"Do you really work in the Pentagon?" Caleb asked. "Can I have a tour?"

"Not today." Inexplicably uneasy, Matt glanced around. "Where did you get your information?"

"I got a snap with your name and rank. A picture," he added.

Matt knew which cell phone app Caleb was referring to. Typically the messages disappeared within a few seconds of being opened by the recipient.

"And you thought I sent it?"

"No," Caleb said.

"The sender have a user name?" Matt asked when Caleb didn't volunteer more information.

"Does it matter?" He hefted the backpack again. "He double-checked who I was and then more stuff came through. Stuff about you. The information was real, obviously."

"Obviously." Matt didn't like the way this was shaping up. "When did you get the messages?"

He cocked his head, thinking. "The first one was about two weeks ago."

That would fit the likely timeline as the compromised information was being sold off. "There were more?" At the boy's nod, Matt asked, "Did you save the messages?"

Caleb's lip curled. "Like I wanna pay for a free app? I made notes, though."

"Good." An itch had cropped up between his shoulder blades. Instinct drove him to get away from the terminal and into a safe space that was out of the public eye, as fast as possible. Rather than pick up the Metro here and head straight for the Pentagon or his condo, he decided to be less predictable. "Where did you keep those notes?"

"The hard copies are at home. I have a file on the cloud, too."

"All right." That would give investigators something to work with. As soon as he decided which law enforcement agency might consider a few random snaps as a crime.

"The snaps were clues sort of," Caleb was saying. "Like I'd get a name or place, maybe a picture. Then I would start digging around online. I didn't do anything wrong."

"Except skip school, take a train alone to a city you don't know and lie to your mom about it."

"She's lied to me, too," Caleb shot back, his gaze full of hurt. "All. My. Life."

"Well, life's about to change," Matt said, wincing. That didn't take long. A dad for ten minutes and he was already quoting his father's wisdom. He kept Caleb close as they moved along the sidewalk, sidestepping tourists. "And three lives are permanently changed now."

"You're mad at me."

Matt had to slow down as Caleb began dragging his feet. They weren't safe yet, though Matt couldn't point to any specific reason why he felt they were at risk. "I'm not mad at you." He was aggravated with whoever compelled his son to take these risks. And he wasn't exactly thrilled with Bethany for keeping him out of Caleb's life this long.

He gripped Caleb's shoulders lightly, waiting for him to meet his gaze. "You were resourceful and smart right up until you skipped school and made your mom worry. Moms don't like that kind of thing."

"You worried your mom?"

"More than once," Matt confessed. "You think I was hatched in this uniform?" Caleb snickered. "That's how I know." Bethany and Patricia had similar standards about child-rearing. No wonder he loved her still.

Whoa. Love? That had to be some transference effect of being around Caleb. Regardless, he'd pick it apart later. Right now, they needed to keep moving. He was sure someone was watching them, although he couldn't spot the tail.

If Caleb reached DC without any trouble, only to get hurt on Matt's watch, on his first day of parenting, he'd never forgive himself. Nor would he ever be forgiven. He ducked into the next storefront, pleased to discover it was a deli. "Hungry?"

They moved to the counter and ordered a couple of sandwiches and soft drinks. It was early for the lunch rush, so they had their pick of the few tables. Matt guided Caleb to a two-top near the back wall and took the seat that gave him a view of the door and sidewalk out front.

While they waited for their food, Matt sent a text message to his office, offering to bring back lunch for everyone. It would give them a place away from prying eyes to regroup and make a plan.

"You look mad," Caleb said.

"I've been told that. It's my thinking face," Matt explained. He wouldn't lump fear or worry onto his son's shoulders. "Your timing is crazy," he said, trying to smile. "We really were going to tell you tonight.

Your mom was convinced the acting out would start tomorrow."

Caleb dragged the drink straw up and down through the hole in the lid, making an annoying noise. Matt didn't react. His little brothers, twins, were five years younger. He could teach master classes on how to ignore annoying moments and get even later.

"How is your soccer season?" he asked.

The noise stopped suddenly. "Now you want to be a dad?"

He'd wanted that from the beginning. "I'd like to get to know you." He would *not* blame Bethany for the estrangement. "You came to me." He sat back, spreading his hands. "Now's your chance. Just you and me. I'm an open book."

Caleb's eyes narrowed as he judged the offer. "Did you not want me?"

"Of course I wanted you," Matt said.

He leaned forward, his voice low. "Then where have you been?"

And now he understood why Bethany hadn't wanted to face this conversation alone. Man up, Riley. Hard questions now equaled a single drop in the ocean compared to what she'd been handling for Caleb's entire life. "There hasn't been a day since your mom got pregnant that I haven't wanted you." The resulting eye roll didn't surprise him, but it prompted a change in tactic. "How did you find out about me?"

"I told you. The snaps."

"Right. And how do you think the sender got the information?"

Caleb's eyebrows dipped into a perplexed frown. "Never thought about it."

"The personnel records for the Military were hacked recently. About the time you started getting messages on that app. The reason there was information for someone to send to *you* is because I've been sending your mother a percentage of my pay as financial support every month since before you were born." He decided not to mention the threatening letter Bethany received last night, but it would be more for investigators to piece together.

Caleb's gaze narrowed as he studied Matt. "So what's wrong with you that Mom didn't think you should stick around?"

Matt supposed that was the easy way to put it, and he wished it didn't feel like the truth. "We met at West Point. We were in the same cadet class there and became friends." Matt couldn't suppress a smile at the fonder memories. "We were young and we cared about each other a great deal," he continued. "Your mom made some really tough choices when she found out she was pregnant. She did what she thought was best for her and ultimately for you." She'd cut him out and left him reeling. "I honored her choices, but insisted on helping in the only way she would let me."

The sandwiches were delivered and Matt asked the server about a to-go order for the office.

"Mom never said anything about going to West Point." Caleb frowned again as he squeezed ketchup into a puddle beside his french fries.

"She was there for three semesters," Matt said. "She transferred to another school when we got pregnant."

"Why didn't you tell anyone I was your baby or anything?"

Bethany had insisted it would be an honor violation

that would get them both expelled, ruining his career and jeopardizing her transfer and scholarship. He'd been willing to risk the potential demotion or discipline. Hell, he'd been willing to transfer with her to a new school. She'd refused, claiming his place was to follow in his father's footsteps. She'd turned down every option Matt offered on the basis of personal responsibility: her body, her rules.

If she wanted Caleb to know all of that, she'd have to share it. He didn't feel it was his place to do so.

"I wanted to," Matt said at last. "And I did my best to convince her to let me be part of your family from the start."

Caleb studied him again, apparently finding the explanation sincere. "Mom can be pretty stubborn."

"Her picture is part of the dictionary definition," Matt agreed, making Caleb laugh.

The unexpected burst of such a happy sound reminded Matt of Bethany. Jealousy flared and flashed through him that she'd had a lifetime with Caleb and kept him out of the loop. Thankfully the bitter-tasting emotion drained out of him almost as quickly as it had appeared.

This wasn't all on her. He could have pressed for his paternal rights and visitation and probably should have. Had they both taken advantage of the easier, ready excuses of his career and her independence? However this had come about, now they had a chance to make a better choice and create a fresh start for their future as a family.

"Why do you keep staring at the window?"

He didn't miss a trick. Matt approved of his observation skills. He thought about shooting straight with him and anticipated Bethany's reaction to that. Their son was only fourteen. He tempered his answer to fall somewhere in the middle. "You finding me now seems tied to the security breach, hack or whatever the official term will be. I don't trust that kind of coincidence. Something feels off."

Caleb twisted around to check for himself, and then turned back and tucked into the food again. "You think I was followed?"

Or sent. He kept that theory to himself. It seemed a little far-fetched, even in his head. "It's crossed my mind."

Assuming this situation was a deliberate setup and put into motion by someone who'd used the compromised information, it pissed him off. Of the three of them, only Matt hadn't been threatened. It infuriated him that some jerk would target the innocent civilians tied to his profile rather than come after him directly.

"Cool. It's like James Bond or something."

Matt should have known. "This isn't a movie, Caleb. If someone used you or manipulated this situation, that stops now."

"So you're sorry I found you."

"No, I didn't say that." His appetite gone, Matt wrapped the remains of his sandwich for later. He couldn't expect Caleb to instantly accept and believe that Matt loved him and had always wanted to be part of his life. "All this time, I've only had pictures and a few annual updates. I've wanted to meet you for some time. You can verify that with your mom tonight over Greek chicken."

"I will."

"Good." His phone chirped with a text message that

the order for the office was ready. "If you're not done, we'll get a to-go box and you can eat with the rest of the general's staff at the Pentagon."

"You mean it? We'll eat inside the Pentagon, really?"

Matt nodded. "Go get a box for each of us. I'm calling for a car."

Caleb jumped up and hurried to the counter and Matt pulled up the app on his phone, only to be interrupted by another text message that the general's car was on the way to pick them up. Although Matt might have protested the assist in the past, today he was happy to accept.

This wasn't a combat zone, but something out here was pushing his buttons. He needed the familiar confidence of knowing he had a team at his back, even if they were all currently in administration roles.

Chapter 3

Bethany stared at the incoming messages and a couple of selfies of Caleb and Matt. Her son was apparently having lunch with General Knudson and his staff in the Pentagon. The boy landed on his feet, every time. Not unlike his father.

As a mom, it seemed as though Caleb's day was looking more like a reward than a disciplinary action for a kid who should have been in school. And as a mom, she knew her son was having the time of his life. With his father.

She wanted to be angry and stay angry, but she just couldn't hang on to it for long. Oh, she was aggravated about Caleb's unauthorized jaunt to DC—and he would pay a price for that—but her heart turned gooey when she saw the father and son together. Their faces were so similar, especially with the matching dimples when they smiled.

Her world had turned inside out in a matter of hours. The idea of the two of them together gave her warm fuzzies, chased by chills she kept bringing on herself. Guilt and regret were her new best friends throughout the rest of the day. Her mind kept traipsing back through all the milestones Matt should have been part of.

Through the years, she'd discarded several opportunities to invite Matt into their lives, all in the name of giving Caleb stability. It had paid off, she thought. He had friends he'd known from kindergarten, a soccer team he traveled with, a normal, healthy childhood without the angst of moving every few years. Yes, she'd given her son so much stability, he thought it would be fine to take a train and track down his dad on his own.

In all fairness, Matt had never complained about the moves or changing schools growing up. Then again, he'd been raised in a prominent Army family and had likely been dialed in about West Point from the womb. Once, she too had planned on a Military career, maybe a husband and possibly, floating in that misty realm of far-off theories, a child someday.

Someday. Not at twenty. Not before she'd tested herself and traveled and become part of something astounding and important. Instead she found herself pregnant and bewildered. Matt had been almost thrilled, while she'd been fighting through sheer terror. Becoming a single mother had never crossed her mind.

He'd proposed, though they couldn't marry while either of them were still cadets at the academy. As much as she loved him, she'd known she couldn't marry him at all. She had to make her own way—for herself, as well as for her child. Following Matt through a career destined for greatness, always waiting at home for news, just felt too passive. She feared he would eventually feel trapped, or she would. And she didn't want either of them to come to a point of resenting the other. That would have been a sorry end to what had started as a good friendship.

Hard as it had been, she'd walked away from Matt, away from her dreams, and into the role of motherhood and new challenges. With Caleb, she'd discovered every day could be astounding in tiny, personal, but no less important ways.

She was straightening her desk when the text message came through that they were leaving the city. Caleb's giddy reaction to Matt's classic muscle car came through loud and clear, along with half a dozen pictures of a gorgeous Chevy Camaro. It was a restored 1967 classic, according to the messages.

Great. As if she needed the man to be any more tempting to either her or her son. *Their son.* She had to start getting that verbiage right.

On her way home, she stopped at the grocery store for the final items to round out dinner. The big news they'd planned to share was out of the bag, but that didn't mean there wouldn't be difficult questions that may or may not have answers. Whatever Matt had already told Caleb, it seemed to have planted him firmly in the idol column.

With that thought, she turned down the aisle and added an extra bottle of wine to her cart. She'd open it later tonight to unwind after Caleb was in bed and Matt was out the door. There were yesterday's cookies ready for dessert, but she added some ice cream to the cart anyway. She could surprise them both with ice-cream sandwiches.

It was bribery, plain and simple, and she was glad she'd thought of it.

When she reached the checkout lane, her cart loaded with too many extras, it looked as if she was hosting a party for a dozen people. Just covering all the bases, she thought pragmatically. She wasn't planning on feeding her nerves at all.

This was their first dinner as a family, and it should be memorable for more than just the bombshell that they *were* a family. Would Matt wait until they were alone to say I told you so? Were he and Caleb already discussing how this situation was all her fault? She could hardly blame her son for reaching that conclusion without any help from Matt.

At home, in her kitchen, with the chicken and vegetables roasting in the oven, she poured a sparkling water instead of the wine she wanted and started on the ice cream sandwiches. Did Caleb hate her now that he knew she'd kept his father from him all this time? He surely felt betrayed, a fact which would make any further lessons on honesty and integrity harder for her to sell.

And she still hadn't heard how he'd found out anything about Matt in the first place. Her queries via text message had been brushed aside with Matt's reply that he'd explain it all in person. Oh, that didn't make her nervous at all.

With dessert individually wrapped and back in the freezer, she stirred up dip for an appetizer tray and set it to chill. Caleb would want something to graze on as soon as he arrived and she assumed Matt would, too. She arranged slices of cheese and cut veggies on a platter and put it back into the refrigerator. When they pulled up, she'd set everything out and add crackers.

With that done, she walked through the dining room and family room, looking for anything out of place. Although she knew she was overthinking it, she couldn't stop. She didn't want Matt to find any reason to criticize the house or her parenting. The house was clean and tidy, thanks to a chore list, ingrained habits and some creative nagging. At last, she turned toward the bedrooms, forcing herself to make sure the guest room was ready if Matt insisted on staying here.

Would he insist? She supposed he'd have to since she had no intention of inviting him to stay over.

She felt heat rising in her face at the idea of Matt sleeping under her roof, just down the hall from her bedroom. It had been years since she'd seen him in person and yet he was still the man she wanted most, the man she held up against all others. And he continued to star in her most erotic dreams. At least that was a secret she could take to her grave, privileged information that never had to be listed anywhere.

The sound of a burly engine in the street drew her toward the big front window in the dining room. A quick chill of uncertainty slid down her spine when the glossy black Camaro with silver rally stripes pulled into her driveway. She was startled to find herself blinking back tears as she watched father and son emerge from the car. Happy tears, she told herself. This *would be* a happy occasion.

Caleb, the backpack on his shoulder, was practically dragging Matt to the front door. Side by side, the resemblance was uncanny, all the way down to their stride. Caleb was lanky, more elbows and knees right now, but already she could see him growing into the charming version of Matt she'd met at West Point.

The years had been good to him. He looked as fit as ever in an untucked soft gray button-down shirt, dark khaki slacks and brown leather boat shoes, with a light jacket in his hand. No wonder she'd been unable to make room for another man in her life. No one else was *Matt*. The man she'd always loved. The man she still loved.

Foolish, she scolded, schooling her expression into something she hoped came across as stern. Her feelings for Matt were impossible and could wait to be examined over that bottle of wine. Caleb was her priority and he needed to know that, happy endings aside, his actions today were absolutely unacceptable.

Hearing another car on the street, she saw Matt turn his head. Following his gaze, she didn't recognize the slow-moving car. The window behind the driver rolled down and the unmistakable barrel of a gun appeared in front of a shadowy figure in the back seat.

A scream lodged in her throat, she raced toward the front door. She heard Matt shout, prodding Caleb into a run as the rapid popping sounds of gunfire chased them. The door opened and Caleb tumbled inside, onto the slate foyer, with Matt practically on top of him. The stained-glass window at the top of her oak front door dissolved in a shower of colorful, glittering splinters.

"Get down!" Matt shouted. He slammed what remained of the door closed with his foot. "Move, move." He urged them back, deeper into the house, closer to the protection of the dining room.

"Caleb!" Bethany dropped to the floor, checking him for injuries. "Are you hit?" What on earth was going on? This wasn't a drive-by shooting sort of neighborhood. "Talk to me."

"I'm fine," he promised.

The coppery tang of blood stung her nose and her hand came away sticky and smeared with blood. "You've been shot," she insisted. "Where?" She reached for his clothing, searching for the wound.

Vaguely, as if she'd been packed in cotton, she heard Matt calling 911, relaying her address and the incident, including details of the car.

"Not me, Mom," he insisted. "It's Matt." Caleb squirmed out of her reach, heedless of the glass scattered across the floor. "Gotta be."

No. The world couldn't be so cruel as to give her son his father and take him away again in the same day. She ignored the slivers of glass biting into her hands and knees as she followed. Matt had pulled himself to a seated position against the wall across from the door.

"How bad?" she asked, lifting away the jacket he'd pressed to his side.

"Grazed." He sucked in a breath as she looked for herself. "Burns a little, that's all."

He wasn't simply being stoic. High on his left side, his shirt was torn, the fabric scorched by the bullet and stained with his blood. "Not too bad," she agreed. "Caleb, go get the first-aid kit."

"Yes, ma'am."

"Stay away from windows," Matt called after him.

"You think they'll come back around?"

He shrugged, winced. "Better to be safe..." His voice trailed off as his gaze locked with hers.

She didn't need him to finish the familiar idiom. Silently, she vowed that whoever had fired a gun at their son would be the only party feeling sorry about this particular incident.

Caleb returned and knelt beside them, the first-aid kit in hand, along with clean dish towels. "Need a bowl of water?"

"That would help," she said.

He nodded and scrambled off again.

"He's great," Matt said as she unbuttoned his shirt so she could get to the wound. "Amazing." He reached out and stilled her hands. "You're an incredible mom. It shows in him." His golden-brown eyes glowed with gratitude and something more she didn't want to consider just now.

"Thank you," she murmured. It was hard to look at him when he stared at her that way, with something that went deeper than simple affection, compassion or pride. How could fifteen years have passed and yet that look still held such sway over her heart and her emotions?

She should say something more, but the apologies she owed him got tangled between her mind and her mouth and once more went unspoken.

"You look great," he said.

She couldn't handle more compliments right now. "You must have hit your head." Flustered, she returned her attention to the wound.

Caleb rushed back, water sloshing over the sides of the bowl he carried. She didn't care. Floors dried and she was far too grateful for the distraction. Carefully, she cut away his undershirt and he leaned back, bracing on his opposite arm to give her better access.

Her first impression of him outside held true. He was still in prime shape, his muscles heavier and his build a bit wider now than he'd been at twenty. An overall maturity, she reminded herself.

She washed the wound and Caleb handed her folded gauze pads that she pressed close to stem the bleeding. "Not sure stitches will help," she said.

"They won't," he agreed, straining for a look. "Just tape it up."

"Police are here." Caleb tipped his head toward the dining room, where red and blue lights gave the room a strange strobe-light effect.

As he spoke, someone knocked on the busted front door. "Police department," a man's voice declared.

Caleb jumped up to answer, but Matt grabbed his arm, held him back. "Let me."

With one hand holding the in-progress bandage to his ribs, he muttered a low curse as Bethany helped him stand up.

Another hard knock rattled the door in its frame. "Police!"

"Yeah, just a second," Matt replied. "Go on back to the—"

"It's my house," Bethany interrupted. There was chivalry and then there was stupidity. He was hurt, not badly, but enough that it mattered. She angled in front of him.

"Beth," he warned.

He'd been the only person in her life to call her that. And he hadn't spoken the nickname that way since she refused his first proposal of marriage. Oh, how she missed this man.

"My house," she repeated and opened the door to a uniformed officer, who was ready to pound on the barrier once more.

"Ma'am," he said at once. "Officer Baker, Cherry Hill Police Department. Are you safe?"

"Yes, we are now. A car drove past and someone fired a gun at my son and his father."

The officer was looking at the damaged door, the scattered bits of colored glass behind them. "Are you injured?" He dipped his chin toward her, the bloodstains on her hands and clothing. "An ambulance is on the way."

"My son and I are fine. Nothing more than a few scrapes and splinters. This is from Caleb's father. He was grazed by a bullet."

"May I come in?"

She opened the door enough for him to see the full extent of the damage. He motioned for his partner to join him. Convinced he wasn't a threat, she made a note of the names and badge numbers anyway, inviting him and his partner into the dining room. It was the closest seating option and, on some wobbly emotional level, it helped her to keep this chaos from spilling into the parts of the house she and Caleb enjoyed most.

She pulled the curtains closed over the window, her only capitulation to the fear rattling through her. The shooter was gone and the danger had passed, but the chills were just starting. As the three of them gave their statements, she didn't hold out much hope that the driver and the gun-wielding passenger would be found.

All of them remembered the car as a dark, four-door sedan. Matt gave them the probable make, though none of them had caught even a glimpse of the license plate.

No, her security system didn't have a camera facing the street. No, Caleb didn't have friends with guns or friends in gangs. No, she hadn't seen the car before.

No one new had moved in recently. No, no, no. The questions only underscored the pervasive sense of helplessness in the air.

At the buzzing of the oven timer, she seized the opportunity and dashed away to take the Greek chicken out of the oven. Matt's voice drifted after her as he answered more questions.

His voice had changed as well, deep and mellow. That solid, sturdy sound had always made her want to lean in close and accept the support he offered. One more reason she'd kept her distance since Caleb's birth. Better to avoid temptation than risk her willpower snapping like a weak thread.

She'd always been weak where Matt was concerned.

"Mom?" Caleb wandered into the kitchen. "You okay?"

"Sure." She smiled at him. "Just debating how best to keep this hot." She covered the baking dish with two layers of aluminum foil and set it at the back of the stove top.

"Matt gave me the get-lost look," Caleb whispered. "He wants us to stay in here."

She bristled, as she'd done when he wanted to answer her door. Yet, he was the one injured and he'd had the best look at the car. He was also a major in the US Army. What he said would carry more weight with the authorities.

"Come here." She noticed a couple of dark stains at the knees of his jeans. "Bring a stool," she added, walking to the sink.

Taking an inventory, she looked over the minor scrapes from broken glass on his knees and palms.

The jeans had taken the brunt of it, though she noticed he had a few deeper slivers. “Roll up your jeans.”

“Seriously?” He rolled his eyes while he cooperated. “I’m fine, Mom.”

“I’ll be fine too if you let me baby you a bit. Please?” Her hands were full of the wet paper towel she was blotting against the various scrapes.

“If it’ll help you.” His sweet grin faded as the police stepped into the kitchen.

“The paramedics are checking on Mr. Riley,” Officer Baker said. “Do either of you need assistance or treatment?”

“No, thank you,” Bethany replied. “Just a scratch here or there, nothing deep.”

“All right. Is there someone to help you with the door?”

She’d forgotten her door would need attention. “I can contact a neighbor.” And call her alarm company to shut down that sensor.

“Good. We have what we need for now and a patrol car is staying behind as a precaution. We’ll be in touch as the case develops.”

“Thank you.” She arched an eyebrow at Caleb and he immediately thanked the officers, as well.

With the paramedics still in her dining room, Bethany turned her attention to the hoodie Caleb wore with the school’s mascot on the front. “This is probably ruined. Off with it.”

“No way. It’s one of my favorites.”

“I know,” she said with sympathy. “Let me see. I’ll try and salvage it.”

He wriggled it over his head, and as the light flashed through a hole in the heavy fabric, her heart stuttered in her chest. A bullet had come this close—too close—to tearing into her baby. No matter that he would soon be taller than she was, he was still her baby. A piece of her heart would always look at him through that soft maternal filter.

"Mom?" Caleb gasped as she drew him in close for a long hug. He patted her back. "You okay?"

"No, but I will be," she answered honestly. On a shaky exhale, she released him. "Go see how Matt's doing." She turned to the sink and started to scrub, knowing she'd only throw out this hoodie. He'd have to find a new favorite, if only for the sake of her nerves. Maybe Matt would give him one with an Army logo.

When he was out of sight and she heard him chattering with Matt, she balled up the hoodie and stuffed it into a plastic bag. Quickly, she carried it to the trash can in the laundry room and stuffed it down deep. Then she called Mr. Payton. He lived a couple houses down and he always volunteered to help with minor home repairs. She and Caleb had learned a great deal helping him help them. He happily agreed to come right over and secure the door for the night.

After she returned to the kitchen, Bethany deliberately began setting out food. Once the door was repaired, they'd eat in here, a casual setting for casual conversation. The dining room was too close to the disquieting mess and the street that now felt dangerous. She didn't pretend to understand precisely what was going on, but she couldn't help making the connection between Caleb finding Matt and trouble following them to her door.

Anger ran in hot and cold spurts through her veins. She wanted a target to strike back and a shield to protect her son. A small, sly voice in her mind blamed Matt, and she shook it off, knowing that was more of an irrational adrenaline-induced reaction.

Regardless, she wouldn't discuss danger and risk around Caleb anymore tonight. And she would not let Matt out of this house until they came to some agreement about what precautions would be put in place for Caleb's safety. She wanted answers, not random platitudes. Her son was her highest priority, and if that meant keeping him away from his father, so be it.

Bethany's immediate fear had burned away, and the cool calm she'd exhibited in the crisis was cracking around the edges. She was furious. Matt could see it simmering under the facade of pleasant conversation she used to cover more sensitive subjects.

It might have helped if he wasn't sitting here in a dark blue T-shirt the paramedics had given him since his shirts had been trashed and bloody. She, on the other hand, had changed into a dark purple shirt that flowed over her curves and snug jeans, and had gathered her hair into a braided knot at her nape. Her gaze turned chilly every time she glanced his way, and he figured the logo on the shirt reminded her of the bullets so recently aimed at their son.

Sitting here, he found her more beautiful than ever, a woman who'd captivated him once and could easily do so again. Thanks to social media, he'd seen pictures of the general changes through the years: her longer hair, changing fashion preferences, new hobbies. None of it made up for seeing her in person, hearing her voice, sharing a meal. The urge to lace his fingers with hers to rediscover that familiar comfort nearly overwhelmed him.

Maybe he should have left and taken a raincheck on this significant event, except he'd spent enough time with Caleb this afternoon and in the car to know where the kid's head was at. Matt didn't think it was fair for Bethany to manage the evening alone. Caleb had serious questions rattling in his head, along with plenty of battered feelings. The best thing he could do was stand as a buffer and keep them from saying things they'd regret.

Though his side ached, it didn't impede his appetite. The paramedics warned him the rib might be cracked, but he knew better, having cracked ribs in training before. Instead, he set out to enjoy what remained of his first night with his family.

He and Caleb devoured everything Bethany set on the table, while she merely pushed the food around her plate. She never could eat when she was mad. He complimented her Greek chicken—perfect despite the delay—and continued swiping baby carrots and crackers through the tasty dip on the appetizer tray.

Their son had endless questions about how they'd met and what West Point was like. Sharing the stories took Matt back to those early days when the excitement for her was as intense as the expectations of the school. Caleb asked about the places Matt had traveled for the Army, soaking up those details, too. It seemed he was fully aware of his mother's tenuous good mood and willing to dance around the more difficult pieces of their family puzzle. Until he wasn't.

"Were you ever going to tell me about Matt?" Caleb

asked his mom as he poked at the last of his salad greens.

Matt endured another cool glance from Bethany.

"Yes." She smiled. "Tonight, in fact."

"No." Caleb took a deep breath. "I mean if the hack or whatever hadn't happened. Would you ever have told me?"

Matt gave the kid points for bravery as he held up under Bethany's stern assessment. "Yes," she replied. One syllable. A complete sentence in itself, but it wasn't nearly enough to satisfy Caleb.

He tapped the tines of his fork against his plate, his gaze locked with hers. "I don't believe you."

She ignored the tapping fork, calmly tracing the side of her water glass with a fingertip. "I understand that. The trust between us took a hard hit on both sides today. Don't you agree?" She arched one dark blond eyebrow.

Caleb's chin came up. "I am *not* sorry I found him. Not sorry about any of that."

"I see." She looked as if she wanted the water to turn to wine or something stronger.

Personally, Matt wouldn't mind something a little stronger than the beer she'd served him. He was starting to feel uncomfortable, an obvious outsider, caught in a family spat. Except, he *was* family and it was past time for him to step up. "Caleb, speak with respect to your mother."

They both turned glares on him. "There have been two of us since day one," he reminded the boy. "I could have pressed my paternal rights and been more involved and I chose not to do that. Don't put all this on her."

"But she—"

"Your mom has always done what she felt was best for *you*," Matt interjected before Caleb stuck his foot deeper into his mouth. "Every decision she made was made in love."

Bethany's eyes dropped to her plate, her lips pressed thin. If they'd been alone, he would dig in, pester or cajole her until she confided in him. He didn't want to employ either tactic in front of their son. Out of respect for her.

Matt lifted his glass in a subtle toast and then took a gulp of his beer. There had to be a middle ground, and one of them needed to find it soon.

"This may not be how I wanted you to find out," Bethany said as if she'd read his mind, "but I'm not sorry that you know. For years I've tried to find the right time and the right words."

"Why didn't you?" Caleb demanded, his voice rising. "How hard could it have been to say, 'Hey, this guy's your dad and he wants to meet you'?"

"Caleb," Matt started to intervene again and Bethany shook her head.

"We were happy," she said, her voice and eyes full of regret. "All of us were happy."

Matt wanted to protest that last bit, though he'd wait for a more private moment. He'd add it to the lengthening list of things they needed to discuss. Caleb couldn't have been too happy if he'd willingly followed a stranger's clues to find his father. Matt sure hadn't been happy with the hands-off arrangement. He'd felt as if a limb was missing all this time. And now, sitting here in her kitchen, he'd call Bethany content, but not happy. Not the way a family should be happy.

Feeling his own temper edge toward boiling over, he volunteered Caleb to help him with the dishes. “Being mad at her doesn’t change anything,” he said, covering the conversation under the sound of running water and cleanup. “You’ve got a right to be upset, as long as you remember she has feelings, too.”

“I know. It’s like I can’t stop being mad,” the boy admitted.

Matt caught the tremor in Caleb’s hands as he loaded the dishwasher. “That’s adrenaline,” he explained. “Takes time to burn through it.” Adrenaline and a healthy dose of latent fear, if Matt was reading the signs right. “We’ll figure it out.”

“You promise?”

“Yes.” He was not going to fade back into the woodwork. Not again. All three of them deserved better.

“I’ve wanted a dad for as long as I can remember.” Caleb’s hands twisted the dish towel, his knuckles going white. “It’s *not fair* that you’ve been out there all this time and I didn’t know.”

Matt saw his son fighting back tears and just pulled him into a half hug. “Life can suck, right?” He could hold the kid for a year and not have enough.

Caleb’s cheek scrubbed against Matt’s shirt as he nodded.

“Well, you know about me now, so good luck getting rid of me.” Matt gave him a squeeze and released him. “Do me a favor.”

“Sure.”

That’s what he wanted to hear. “After dessert, go find something else to do so I can talk to your mom alone.”

“About me?” Caleb eyed him closely.

"Among other things," Matt said with a wink.

"Fine." Caleb's eyes clouded over. "Will you stay here tonight? Please?"

"You'd feel better if I did?" He waited for Caleb's affirmative nod. "Well, I'll let you in on a secret—I was already planning on it." Now that he had his family within reach, he wasn't about to leave them vulnerable to any threat. Tonight's drive-by wasn't some random occurrence.

"What about your job?"

"General Knudson and I will figure it out. This falls under the exceptional circumstance category. You just worry about getting some rest. What time does the bus come tomorrow?"

"It doesn't," Bethany said, walking up behind them. She pulled the ice-cream sandwiches out of the freezer. "Caleb was suspended for two days for truancy."

"What?" Caleb's voice cracked. "I have a history midterm on Thursday." He turned to Matt. "When you're suspended, you don't get credit for homework or assignments or tests. Man." He covered his face with his hands. "I am so screwed."

"Consequences," Matt and Bethany said in unison.

"Come on." He flung a hand toward Matt. "I had a good reason!" Neither one of them reacted. Caleb's shocked gaze shifted from one parent's face to the other and back again. "Oh, this? This is perfect." He grabbed two ice-cream sandwiches from the plate on the counter and stormed off, down the hall.

"Think he'll try to sneak out?" Matt asked.

"Won't get too far with the security system on." The first hint of a grin teased her mouth at one corner. "I had the windows wired when he started middle school."

The amused tilt of her lush mouth tempted him. He reeled in his desire. "Not to mention the cops keeping watch outside." He tipped his head in the direction of the driveway. "Did we just have our first united-we-stand parental moment?"

"And rocked it, I think." She raised her fist for a bump.

He chuckled and bumped, mindful of the small scratches. "Good. Go, us." He took her hand and pressed a kiss to her knuckles. Her hand was still a perfect fit in his. "Thank you."

"For what?"

Everything. Letting me stay for dinner. "Caleb," he said. "Your compassion, to start. The fabulous food. I could go on and on." Reluctantly, he let her tug her hand free. "You really should have eaten more."

"I will." She slid a bottle of red from the rack. "I should be thanking you."

He took the corkscrew from her hand and opened the bottle for her. "My turn to ask. For what?"

"For not throwing me under the bus earlier. We both know he didn't know you because of my choices."

Her admission left him speechless, and the way she peered at him from under her dark lashes took him back to the days at West Point, when he would sneak a kiss when they'd walk up to the cemetery.

She used a nifty aerator to pour the wine into the glass. "Saves time," she said with a smirk. "Want a glass?"

He turned to the refrigerator for another beer. Pulling himself together, he handed her one of the plain cookies she'd added to the plate of ice-cream sandwiches. "Hear these go great with any kind of wine. And chocolate is good for stress."

Her lips quirked into a faint half smile. "Even when the chocolate is delivered by the *source* of my stress?"

"Me?" He counted it a victory that she wasn't trying to toss him out. "I'm not your only source of stress."

"He has every right to be mad at me," she murmured, gazing toward the other side of the house and, presumably, Caleb's bedroom.

"And me," he insisted.

She shook her head. "You're the father he's always wanted. I'm just the mom he's always known."

He wanted to soothe her, to gather her close and kiss away every doubt clouding her gorgeous eyes. He wanted to be the man she would let into her life from this moment on. "We don't know what kind of dad I am."

"I think we can safely assume you'll be father of the year," she murmured.

If she believed that, why had she been so determined to shut him out? "Are you seeing anyone?" he asked.

"No. You?"

"No." He managed to keep the single syllable under control as relief flooded through him.

She pinned him with a skeptical gaze over the rim of her wine glass. "Then it was work that kept you out so late last night?" She turned toward the family room, turning out the kitchen light. "That doesn't sound like General Knudson's style."

Through the JAG office communications, he'd made sure Bethany was aware of every assignment throughout the course of his career. He hadn't expected her to know anything about his current boss. "He makes us go out as a group for the football games on Monday nights."

"Ah."

That sounded a lot like her "oh" from last night, and it put him on the defensive. He shot a glance down the hallway. "I was late getting home because of a prank when we left the restaurant." He couldn't call it an outright attack, not in light of what had happened here. "We had to file a police report. It was a mess."

"What happened?" The sincere concern shone in her eyes as she tucked her feet under her on the couch.

"A car came screaming through the parking lot and the driver lobbed a baseball into his windshield." He settled into a low chair, facing her. "It sent us into a protective response, which was probably a good show for anyone in the area."

"A drive-by with a baseball?" she asked, incredulous.

"Guess so. We didn't know that was the end of it at the time," he said, defensive again.

"No, what caught my attention was the similarity of the attack," she insisted.

She was right. "The driver wasn't in such a hurry here." Not until the bullets were fired; then the tires had squealed as the car sped away. "I meant it when I told Caleb I was staying the night," he stated.

"We'll all rest easier if you do." Her lips twitched to the side. She never could lie without that particular tell.

It was nice to see some things didn't change. "You don't want me to stay."

She sighed, rolling her wine glass back and forth

between her palms. "It's a reasonable expectation, especially under the circumstances."

That much was true. "I want to be a part of his world, Beth."

"I know." She reached back and unpinned the braid so it fell over her shoulder. "You should have been long before now."

Her admission startled him out of a vision of threading his fingers through the silky mass. "How are we going to work it?"

"Day at a time, I guess." She set the wine glass aside. "Did the two of you make some sort of pact not to tell me how he found you?" Despite the weariness oozing from her every motion, her eyes blazed now.

"No, but maybe we should have." Once more, he glanced around for a liquor cabinet. A shot of whiskey would make this story easier for him to share. Probably make it easier for her to hear.

"Tell me," she ordered.

Matt would rather open a vein than add to her worries. He leaned forward, elbows propped on his knees. "He told me he got hints through a social app on his phone. The one where the messages disappear," he added before she could race to his bedroom and confiscate his device. "Caleb would take the hint and start digging and eventually, he learned I was working at the Pentagon. He planned it well when he came down to confront me."

Her face had gone pale. "You sent him hints, put all this in motion?"

The accusation was like taking a knife to the gut. "No." Matt jerked back, palms raised in surrender. "Absolutely not. You know me better than that."

"Do I?"

"You *do*." He struggled to keep his cool and keep his voice low. "From what he told me, the messages came through a couple weeks ago. About the time of the personnel office breach, but before they found it or announced it. I assume whoever bought the compromised information is trying to embarrass me or harass us. I can't figure out why, though."

"Or maybe they want to kill you." She flicked a hand toward the front door. "If I don't finish the job for them. You brought them here."

"Bethany, come on, I didn't put any of this into motion." Though he'd be hard-pressed to prove he was innocent of instigating Caleb's search for him. "If I'd wanted to introduce myself, I could have done it a dozen times by now. Legally or by being a jerk and showing up to a game or school event."

"You're right. Sorry. I'm just unsettled."

He wanted to hold her, as a friend, if nothing else, just to reassure them both that they'd get through this. As a family.

"I'd imagined this night going so differently," she muttered, rubbing at the furrow between her deep golden eyebrows.

"Me too." He'd been hoping for at least a brief hug as thanks for bringing Caleb home safely. He didn't need or want a hero's welcome, just a friendly one.

His fantasy of walking into her open, welcoming arms had begun halfway through his first deployment as his fellow soldiers talked about their family interactions. He'd had vivid dreams about finding her smiling face in the crowd, at the airport, lingering at the edge of the unit picnic. When he'd returned with his unit and their families rushed them as soon as the formation was dismissed, he'd caught himself looking for her. It had been ridiculous and illogical, yet he couldn't seem to stop.

What would she do if he told her all of that now? He knew the answer. Despite any potential mutual attraction, the ever-practical Bethany would focus on problem-solving and keeping Caleb safe. Giving himself a mental shake, he dragged his thoughts back to the present. "What did your supervisor say when you showed him the letter you got last night?"

She blinked rapidly, as if she too had been lost in thoughts of what might have been. "Not a lot he could say. We turned it all over to the security team. I've been wondering how exposing my financials turns into a drive-by, and I keep coming up empty."

"There's no logic to it. Someone is jerking us around." Matt pushed himself out of the chair and started to pace the width of her family room. All the curtains had been drawn and he felt cocooned, but not in a good way.

"Manipulating Caleb to find me, threatening you outright."

"Hardly a threat," she said. "Whatever it looked like on paper, you know it wouldn't have been a real problem."

"I'm not sure which matters more, the threat or the outcome," he admitted. "You and Caleb were approached directly. Whoever did that left me out of it..." His voice trailed off while he struggled to contain his temper. "Unless that dumb baseball was meant for me instead of General Knudson." The possibility hadn't occurred to him until the words left his mouth.

"But why?" she asked.

"We're all in one place. All three of us scared and distracted by what couldn't have been a random crime. When I picked up Caleb at Union Station, I felt like we were being followed, but I couldn't prove it."

"Why?" she asked again, coming to her feet, as well. "Who would care about the three of us enough to go to this much trouble?"

"No idea. Have you been seeing anyone new?" She shook her head. "Working on any sensitive contracts or audits?"

"No." She stepped closer. "Matt, you're scaring me."

Her scent enveloped him, stirring more sweet memories. This wasn't the time. "Has anything changed with Caleb? Friends, teachers, coaches?"

"Nothing like that," she replied. "What are you thinking?"

"We've been pushed together, according to someone's agenda, and I don't really want to sit around and wait for that someone to make the next move."

"What do we do?"

"Whoever took those shots at us when we arrived had either been waiting or followed us," he said, thinking out loud. "I didn't see any kind of a tail, and I was watching."

She gestured for him to continue. "The police told me they found a couple of nine-millimeter slugs and casings outside. Not the most effective weapon for a drive-by scenario."

"Shouldn't we be thankful for that?"

"Yes. We should also be on the lookout for more serious trouble until we know who's behind this and what they really want."

She sat back into the arm of the couch as though

her knees had given out. "You really get all that from a vague threat and the messages Caleb received?"

"If the baseball was for me instead of the general, that's all three of us being harassed in one form or another and now we're all together, under the same roof."

"Who would want that?"

He did, but not for criminal reasons. "I don't know, but considering our past as a couple and our present careers, I think it's time to get the Army involved with an official investigation." He rubbed at the tension in his neck. "And I thought telling my mom would be the worst part of the breach."

"Still might be." She smiled up at him. "How are your parents doing?"

That smile created a strange ripple of hope around his heart. "Great. Dad retired a couple months ago. They built a house on the beach down in North Carolina and they take the boat out every chance they get."

"Will they make demands when they hear about Caleb?"

"They'll definitely want to meet him," Matt replied. "If you'll allow it."

Her gaze fell, but she nodded.

"Would it be easier if I called them now? I'll put it on speaker and you can hear Mom rip into me," he offered.

"That is tempting."

He pulled out his phone, determined to show her he meant it. When she saw the time display, she stopped him with a touch before he could dial.

"If you call now, she'll think it's an emergency."

"Right." He was already bucking for worst son of

the decade, so why compound it by adding even one moment of unnecessary worry? "Tomorrow then?"

"Over breakfast," she suggested with a chuckle.

"What time do you head to the office?"

"Normally I leave right after Caleb catches the bus. I knew about his suspension before I left the office today, so they're expecting me to work from home."

That actually worked better for him. He'd been wrestling with the best way to convince her that they should stick together until they had more information. "Caleb said his fall break is next week."

She nodded. "They're out starting this Friday."

"And he's suspended tomorrow and Thursday."

"That's right." She sipped her wine.

"So there's no reason you can't come stay with me in Washington for a few days."

Carefully, she set her wine aside again. "No."

"Good," he said, deliberately misinterpreting her answer.

"No, Matt. I mean we're *not* doing that." Her eyes wide, she seemed on the verge of panic. She hadn't shown this much when the bullets were flying.

He crossed the room and, contrary to all of her signals and his common sense, he drew her into his arms. She resisted, her body stiff, her hands curled into fists trapped between his chest and hers. He didn't let go, just swayed a little. On a shuddering breath, she melted into him, her palms relaxing, smoothing over his chest and slipping around his waist until she was holding on to him.

This. Her. He'd missed this comfort and warmth since she walked out of his life, pregnant with his child.

"I've missed you," he said, pressing a light kiss to her hair, breathing her in.

She popped out of his embrace as if he'd scorched her. "We can't go to DC."

He didn't like the finality in her tone. "We sure can't stay here like a flock of sitting ducks." He shoved his hands into his pockets before he reached for her again.

"If we go hang out with you, it will feel like a reward to Caleb." She plucked up her glass and his bottle and retreated to the kitchen. "The time you had today was reward enough for his outrageous behavior."

He stalked after her. "Better that than risking more injury when I'm three hours away."

She spun back to face him. "We have managed just fine so far. No one ever fired a gun at us until *you* showed up."

The jab found its mark and left him reeling. It must have showed on his face, because she immediately apologized.

"Don't." He waved it off. It was a logical train of thought that originated with him—the breach, the threat, the drive-by. "You have every right to be upset." He could handle her anger, even be the scapegoat she needed, as long as he let her take point on their safety.

Besides, he didn't want her apologies; he wanted to claim his family. Couldn't she see how good things could be for all of them if she'd just bend an inch? *Of course not.* It wasn't her job to bend, he reminded himself. It was his job to provide. Maybe he really was mired in the past, while she'd successfully moved on.

Frustrated, knowing this wouldn't get resolved tonight, while they were both so raw, he stalked through the parts of the house he'd seen and checked the doors.

Back in the dining room, he nudged the curtain back just enough to verify the police were still there. "Any other exits?" he asked, returning to the kitchen.

She shook her head.

"Good night, then." He walked over and stretched out on the couch.

"We have a guest room."

"Good to know. This is fine." This was better. The cops might have the place covered outside, but he intended to plant himself firmly between any threat and his family.

"Matt?"

He opened his eyes to find her watching him from the hallway. "Go to bed, Bethany."

"Why didn't you ever get married?"

He should tell her the truth. She was the only one he wanted to build a life with. He would have confessed if he hadn't been so tired. Instead he gave her an answer she expected, one that worked best for the current quagmire that was his personal life. "Guess I just never found enough time. What about you?"

"The same," she said, her lips giving away the lie.

"Get some rest," he suggested, closing his eyes again.

He waited until he heard her soft footsteps moving down the hallway. He waited another twenty minutes after that. Then he started sending text messages to a friend in the Pentagon who might be able to commandeer surveillance feeds and closed-circuit cameras in this area to give them a better lead on the shooter. The local police would be doing the same thing through their sources, but he didn't care. His friend would be faster and would share the results right away.

Despite taking every possible proactive measure, Matt had trouble falling asleep. It wasn't the furniture or the circumstance. It was the awareness that Bethany was just down the hall and still maddeningly out of his reach.

Chapter 4

Bethany had expected Caleb to sulk when she woke him at the normal time, greeting him with a kiss and a list of chores to fill the next two days. She reminded herself she was grateful he'd stayed in his room and was still speaking to her.

She hadn't expected to find Matt in a similar mood.

Oh, the apple didn't fall far from the tree, she thought, watching the man glare at her kitchen countertops. His feet were bare and his hair was damp from a shower. She marveled that, on him, the wrinkled khakis and T-shirt the paramedics had given him somehow looked stylish.

"What is it you need?" she asked from the opposite side of the island.

"Coffee."

Mentally, she cringed. As a tea drinker, she didn't stock coffee. It was the one thing she hadn't thought of at the store. Because she hadn't thought he'd stay over. Cautiously, she approached him and opened the drawer where she kept the pods for her brewer. "I have black tea."

He glared at the pods in the drawer. "Tea is not coffee." He put a bite into each word.

Poor man. Unable to resist, she rubbed his shoulder. "I'll go out and—"

"No." He sidestepped away from her touch. "Thank you." He gave her a patently false smile. "Tea works."

She couldn't let him break the news to his mom about having a son without the buffer of his morning coffee. "Hold on." She sent a text message to her next-door neighbor and received an immediate reply. Less than five minutes later, she heard the knock on the back door.

She went to answer it, Matt's clean-soap scent shadowing her as he followed. When she reached to turn the deadbolt, Matt slapped a hand against the door. "Ask who it is."

She stared up at him, trying to ignore the appeal of his sculpted arm. "It's Tina, with coffee for you."

Matt didn't move. "Ask anyway."

"Who is it?"

"Tina. I have the coffee pods for you, Ms. Trent."

She unlocked the door in a rush, smiling through gritted teeth as she struggled to open the door wider against Matt's stubborn weight. "Thank you." She took the small sack of coffee pods.

"Is Caleb okay?" Tina was in a few of Caleb's classes at school. "I heard he, um, skipped yesterday."

Bethany was sure she'd heard it from Caleb himself. She made a mental note to confiscate his cell phone. "He's fine," she assured her young neighbor. "Though he'll be grounded for quite some time."

"I bet." Her eyes went round as she caught sight of something over Bethany's shoulder. Matt, no doubt. "Well, okay. Have a good day, Ms. Trent."

"Thanks again." She hoped the words reached the girl before Matt shoved the door closed. "That was rude."

He shrugged and nipped the sack out of her grasp.

She managed not to laugh as he scowled at her brewer, looking rather desperate for it to finish. Or when he inhaled the aroma he found so appealing as if he'd been spared a fate worse than death. Grumpy or not, she enjoyed his presence in her kitchen and she'd slept better knowing he was here.

That sense of ease was the perpetual risk with Matt. Not to mention the desire that pulsed through her whenever she looked at him. If she didn't keep the boundaries clear, the center of her life would slip until she and Caleb were orbiting around him. Matt needed time with his son, but he didn't need her leaning in too, dragging him away from all he was meant to do. And she'd worked too hard to toss away her career and goals in favor of following him around the country or the world.

Caleb wandered in, eyeing them both with open suspicion and offended-teen hostility. "You're still here," he said to Matt.

"Told you I would be," Matt replied, taking his coffee to the table.

Bethany didn't say a word. Clearly this was Caleb's new attempt to get in his digs about her lie of omission. Fighting about water under that bridge was a waste of energy, and Bethany needed all of her resources to keep her hands off Matt.

When he'd held her close last night, she'd been so tempted to take the comfort he offered. She'd nearly admitted her longing for him had never faded. Thank goodness she'd kept those words inside. Leaning on him now seemed like too much added burden for the man who was carrying a heavy load already.

I missed you. His words had echoed in her head all night and sparked dreams she wished could come true. She yanked herself back to the moment as Caleb poured cereal into a bowl. "Matt told me about the messages you received. I'd like to take a closer look at your cell phone."

"He did that yesterday, at the Pentagon," Caleb said.

She held out her hand. "Just give me the phone."

"Why?"

Bethany didn't dignify that with a response.

From the table, Matt snorted. "You're old enough to know nothing changes her mind when that look sets in."

She managed not to grin at his remark. On a gusty sigh, Caleb slapped his cell phone into her palm. "Thank you." She dropped the device into her purse. Once she'd checked his social apps, she'd give it back to him, with a lecture if necessary. "Would you like eggs or pancakes for breakfast, Matt?"

"Coffee works. We should get going ASAP."

She caught the glint of triumph in Caleb's eyes. "We have time for breakfast."

"Eggs, then. If it's no trouble."

"Not a bit." Grinning, she settled onto a counter stool. "Caleb, you're up."

"Aw, man." He froze, gallon of milk in hand. Shaking his head, he put the milk back.

Matt raised his coffee mug to her in a silent toast of approval. "Sure he won't poison us?"

"He's a good cook and enthusiastic about it most of the time," she said. "Besides, I keep all the hazardous materials locked up in the laundry room."

Caleb shuffled his feet as he gathered utensils and ingredients. "Stuff tastes better when I get to fix what I want."

"And yet, that's so rarely how life goes," Bethany pointed out pleasantly.

"You want pancakes?" Matt asked. "I could be talked into pancakes."

"We're having eggs," Caleb grumbled. "Make one mistake. Sheesh."

"We all make mistakes," Bethany said, sliding around him to brew another cup of tea. "It's how we handle the consequences that makes the difference."

She turned at the sound of a cell phone humming. Matt's, she realized. He was staring at his phone as if it was about to bite his hand. When he lifted it, she saw Patricia Riley's face on the display. She caught his eye and shook her head, but he hitched a shoulder and swiped to answer, putting the call on speaker immediately.

"Hey, Mom. You're on speaker."

"Hello. Where are you?"

"I'm sitting in Bethany Trent's kitchen. Her son is making us breakfast."

"Is there a chance we could talk privately?" Patricia asked.

"Not if it involves either of them," he said.

Bethany's face was turning a thousand shades of

red. Even if she hadn't felt it happening, Caleb was snarky enough to point it out.

"You look like a cherry tomato, Mom."

"Oh, hush." She added a splash of milk to the bowl with half a dozen eggs in it. "Whisk."

"Bethany?"

"Yes, ma'am. I'm here."

"I apologize for my son's outlandish behavior. It's hardly the example you'd want him to set for your son, I'm sure."

"Not gonna work, Mom," Matt said.

He sounded firm, but Bethany caught the subtle fidgeting. He wasn't happy about defying her or behaving rudely in front of Caleb.

"Fine." Resigned, Patricia explained the purpose of her call. "Your father and I received some disturbing news from General Knudson last night. When you have time to speak privately, call me back."

"Hang on, you win."

Matt carried his coffee and his phone out of the kitchen. A moment later, the security system announced his movement as he went out through the front door. She felt a little sorry for him and more than a little responsible.

"Yikes," Caleb said. "She sounds mad."

"That's your grandmother, Patricia Riley," Bethany said. "I imagine when you meet her in person, she'll be far nicer to you."

"Why?"

"Because you're her first grandchild."

"I'm practically an adult."

Bethany nearly dropped the small pitcher as she added cream to her second cup of tea. "Adulthood is more than height and age," she said. "You have a ways to go yet before you hit reliable and responsible status."

"So what is Matt's family like?" Caleb asked, pouring the eggs into the hot pan.

"Tight," she said. She only really knew them by reputation and from stories Matt had shared during their time in school. "They'll be excited when they hear about you. I'm sure they'll want Matt to introduce you as soon as possible."

"Won't they want to meet you?"

Imagining the awkwardness of that kind of meeting made her palms damp. She'd kept Caleb from his father and extended family. The Rileys frowned on that sort of thing. "I met his parents when we were at West Point. His dad finished his Army career as a general. His mom was a nurse. They recently retired." She did not want to go any further down this road. "I liked them a lot," she said, hoping that put an end to it.

"He said he has brothers and sisters?"

"Yes. Two of each," she remembered. "Watch the eggs."

"That's a big family."

She agreed. Caleb had been six the last time he'd asked why he didn't have siblings. She'd explained families came in all sizes. It had been enough of an answer for him at the time, though she knew how much he enjoyed the action of his friends who were part of bigger families. If she'd married Matt at twenty, would there have been more children? Probably. At twenty, an only child herself, the idea of being resigned to Army wife and motherhood felt stifling.

There had been a handful of moments through the years when she wondered if she'd made a mistake by not settling down with him. Then she'd get word of Matt's next post or deployment and she'd remember why she'd chosen this path. Maybe Patricia Riley had effortlessly juggled the duties of her career with those of being an officer's wife and mother, but Bethany had never been able to see herself rise to that particular challenge.

Matt stared into the empty coffee cup, wishing it would magically refill. He wouldn't go back in the house until his mother had finished her rant. He held the phone back from his ear as his mother continued her lecture. Wasn't she supposed to be sharing why Knudson had called them?

Apparently not yet, he thought as she hit the bonus round of the family, duty and honor talk. It wasn't anything he hadn't said to himself time and again where Bethany and Caleb were concerned. She had to know that, she'd been the one to drill those values into his head from the cradle.

"Mom," he interrupted, exasperated. "I'm sorry you found out this way—"

"Or are you sorry I found out at all? I was listening for your call all night long."

The hurt was coming through loud and clear now. "Mom, it wasn't like that. Bethany had her reasons for raising him alone." Was he going to have to face all of his faults today?

"Of course she did. You should have been able to overcome those reasons."

His mother's aim with the guilt arrows was dead-on today. "I tried." He'd bought a ring. "I proposed."

"You did? *When*?"

"When she told me she was pregnant." That was the

first time. There had been others. Somehow Bethany always managed to make marriage to him, life with him, sound like a fate worse than death. "She had a different plan." And she'd done one hell of a job executing that plan.

"I want to meet my grandson and speak with Bethany. You know I was fond of that girl from day one."

"I know." And he'd never stopped believing they would have been close friends, given the chance.

He'd liked Bethany from the start, as well. It wasn't exactly love at first sight, but that layer of affection had grown out of his initial respect and fast friendship. Once he'd looked at her through a different lens, he couldn't shift the focus back to a platonic view. At the first kiss, he'd known she was where his heart would stay. If only he'd known how much it would hurt to be right.

"I'll make sure you get to meet Caleb. It's going to take some time. We're all adjusting here." He explained how he and Bethany had planned to speak with Caleb last night and then share the news with his family. "Things changed in a hurry when Caleb came to Washington to find me."

"I'm putting you on speaker," she said. "Your father needs to hear this."

"Hi, Dad." Matt didn't bother arguing, just moved on with the recounting of last night's drive-by. "General Knudson wasn't happy when I informed him of the incident, but I don't understand why he'd call you?"

"We do go back a ways," Ben Riley answered vaguely.

"And?" His dad was on a first-name basis with

nearly every officer at the highest echelons across the various Military branches.

"He called us as a courtesy as soon as he realized he couldn't keep the story quiet," Ben continued. "He wanted to let us know you weren't seriously injured. When we pressed him about why you were in New Jersey, he told us Caleb was your son," Ben said. "Not a big surprise once your mother recognized Bethany's name. He wasn't sure when you'd be able to call, and he thought we should hear the news from a friend."

Matt desperately wanted another jolt of caffeine. "If I'd thought the incident last night was newsworthy, I would've called."

"You didn't see the news," his mother said under her breath.

"No, I was tangled up with the fallout here." Trying to figure out if there was room to carve out a place for himself in Caleb's life.

Behind him, the door opened and Bethany handed him a fresh mug of coffee. If he hadn't been in love with her already, that would have done it. He gave her a nod of thanks and got a quick smile as she ducked back into the house.

"What did I miss?" he asked when his parents hesitated.

"Someone sent a cell-phone video of the drive-by shooting to the media."

"What?" He couldn't have heard her correctly. No one else had been on the street at the time. He stared out at the street as he thought it through again. The shooter had rolled up only a few moments after he and Caleb arrived. The window behind the driver had rolled down and the street was clear when the bullets started flying.

"Knudson tried to suppress the video and the story," Ben said. "Unfortunately your face was easily identified and confirmed. Caleb's face was hidden by your body and his name was protected, since he's a minor."

"This was on national television?" Matt asked, incredulous. That made no sense.

"Yes," Patricia replied. "Breaking news on all the late-night broadcasts. I was so grateful for the general's call so we could let your brothers and sisters know you were safe. The video…well, it was disturbing, to put it mildly."

Great. He could envision his dad comforting her. He wanted to blast the news outlets, though it wouldn't do any good. No mother should have to watch her son being fired on, and now both Patricia and Bethany had endured it.

"Mom, I'm really sorry." He focused on the one thing he'd tried to control. "I swear Bethany and I planned it so you'd hear about Caleb from *me* first."

"It's okay. I believe you, sweetheart. They painted you as a hero for saving him. General Knudson said you weren't injured. Did he soft-pedal that detail?"

Matt chuckled at how far down the list that question landed. "Only a little banged up. Whoever opened fire used a pistol and didn't have the best aim." He twisted around to look at the cardboard and plastic that qualified as a temporary repair on the door. Bethany would never agree to go to DC until this was fixed. "Her front door got the worst of it."

"Well, that's a plus," his mom said. "Naturally, I'm

less than thrilled with the way this has come out, but I'm confident you'll deal with this properly."

He didn't need her definition of that term. She expected marriage and a family unit including Caleb at the next Riley family function, followed closely by duty and honor. He glanced at his 1967 Camaro in the driveway. It didn't seem all that out of place. The patrol car on the street—that bothered him.

"Mom, you do remember it takes *two* willing people to make your idea of 'properly' work out."

"Don't sass me." Her voice slid toward impatient. "I believe in your powers of persuasion and I expect you to apply yourself so I can meet and get to know my grandson."

"Patricia," Ben scolded gently. "Let us know what works out," he said. "We can always come up there if it's easier for the three of you."

What would be easier would be having some time to figure out this new dynamic for the three of them before stirring in all the extended-family expectations. He didn't bother pointing that out.

"First we're going back to Washington." He'd feel safer there, with a team he trusted and Military support to watch his back. "I'm hoping we can sort out a few things, starting with security. This must be tied to the data breach of the personnel records, though I don't understand why anyone would care so much about exposing the existence of my son."

"What about the weekend?" Patricia asked. "Can we come up to see you this weekend?"

"Mom." His two-bedroom condo was way too small for that kind of family reunion. "Caleb has fall break next week. If I can convince Bethany to spend a few days at the beach with you guys, will that work for you?"

"Yes, definitely. We'll—"

"We'd like that," Ben interjected before Patricia got too caught up in her plans. "Just keep us posted, son. You know where to reach us."

"Thanks, Dad. I'll be in touch."

He ended the call, his gaze on the street. He didn't see the street in the bright morning light, his mind caught up in recreating last night. Either they'd been fortunate enough to be randomly targeted by a poor marksman or they'd been played, moved to this location by an expert.

Matt wasn't sure where they'd find any evidence to point them toward one theory over the other, but it was past time to start digging in.

In his private office, the door locked against an untimely intrusion, he donned his headphones and replayed the witness video and late-night news reports. Utter perfection. He made a mental note to give the man running this op a raise.

His technician had pulled the 911 call for him. Matthew Riley had kept it together admirably. Well, that wouldn't last much longer.

He'd wanted the full injury report from the ambulance, but those files proved trickier to pull and he had to rely on word of mouth that no one had been injured seriously enough to be transported.

A shame. He'd hoped for something more sensational, more distracting, to keep the talking heads rambling. Ah, well, moving too fast wouldn't be nearly as satisfying in the long run.

He replayed the original broadcasts from each major network as the various anchors related the story, painting a hero's halo over Matt Riley's regulation Military haircut.

Oh, how the mighty would soon fall.

They were scrambling and he considered that a good start. Before he was done, the Riley family would be drenched in a collective cold sweat, paralyzed with fear. When he took them to their knees, had them at his mercy, that would be the triumphant moment when he would taste the *real* victory.

His mind on that prize, he picked up the phone and gave the order to unlock the next part of his plan.

Chapter 5

Bethany wished she could claim Matt had bullied her into leaving her home and taking an impromptu vacation from work. He hadn't. He'd been patient to the point of annoying as they discussed and debated the potential fallout of each option.

If she wouldn't leave the house, he vowed to stay through the weekend and make sure she had a security detail that measured up to his standards before he left. Whether that detail would be official or unofficial had never been answered to her satisfaction. She dreaded the idea of having bodyguards hovering. Caleb thought it would be cool.

That had pretty much been the deciding factor for her. She didn't need her fourteen-year-old thinking they were living out some sort of action movie script.

She'd tossed out the excuse of work, knowing it wouldn't hold up. She had plenty of leave and vacation time built up. After looking up last night's dramatic news reports online, she wasn't surprised that her supervisor encouraged her to take every precaution for herself and her son.

Their son. With Matt underfoot, she clearly needed to adjust sooner rather than later. He'd filled her in on the call with his mother while Caleb worked through the long list of chores she'd given him.

When Caleb finished raking up leaves in the backyard, she took pity on him and let him ride along with Matt to buy a new front door. The busted door had been her last viable reason to stay here when Matt wanted them in DC.

As Matt and Caleb loaded the Camaro with their luggage and she locked that new door, she glanced up into the eye of the new security camera the alarm company had added for her. How much more would her life be irrevocably altered before they came home again?

The evening dinner rush had passed by the time they stopped to indulge Caleb's request for authentic cheesesteak sandwiches in Philadelphia. The delay wasn't nearly long enough to quell the butterflies swirling in her belly.

Too soon they were navigating the notorious congested streets of Washington as Matt pointed out various monuments and sites. Her nerves reached an all new high as he ushered them into his building on the channel and up to his condo. Naturally, Caleb was enamored with anything and everything about Matt's world. Since she'd always had the same problem, she wondered if maybe it was a genetic predisposition.

Matt gave them the full tour of the space and then encouraged them both to settle in while he went to his bedroom for clean clothes. Caleb dumped their suitcases into the guest room and then went straight to the entertainment center, checking out the game system Matt mentioned.

Bethany turned a slow circle, trying to get comfortable with the idea of staying here. A big island divided the kitchen from a large, open living area that seemed even bigger with floor-to-ceiling sliders that opened to a balcony and a stunning view. The bedrooms bracketed the living area. The kitchen had been recently updated with stainless-steel appliances and granite countertops.

Matt returned a few minutes later in well-worn jeans and a long-sleeved T-shirt with a character she recognized from one of the video games Caleb enjoyed. Confirming her son was distracted, and more than a little concerned he was getting off way too easy after yesterday's stunt, she motioned Matt to join her in the kitchen.

"What do you expect?" she asked.

His expression shuttered. "Can you be a little more specific?" He reached into the refrigerator for a beer. "Want one?"

"No, thank you." She wanted answers. It was clear his mind had been churning since his talk with his parents. Was getting them out of her house a strategy to lay groundwork for a custody claim?

"Can you narrow it down for me?" he prompted.

She couldn't outright accuse him of making the self-serving choice. As insecure as she was about his real intentions, that had never been Matt's style. He was consistent and reliable, and for the entirety of Caleb's life, he'd respected her wishes.

"What do you expect to happen?" she began. "You

said we're safer here than in New Jersey. I'd like to understand why you believe that."

He arched an eyebrow. "We talked about that before we moved."

They had, yes. Still, she gulped. This wasn't a *move.* It was temporary. Had to be. She'd never considered herself a coward before. She prided herself on being strong, direct and doing what was necessary, even if it wasn't fun in the moment. So why was she standing here, dancing around her real issue?

He leaned around her to confirm Caleb was finding his way through the gaming console. "As I said, it's about resources," he said. "Here, there's a camera on every corner. At your place today, I wanted to send Caleb inside every time I saw a dark sedan roll by. That's counterproductive when we're trying to sort out what's going on."

"If anything is going on."

One dark eyebrow rose and the other lowered.

"Right. You expect more trouble," she said, summing up that expression.

"You're not here as bait, Bethany. I wouldn't use either of you that way. We're here because this is where we have the best chance of figuring out the problem."

"And what about us?"

"*Us* as in you and me?" His gaze locked on her, hot and interested. "Is that an invitation?"

She backpedaled. "I meant *us* as in what are Caleb and I supposed to do while you're fixing the problem?"

He watched her steadily as he took a long pull from the beer bottle. Setting the bottle aside, he took a step toward her. "It was only a few hours ago that we discussed all of this."

"I-I know." She backed up, hit the counter. Her hands curled around the cool edge of the granite. "I'm second-guessing, that's all. Stress." First stuttering and now she couldn't get her thoughts into coherent sentences. She tried to wave it off but didn't think she'd quite sold it when his brown eyes went darker still.

He prowled closer. "Which part concerns you most? The sticking with me for safety, or maybe it's just the idea of sticking with me?"

The last one, a small voice in her head cried out. But she wasn't that overwhelmed nineteen-year-old anymore. She was a grown woman, a mother with a son and an established career. No matter the circumstance, Caleb's safety was her top priority.

She planted her hand in the center of his hard chest. His heart kicked, his chest swelled as he sucked in a breath. He leaned into her touch, as though his heart was drowning and she was the lifeline. Good grief, her imagination needed a dose of reality.

"Bethany," he murmured.

The blood rushing through her ears was so loud, she saw him speak her name more than she heard it. The blatant need in his brown eyes triggered an answering need in her. Any reply she might have given went up in flames when he lowered his firm lips to her mouth. Lightly at first, she recognized the spark and heat just under the surface, waiting for an opening to break free and singe them both. Her hands curled into his shirt, pulled him closer. Oh, how she'd missed this. She'd thought time had exaggerated her memories and found the opposite was true when his tongue swept over hers, as he alternately sipped and plundered and called up all her long-ignored needs to the surface.

Our second first kiss, she thought. As full of promise as the *first* first kiss had been when they were kids.

"Oh. Ah. Sorry. Never mind." Caleb's voice, choked with embarrassment, doused the moment as effectively as a bucket of ice water. Footsteps swiftly made their way back to the living room.

She muttered an oath.

Matt's head lifted but that was all. His palms still warmed her waist, his fingers kneading a little. He stared at her, his eyes roaming over her face as if seeing her for the first time.

She sympathized. It took more willpower than she anticipated to release her grip on him, to smooth the wrinkles she'd left in his shirt.

"Stop," he warned. "Unless you want me to start over."

Oh, she did. "We can't." She tried to wriggle out from between him and the counter at her back, and only teased them both. "We can't send him mixed signals."

"Agreed."

"Matt." He showed no inclination of letting her out of this corner. "I need to go talk with him."

"This was the expectation you meant."

No sense denying it. "Well, yes."

"I didn't *expect* this." He traced her eyebrow, cheek and jaw with his fingertip. "But I won't lie and say I don't want it. You."

She wouldn't lie to him either, so she kept her mouth closed, her eyes aimed somewhere in the vicinity of his chest. It could have been one minute or ten before he moved aside and she escaped the kitchen.

She found Caleb on the floor of the living room, leaning back against one couch, his eyes locked on the racing game filling the big-screen television. He leaned into the curves, hands twisting the controller like a steering wheel.

She walked over, sat down close enough to touch him, though she didn't. "Did you need me?"

"No."

The flat answer reminded her he was embracing his teenager status. "Caleb."

"No, ma'am."

For a slow count of ten, she watched him navigate the ridiculous track on the screen. As his character crossed the line first, he stretched out his legs. Before she could suggest they talk, he flipped through the options and started the next race.

She waited through another race, another win. Matt came in, beer in hand, to watch as well. When she caught Caleb's grin when he took out an opponent with some dastardly trick, she dared to try again. "What did you need?"

"Nothing, Mom. Forget it."

Matt caught her eye, signaled to let him try. She indicated he could have at it, oddly comforted that they could still communicate so well without words.

Matt started with a couple of comments about the game. When the stats came up for Caleb's latest win, Matt sat forward. "Are you playing that on the easy setting?"

"No," Caleb replied, indignant. "Don't you recognize the high-test levels?"

Matt stretched out his hand. "Hand me a controller and I'll wipe the track with you."

Within five minutes, the two were jeering and cackling, both of them promising certain death to the other.

She could almost hear the snap, like the last piece that completes a puzzle, as her long-abandoned wishful thoughts dropped into place. She hadn't known how nice it would be to believe, even for an evening, that they were a family capable of careless fun.

"So, why'd you barge into the kitchen?"

"Just wanted a soda," Caleb said.

"Mmm-hmm." Matt's character took a shortcut through a tunnel. "Look out, loser." With the press of a button he launched some sort of projectile at his son's racer.

Caleb smacked his controller and the bomb, or whatever it was, bounced harmlessly to the side. "You got nothin'." He sneered as he hit a ramp and launched himself back into first place.

"That so?" Matt's character came out of nowhere, sideswiped Caleb's, and took the race.

Sputtering, Caleb whirled around. "What was that?"

"All's fair in love and gaming." Matt spread his arms wide, his smile smug and superior.

The images on the television shifted, replaying the last few seconds of the race to Caleb's theatrical dismay. "Sore winner," Caleb accused.

"No such thing," Matt said. "I am the epitome of fairness and compassion."

The utterly false statement and the grandiose way he'd delivered it left her and Caleb laughing. Maybe her son's current theatrical tendencies were genetic, too.

"One more round." Caleb turned to her. "You want in?"

"Sure." She knew how to get in the way and make her character a nuisance for both of them. "Is there a third controller?" She'd given up on maintaining the pretense about Caleb being grounded. He needed to get to know Matt, regardless of the catalyst that had put this into motion and brought them together.

"You gotta watch her," Caleb warned as he hooked up the controller for her. "Mom likes to hang back and pretend she doesn't get it, and then wham!"

"Duly noted, thanks," Matt said. When his eyes met hers, she could see him putting the warning into a decidedly personal and inappropriate context.

She started to protest and decided that gave everything that had transpired in the past few minutes too much weight.

"So, what did you really need?" Matt asked Caleb. "Earlier."

"A soda." His shoulders rose and fell. "And to see if you'd come race with me."

"Cool," Matt replied. "Go on and get a drink while we wait for her to set up."

Caleb didn't give her a chance to contradict Matt. He scrambled up and dashed to the kitchen, returning with a can of his favorite soft drink.

The two of them waited, boldly scheming against her as she chose her character. She came in dead last on the first race, beaten by Caleb, Matt and every computer-generated player, too. As she got a feel for the track, she made them pay in the next round. They were halfway through the third round when Caleb lobbed up a verbal bomb.

"So, why were you kissing Mom?"

Her character skidded off the track, but Matt stayed the course. "Seemed like the right thing to do."

"Why?" Caleb persisted.

"She wanted me to kiss her."

Shocked, she dropped the controller and it bounced under the end table. "Matt!"

"Bethany!" he mimicked.

"This isn't an appropriate topic," she protested, coming in dead last again.

Caleb faced her. "He's not the first guy I've seen you kiss."

It was a wonder her cheeks didn't just go up in flames. "That's enough," she said, pleased that her voice was steady. Caleb opened his mouth to argue and she halted him with a raised finger. "Matt is your father. Your existence makes it obvious we have an intimate history."

"Yeah, so?"

"Caleb," Matt warned. "Show some respect."

Caleb's eyes revealed his turmoil; he was angry with her and not yet sure where Matt fell in the parental hierarchy. She sympathized with his confusion, though she couldn't allow this to become a communication habit. At four, he'd asked Santa Claus for a daddy for Christmas. She'd reached out to the JAG office and learned Matt was deployed, not planning to be in the States over the holidays. Year by year, she'd given him more age-appropriate details about his father whenever he'd asked. Never a name, only the reasons they decided not to be a normal family.

Hurt and angry, she searched for a more positive response. "As I said last night, your father and I were young and we cared for each other a great deal. Matt and I chose to have separate lives for good reasons." She couldn't rebuild the trust between them if she didn't give him the truth. "Being together stirs up those old feelings," she admitted quietly. "Neither one of us is seeing anyone, so no one was hurt by our kiss. Not even you.

"Maybe this would have been easier on all of us if I'd told you earlier, given you two a chance to know each other sooner. For that, I apologize." She handed him her controller and stood up. "*Only* for that."

She walked away, pausing at the wide archway that led to the guest room. "Be sure you're in bed by eleven, Caleb."

She chose to take his mumble as agreement and closed herself in the room they would share during their time here with Matt. If her hands trembled and tears threatened, that was her problem and certainly not the first time she'd felt shaky during this journey called motherhood.

"That was rude." Matt turned off the game system and braced for a tantrum or a protest. "You owe her an apology."

Caleb surprised him. Instead of fussing or making excuses, he slumped back against the couch and balanced his hands on his drawn-up knees. "Do you love Mom again?"

Matt studied his son's face, seeing the traces of Bethany despite the puzzled expression. Bethany had been brave, so he could be, too. "I'm not sure I ever stopped," Matt confessed.

"Will you move in with us, or will we move here for real?"

If only it were that easy. "That's probably rushing things," Matt said. "Sometimes loving a person isn't enough."

"You're just saying that because I caught you making out."

"It's a factor, sure." Matt winked.

Caleb rolled his eyes. "Be serious."

"I am." Matt wouldn't insult Caleb with anything less than straight talk. One more parenting tip he'd picked up as Ben and Patricia's oldest, he supposed, as well as from Bethany's example. "You know we've talked through the years?"

"Yeah, you've said." He started picking at one of the healing scratches on his hand.

"Right. It hasn't been easy to stay out of your life," Matt said. "You're on my mind every day. Seriously," he added at Caleb's derisive snort. "No matter where I was working or training, you were on my mind. I can't tell you how hard it was to listen to other soldiers brag on their kids and not be able to jump in and set them straight." To honor Bethany's wishes and protect their secret, he'd never carried a picture of Caleb. He supposed now he could. "Naturally, thinking of you meant I was thinking of your mom, too."

"So you kissed her because she's the one that got away."

Matt didn't care for that confident tone. "Where did you get an idea like that?"

"School." Caleb shrugged.

Matt couldn't remember thinking about much more than cars, sports and girls—in that order—when he was fourteen. And at that age, his thoughts about girls didn't run as deep as "the one that got away."

"Are you going to marry her?" Caleb asked.

"Now you sound like my mom," Matt replied. He

didn't need two lectures on that particular topic on the same day.

"Well? What did you tell her?"

Matt forced a smile when he wanted to grind his teeth. "Takes two people to answer that question," he said. "Three, in this case, counting you."

"I get a vote?" Caleb hopped up on the opposite couch. "Why?"

"Your mom has always put your needs first. That won't change." In fact, Matt intended to make sure she could count on him to be a benefit in their son's life. While Caleb chewed on that, Matt changed the subject. "My mom and dad are eager to meet you."

"It's kinda cool thinking about having more grandparents," Caleb said.

By Matt's count, everyone except Bethany thought Caleb meeting his family was a great idea. If she didn't open up soon, he'd have no choice but to start digging into why she was so resistant to the idea. "When we meet them, promise not to let it all go to your head."

"What do you mean?"

"My mom's likely to smother you with attention, questions, cookies, the works. Think you can handle that?"

He lifted his chin. "I'm tough."

"Are you? I hadn't noticed," Matt joked. "It could feel like a gauntlet, especially if you factor in my brothers and sisters."

"You think they'll like me?"

"Absolutely." He'd never been more certain of anything in his life. "I'm sure they can't wait to dote on you. My parents are pretty ticked off with me about keeping you a secret, and my siblings are likely to be mad at me, too. Anything bad they say about me is a lie—remember that."

Caleb laughed. "Were you ever tempted to tell them?"

"Yes." He'd lost count of the number of times he'd picked up a phone or started an email for precisely that purpose. "Every time your mom sent me one of your school or soccer pictures."

"You have all of those?" He glanced around the room as if trying to spot any proof.

Matt nodded. "The pictures would be out if my family didn't drop in unannounced so often. I gave your mom my word I wouldn't tell them until she gave me the all clear." He stopped, realizing this wasn't an issue anymore either. "Wait right here."

He all but ran to his bedroom closet and rooted out the box filled with all the pictures and highlights Bethany had sent him through the years. Matt came back and sat down next to Caleb, placing the box on the coffee table. He removed the lid and Caleb's eyes went wide.

"Wow," he said.

Matt stood up and crossed the room, choosing two framed pictures from the bookshelf. One held a print of his parents on the boat—the first trip they'd taken after his dad retired. The other was a picture of the Riley clan, all of them disheveled and grinning after the annual Thanksgiving touch-football game. "Is your phone handy?" Matt asked, taking the pictures out of the frames. Caleb pulled it out of the front pocket of his hoodie. "Take a good picture of both of these until we can get you frames for the real photos."

"You mean it?"

"Unless you don't want them."

"No. I mean yes, please. I want them."

"Then they're yours," Matt said. His heart about to burst with happiness, Matt added Caleb's latest pictures to the frames. He carried both back to the shelf and reorganized things to make Caleb front and center.

"Thanks, Matt."

"My pleasure." He smiled, though it stung to have his son call him by his first name. He didn't blame Caleb, but he hoped that, with enough time, he'd hear his son call him Dad.

He returned to the couch and pulled out pictures one by one, urging Caleb to talk about the highlights of each school year and each soccer season. The conversation transitioned to sports and his favorite classes—science and history—and when Caleb started to yawn more than chatter, Matt sent him off to bed.

Tomorrow would be a long day. He'd called before they left Bethany's house and discussed how to proceed with Knudson. The general had called him back after he scheduled a meeting with investigators and security to review how the breach and recent incidents might be related. They would also assess the risks and solutions to keep all three of them safe moving forward, until they pinned down the source of the trouble. He knew he couldn't keep them tucked to his side indefinitely, no matter how right it felt. For tonight, he'd enjoy another night of being under the same roof with Bethany and Caleb. Almost like a real family.

He paused before he shut out the lights in the living room, marveling at how good it felt to have Caleb's pictures out where he could see them.

Sensing movement in the hall, he turned to scold

Caleb and found Bethany standing in the shadows, watching him. Wearing loose knit pants decorated with cartoon owls and a red thermal tunic, she couldn't be more tempting if she'd strolled out here in sheer lingerie. She'd braided her long hair, leaving her face unframed, and her fingers toyed with the placket of her top, her eyes wide.

He held out a hand, beckoned her closer so she could see the new pictures. "Look."

Her brow wrinkled a little as she stepped into the light. When she noticed the pictures, her eyes filled with tears, though none spilled over her lashes.

"You always know just what to do," she said, her voice as soft as silk.

He decided not to argue.

She wrapped her arms around her waist. "I've wondered for years how much damage I was doing to Caleb and tried to pretend you weren't suffering at all."

Unfortunately, *suffering* was an accurate assessment. The way she was beating herself up enough for both of them made him go with the kinder response. "Caleb isn't showing signs of being anything less than a well-adjusted kid."

Her lips curled into a soft smile. "I have extra pictures at home. I'll send them to your parents when we get back."

"That's the right way to suck up to my mom." As he had hoped, it made her laugh. She clapped a hand over her lips to smother the bright sound and glanced over her shoulder as if expecting Caleb to catch her again.

Matt drew her over to the couch, simply to keep himself from scooping her into his arms and carrying her to his bed. "Don't take this the wrong way." Unable to resist, he slipped an arm around her waist and enjoyed the sweet feeling. "I've wanted to display his pictures from day one."

"I know." She leaned her head against his shoulder. "If you want to take him next week, for his fall break, you should."

Yes, he absolutely wanted to take Caleb. Not just for a week or every other weekend. He wanted the day to day, with Caleb *and* Bethany. Anything less felt incomplete, wrong. It was the reason he'd never pushed for partial custody. After all she'd done to protect his place in West Point and subsequently his career, he couldn't bring himself to do anything that would upset her.

"We can talk about it," he hedged. She tensed, sidled away. He let her go, though it cost him. "I definitely want time with him," he assured her. "I'm not willing to break up the band before we clear up the threats." And he wasn't quite ready to trust anyone else with her safety.

"Thanks."

Gratitude wasn't what he expected. "I haven't done much. I'm counting on the investigators to find the lead."

Her hands smoothed over the back of the couch. He envied that leather upholstery. "You've stepped up without any judgment," she said. "I shouldn't be surprised."

Feeling as if they were at the edge of an important revelation, he waited for her to elaborate. Would she finally explain what she needed from him to keep him around?

"We've been tossed into a challenging situation,"

he said when the silence became uncomfortable. "This time we'll get through it together."

"All right."

He wished he could erase the dark smudges under her eyes, the small lines of stress bracketing her mouth. "Go get some sleep," he suggested. "We all need to be fresh for the interviews tomorrow."

She studied him for a brief eternity and then finally walked back to the guest room without another word.

He watched her go, wondering what she thought she saw in his face. For so long, he'd blamed himself for being the wrong guy, the guy she wouldn't trust to provide for her and their son. Either she was more trusting now that Caleb was older, or that had never been the real problem.

Matt headed to bed, his mind mulling over recent events. As much as the threats and bullets sucked, he found the silver lining in the circumstances that gave him another chance to be the father he wanted to be.

Chapter 6

Despite a restless night, Bethany rose early to shower and dress before she woke Caleb. She kept it simple, choosing black slacks and a soft white shirt. She left her hair down and saved the pumps and blazer until they were ready to walk out the door.

Determined to make a hearty breakfast for all of them, she hurried to the kitchen, only to run into Matt, who was waiting impatiently for his first cup of coffee to brew.

He turned, a self-conscious smile on his face, and her hormones danced a happy jig at the sight of that lone dimple in his cheek. Along with the rest of him. The morning greeting died on her tongue and she bit her lip to keep from sighing over the view. Hair dark and damp from a shower, the crisp scent of his soap lingering on his skin. He'd clearly pulled on the sweatpants just to grab a coffee before he dressed for the day.

"Did you sleep okay?" The dimple disappeared as his smile faded.

She nodded. "I-I was going to make breakfast."

His brown eyes lit up. "Really? That would be fantastic." His coffee done, he picked up the mug while watching her. "You look great."

She had no idea what she was wearing, too busy staring at the carved expanse of his chest, which was dusted with dark hair. "Thanks." Her fingertips tingled. She pointed to the fresh bandage, stark white against his skin. "How is that healing?"

"No worries." He stepped away from the brewer. "All ready for you." He lifted his chin toward the cabinet. "Mugs are up there." His gaze skimmed over her, his slow smile warming her as effectively as a touch. "You brought tea, right?"

"Yes." She cleared her throat and moved toward the brewer, wishing he would give her a smidge more space. Forcing her mind away from the temptation he presented, she reminded herself they were here, playing house, because someone had shot at their son. Unpleasant as it was, she had to remember she wasn't here for second chances. "Any requests?" She caught him staring at her lips. "For breakfast," she clarified quickly.

"Whatever you're in the mood to make," he said, grinning. He leaned in, kissing the corner of her mouth and taking his coffee and sexy body to his bedroom.

Dazzled, she nearly followed him.

The brewer sputtered, giving her something much safer to focus on. Sipping tea, she found the ingredients for a fast skillet hash. Caleb and Matt emerged from the bedrooms at about the same time, cued by the savory scents of fried potatoes and sausage, she was sure. They set the table while she served.

"You can expect today to be more formal than yesterday," Matt said to Caleb. "They're going to pick apart everything we've done—all of us—for the last few weeks, probably more, looking for any clues."

Caleb nodded, his eyes downcast. "I didn't mean to make such a mess by looking for Matt."

Bethany rubbed his shoulder. "This isn't your fault."

Matt reassured him, as well. "Someone used you, son. It's up to the investigators to dig in and it's up to us to give them what we can. I want you to be prepared for anything."

Bethany knew that warning was meant for her, too. Although she and Matt had lived apart for fifteen years, someone was coming at them directly, using information they shouldn't have. It would be a natural assumption that the culprit had a personal connection.

Though the overall mood was subdued as they ate, she couldn't help appreciating how sharp Matt looked in his uniform, the Army's current equivalent of a business suit. Caleb, in khaki slacks, a white button-down shirt and a tie in his school's colors of black and red, was dressed more appropriately today for a visit to the Pentagon.

"Have you apologized?" Matt asked Caleb, surprising her as they polished off breakfast.

Caleb's eyes went wide. He swallowed quickly and wiped his mouth with his napkin before turning to her. "Mom, I'm sorry for being rude last night."

"Thank you."

"I know it's not really any of my business who you kiss."

"Caleb," Matt said, exasperated.

Bethany however had caught the glint of humor in Caleb's eyes and just shook her head. "Get it out of your system now," she said. "I doubt the investigators will appreciate your jokes."

"You got it." He slid out of his chair and cleared the dishes, even loading the dishwasher. "I'll clean up while you finish getting ready."

She recognized the strategy of sucking up, but she'd rather count her blessings than argue. It would help to go into this meeting on the same page, without any additional family drama.

When they were ready to leave, Matt surprised her again, calling for a car service rather than taking the Camaro. Caleb was bummed about the choice.

"Why don't you drive?" he asked when the driver stopped at the front of the building.

"Because I love my car," Matt stated. He opened the back door for Caleb and Bethany, and when they were settled, he sat up front in the passenger seat.

The driver made quick work of the trip and as they approached the main entrance, Bethany experienced a blend of pride and trepidation. She'd visited the Pentagon for business on several occasions, but the vast complex never failed to impress her. Beside her, Caleb's nerves were evident as his hands gripped the notebook he'd brought along for the investigators. She nudged him as the car pulled to a stop and when he glanced over, she smiled encouragingly. As she'd hoped, a little tension eased from his young shoulders.

Matt guided them to the security desk and showed his credentials. Due to her clearance for work, Bethany had an active standing visit request, though she'd never thought to use it for what amounted to a family meeting with the potential for a criminal investigation. She showed her ID and entered without any issue.

Matt had arranged for Caleb's visitor pass yesterday, smoothing the path for today's visit as well. Her son's eyes were huge, and yesterday's excitement over things like finding Matt and potential bodyguards was tempered now as they made their way to the conference room General Knudson had scheduled for the appointment with investigators.

The meeting was necessary, she reminded herself, her stomach twisting while they questioned Caleb. Her son had been manipulated and shot at in front of his home. The other threats seemed weak in comparison. She listened as he laid out the timeline of when he'd been contacted through the app, and how he'd logged and resolved the clues provided. All the way up to his solo trip yesterday to track down Matt.

The investigators took his notebook as evidence, along with his usernames and passwords for his social media accounts. They had her authorize them to search through the cell phone records as well, and then they announced a short break.

Edgy, she left her chair for the tea service near the door, sneaking a peek at Matt as she passed him. Where would their son be now if he hadn't found him at Union Station? Her stomach pitched. The important thing was that Caleb was safe and they would keep him that way.

Together.

She wasn't thrilled to share how completely off her motherhood radar had been with a room full of strangers, or even Matt. The failure left a bitter taste in the back of her mouth that even sweetened tea couldn't erase. "I thought you were struggling with something at school," she said, giving his shoulder a squeeze as she returned to her chair. "I wish you'd come to me with this sooner."

"I know." Caleb frowned a little, picking at a scab on his hand. "Doing the searches was kind of like solving a puzzle. Besides, I've asked you about him," he said. "I didn't want another hero story. I wanted to know who I am."

"You're my son." She couldn't keep the words inside, couldn't keep the pain from her voice.

"I know." He sounded as miserable as she felt. "Sorry, Mom. Again."

"Stop. We can't change yesterday. We can only decide how we manage today so tomorrow is better." It was a philosophy she'd adopted from one of his soccer coaches a few years back, when the team started showing frustration over their performance on the soccer field.

"Right." He smiled, the dimple flashing briefly before the questions resumed, this time focused on her.

The original letter she'd received was still with the crime lab for processing, but they had a copy of it here with the rest of the file. Impressive, considering she'd given that to authorities in New Jersey. No doubt Matt's influence made this situation a top priority.

"I don't understand who could possibly be this concerned about Caleb's father." She bumped Caleb's knee with hers, gave him a small smile. "Other than Caleb." Somehow she'd make up for keeping his father away and they'd all get their lives back on track again.

She regretted voicing her opinion as she suddenly found herself answering pointed questions about her most recent romantic relationships in front of her son and his father. There hadn't been anyone serious in the last three years.

She wasn't exactly embarrassed by that fact; it just felt as if all of the sharing was only going in one direction. Presumably, they'd soon put all of these questions to Matt, as well. On the other side of the conference table, he maintained a perfect poker face. What upset her most was that her lack of a personal life didn't bother her. Not until she had to spell it out in front of him. And that wouldn't have mattered at all if she wasn't still so hung up on him.

That wasn't much of a secret either, considering how she'd responded when he'd kissed her.

Exasperated with herself, she left the table and went to stand at the window when they were done asking her about her friends, associates and whom she'd met on recent travels. Outside, the trees were turning colors, and as she watched them sway with a gentle breeze, she felt like she too was at a seasonal crossroads.

That kiss he'd laid on her yesterday made her lips tingle even now. Worse than Matt's flat-out declaration of his desire was the persistent tenderness and care he showed her at every turn. The way he insisted Caleb respect her, despite their son's understandable anger. With Matt pursuing his career, she'd given up on finding another man who could be her partner, as well as a good father figure for Caleb.

Then Matt had fallen into her foyer, demonstrating willingness and aptitude for both roles. When would she get past this childish longing to lean on his strong shoulder?

She tried to concentrate on his responses as the investigators quizzed him, starting with the baseball message on Monday night. It seemed to be up for debate as to who was the real target of the vague threat scribbled on the old baseball.

Neither the Metro police nor their counterparts in Virginia had found a fingerprint on the ball or a lead on the car. The Cherry Hill police had reported a similar dead end, unable to track the dark sedan after the driver had left her neighborhood.

Today's investigators didn't appear to be any closer to a motive than the other authorities. Nothing in her recent past or his had sparked a theory of who might be orchestrating these events. It was too early in the process to be impatient, yet she couldn't bear the idea of looking over her shoulder indefinitely. Being cautious, even vigilant, was fine, until paranoia kicked in.

"Are we sure the drive-by wasn't random?" she asked Matt when the meeting broke up so they could all have lunch.

"In your neighborhood?" Matt shook his head. "Not a chance."

Caleb was distracted, thoroughly involved in a conversation with one of the two Military policemen General Knudson had assigned to the three of them as an extra precaution.

She thought about all they'd discussed with the investigators. "Matt." She slowed her stride, resting her hand on his arm. "Someone drew Caleb out where anything could have happened."

"He's safe," Matt said. "We'll keep him that way."

"Yes, of course, but that isn't my point."

Matt stopped short and drew her to the side of the hallway. "What is?"

"I know you've considered the idea that all of these

incidents are about *you*. What if the goal was to bring you out into the open or bring you and Caleb together? The two of you were followed and attacked at the house within hours of Caleb finding you."

He scowled, his gaze moving up and down the hallway.

"You've thought the same thing," she pressed. "I knew it."

"Based on the timing, sure," he said. "Based on the message and where it was delivered, it's questionable."

"But not out of the realm of possibility."

"The investigators will figure it out," he said.

She clutched his sleeve. "Who would do that?"

He shook his head. "I don't know."

She saw Caleb look back for them and she and Matt moved to catch up. "We need to find time to talk about this without extra ears," she said under her breath.

"He can handle whatever we need to discuss," Matt said. "Probably best not to hide anything anymore."

The mild rebuke set off her temper like a match to dry leaves. "Whether or not he can handle it isn't the point. He shouldn't *have* to. I don't care how tall he is, he is still a child." She turned sharply, hiding her next words from Caleb. "You don't get to waltz into his life and start deciding what's best for him. You don't even know him."

Any warmth in his brown eyes went glacial and his expression shut her out as her words sunk in. *Oh, crap.* "Matt, I'm sorry."

He stopped her apology with one brutally indifferent look. "You've been clear about my role." His fingers curled around her elbow, his touch polite and cool as he guided her toward Caleb and the two MPs waiting with him to sign out.

Crap. He'd done everything right, honored her every request. She had to stop letting fear run away with her mouth. "Matt, please listen." If she could take the words back, she would. If she could rewind fifteen years, she'd do that too and give him the chance at fatherhood he'd begged for.

"Later."

She recognized that look. Of course he meant that he'd listen later, most likely at some point in time after the world stopped spinning. Well, she'd insist they talk at the first opportunity. For Caleb's sake. No, she had to be honest and hold herself accountable.

She hid her trembling hands in her pockets as they signed out to leave the building for lunch. They were nearly outside when someone called Matt's name.

They all turned, flanked by the MPs.

"Major Riley."

"Major Gadsden." The men shook hands and then embraced like old friends. "How you feeling?"

"Hundred and ten percent." The reply came with a wink and a smirk.

Bethany studied the newcomer. He had an inch or two on Matt, was lean as a whip and radiated a quiet confidence. Based on the various insignia on his uniform, she recognized he was one of the Army's elite.

"Alex," Matt said. "Meet Caleb and Bethany Trent." He turned, raising an eyebrow in query, still asking her permission. She gave a tiny nod. "My son and his mother."

Alex's tawny eyebrows jerked up toward his hairline. "Son? Interesting." He smiled broadly. "You're a little tall for a newborn." He reached out to shake Caleb's hand, and then Bethany's. "Pleasure to meet you both. Congratulations, man," he said, slapping Matt's shoulder.

"Thanks," Matt replied, a muscle twitching in his jaw.

"Should I go grab cigars?" Alex asked, utterly unrepentant. His gaze darted between her and Matt. "I'd love to hear the whole story."

"We were on our way to lunch," Matt said. "Do you have time to join us?"

"Sure." Alex walked with them outside and toward a car the MPs must have ordered for them.

Matt gave the driver the name of a restaurant and slid across the back seat. Caleb followed and then Bethany. Alex sat up front. Bethany figured Matt was tremendously relieved to have bumped into a friend as a buffer. She couldn't blame him.

Driving off, Alex commented on the security team on a motorcycle and in another car following them. "I'm guessing this escort and red-carpet treatment is one of the perks of working for General Knudson. You're not going soft on me, are you Riley?"

"You wish," Matt drawled.

Caleb started to pipe up and she tapped his knee to keep him quiet. The men were friends and it was up to Matt how much he wanted to share.

"I can't believe it. You're a glorified desk jockey." Alex shuddered and winked at Caleb. "I'm still rated for fieldwork," he said, clearly boasting for maximum effect.

"What kind of fieldwork, Mr. Gadsden?" Caleb asked.

"Major," Bethany corrected him quietly.

"You know, I like the sound of Uncle Alex." He grinned brightly. "Your dad and I go way back."

Bethany wondered if the two men went back far enough that he'd confided in Alex about Caleb, though his surprise at the introductions had seemed real. She was curious that he was taking their sudden appearance so well.

"We met in Airborne School," Matt explained.

"He wasn't this gloomy then," Alex assured them. His shrewd gaze landed on Bethany. "How did *you* meet Matt?"

"We met while he was at West Point." It seemed the most neutral explanation.

Alex opened his mouth to ask something else and Matt cut him off. "How long will you be in town?"

"I've got some irons in the fire," Alex replied. "Figured we could talk about it over a beer tonight if you're game."

"Why not come over to the condo for dinner?" Bethany offered. "I'll cook."

"Greek chicken?" Caleb asked.

"Hush." She elbowed him lightly. "I was thinking chicken parmesan."

"Please!" Caleb bounced a little in his seat. "Hers is the best."

"With a salad," she added.

He deflated a smidge, and then brightened again. "And garlic bread?"

"Please?" Alex chuckled. "Come on, Dad." He sent an overblown pleading look Matt's way. "Say yes."

Bethany could see the wheels turning in Matt's mind. Over her earlier insult or the general trouble, she wasn't sure. Did it even matter? She needed to find time to clear the air, even if admitting what scared her left her vulnerable to him.

"Caleb and I can amuse ourselves elsewhere after dinner while you two catch up."

Matt exchanged a long, speaking look with Alex and made his decision. "Dinner at the condo is fine." The car pulled to a stop at the corner closest to the restaurant to drop them off. "For now, let's grab a burger before we have to get back in there."

With the security team keeping watch, Matt should have felt safe, but he didn't. Alex alone was more lethal than a platoon of MPs and yet Matt couldn't relax and enjoy the food and conversation. His restless anxiety went deeper than the recent security issues. He tried chalking it up to having family close enough to touch. They were his responsibility now, whether they wanted to be or not.

He snuck a glance at Bethany. Yeah, he had a family all right. And like the family he'd grown up with, she could drop him more effectively with a few well-placed words rather than the weapons he knew how to defend against.

Shifting in his seat, the healing wound on his ribs complained, making him wince.

"Are you okay?" Bethany queried, low enough that only he could hear.

"Fine," he muttered. She backed off and somehow he felt like an ass.

Alex was right. He was gloomy. Well, too bad. He was entitled. For years, he'd prayed Bethany would relent so he could get to know his son. Now that she had, it wasn't going at all as he'd envisioned. Threats or not, he hadn't expected to get slapped for stepping up.

Maybe she didn't want to accept it, and maybe it was a burden, but their son could handle them being open about the dangers and plans. Look what had happened when they'd let him draw his own conclusions.

Caleb had inhaled his burger, and after a brief discussion, he and Bethany had gone to the ice-cream counter at the back of the restaurant to order milkshakes for all of them. It was a gorgeous day outside and Matt wanted Caleb to have a few memories of DC that didn't involve Pentagon conference rooms and investigators.

"So, Miss Trent is the one who's kept you tied in knots all these years?" Alex's gaze followed mother and son as he popped the last fry into his mouth. "Any potential?"

"No idea," Matt lied, thinking of that kiss. He swallowed a sigh. There was potential, if the way she'd ogled him this morning was any indication. Too bad sex wasn't all he wanted. Regardless, they wouldn't make any progress until Bethany let down her guard. "It seems one-sided," he said. "Factor in the catalyst for our reunion was a security breach, and it's just layer after layer of bad timing and distorted expectations. He's nearly fifteen." Matt balled up his napkin in his fist. "I've missed everything."

"Not true," Alex countered. "The kid is smart, athletic and polite. She raised a mini version of you, man."

And she'd made it clear she intended to finish the job on her own. "Whatever." This wasn't the time or place to get into all of that.

Alex changed the subject. "About that catalyst." He

double-checked they wouldn't be interrupted and then slid his cell phone across the table.

The display showed a picture of Matt, Bethany and Caleb at the restaurant in Philadelphia, where they'd stopped for cheesesteaks. Whoever had taken the picture had either been just outside the restaurant or using an excellent telephoto lens. Though it was a logical assumption that he'd been followed—at the very least to the house—he hadn't forgotten the same sensation of being watched from the moment Caleb arrived at Union Station.

"Where did you get this?" Matt asked through the dread pooling in his stomach.

"Your dad received it," Alex said. "He asked me to come up here to help you unravel what's going on."

Matt smothered a violent oath behind his hand. "Let me guess, the picture came through, along with some vague threat about making him pay."

"Pretty much." Alex sat back in his chair. "What do I need to know?"

This is the second time in two days his parents had been dragged into this, first by the media and now directly. Matt looked around the restaurant, searching for anyone taking undue interest in them. "He reported it, right?"

"He did. After he sent a copy to me. It should catch up with the investigators by the end of the day. I'm here to help devise and execute a plan as needed."

Seeing Caleb and Bethany heading back to the table, loaded with treats, Matt forced a smile to his face. "You know, I thought the worst of this breach would be the potential for identity theft."

"Right there with ya," Alex muttered. "I'm not sure

I believe in such a thing as online security or integrity anymore." He turned and gave mother and son a big grin. "But that right there is the silver lining."

Matt agreed. "Better believe it." He picked up the tab for the meal and then the four of them headed out to the park, milkshakes in hand, the security team sticking close.

As they walked along the trail, he did his best to avoid Bethany without being too obvious about it. Alex picked up on his intention and monopolized her attention, leaving Matt and Caleb to chat uninterrupted.

Still, his attention naturally drifted toward her like a moth to a flame. Since she'd left West Point to have Caleb, he'd been forced to put their relationship away, all his dreams stored on a shelf in the back of his mind, where he could ignore it at least half the time. Much harder to keep that box shelved when she was within easy reach. Her smile hadn't changed and neither had his pleasure when she shared that smile with him.

Right now, she was laughing at whatever nonsense Alex was spouting and Matt felt a ridiculous spurt of jealousy.

What could he do to convince her to give him a real chance? They were older and still attracted to each other. He'd never gotten over her and he'd experienced a perverse satisfaction when she told the investigators she hadn't been seriously involved with anyone for some time now.

Did that leave an opening for him, or was he getting lost in another pipe dream? Pipe dream, he decided. Her priorities hadn't changed. She remained as independent as ever, career-minded and determined to give Caleb a normal, suburban life. He didn't want to change any of those things about her; he just wanted to be welcome within that tight, protective circle.

He wanted the right to state his opinion about what was best for his son.

Matt glanced at Caleb, who was chattering away about an upcoming soccer tournament in Maryland. His brown hair was tousled, shot with gold from all his time on soccer fields. He was lanky and, though it probably wasn't possible, it seemed as if he'd grown an inch since they met on Monday.

"This will all be over by then, right?"

Matt couldn't make that promise. "I hope so. Either way, we'll have a workable solution established by then."

"Awesome." He slurped at his milkshake. "Will you come watch me?"

"I wouldn't miss it," Matt replied immediately.

Caleb's happy smile rivaled the sun shining overhead. "Great! I'll tell Mom." He jogged ahead to share the news with Bethany and she managed to get in a quick hug before he turned and jogged back.

Matt's pride and love for his kid swelled in his chest. Yeah, whatever success he might or might not have rekindling a relationship with Bethany, Caleb was his silver lining. He might have missed fourteen years, but he could make sure he was around from this point forward.

In those few seconds when Caleb was loping along the path alone, Matt saw the red dot of a laser sight on his son's chest. He opened his mouth to shout a warning only to see a second red dot appear dead-center on Bethany's back.

No! "Gadsden!" He tapped his chest and motioned for his friend to shield Bethany as he moved to shelter Caleb.

Noticing the dots as well, the security team closed around them, calling the situation in and requesting backup. Their swift response assured Matt he wasn't seeing things induced by paranoia. The menacing dot held steady on Caleb, no matter what Matt tried. He spun in a circle, trying to locate the origin of the laser. In the daylight, it was nearly impossible.

He simultaneously sought the source of the threat and a place of safety for his son as chills skated over his skin. He'd known fear in combat, had felt helpless multiple times and fought through both for the sake of the mission and his men.

This was different. He wasn't on a battlefield, surrounded by a team of trained and willing soldiers. This particular threat against his innocent family in broad daylight outraged him. There were high-rises on two sides of the park. To keep this kind of angle, the shooters had to be nested on an upper floor.

"Matt, you're clear."

He turned toward Alex's voice. Security had managed to squeeze them together between a cluster of trees and an open basketball court with access to the bordering street, cutting off the angle of the laser sights.

Bethany and Caleb were pale, but protected. Matt began to stand up, intending to circle around and confirm they weren't in imminent danger, when Alex stopped him with a look.

"No more signs of sights?"

"You're clear, man."

Bethany's dark brown eyes were brimming, her lashes spiked with the tears she couldn't hold back. Caleb's hands shook, though he tried to hide it. Matt wrapped the two of them in his arms and just let himself hold on.

They were alive and they would stay that way.

Two black SUVs arrived, both emblazoned as the property of the US Army. A team in full gear, from helmets to bulletproof vests, weapons at the ready, poured out of one vehicle and surrounded them.

They were shepherded into the first vehicle, where a driver and two armed guards waited. The doors had barely closed when the driver sped away from the scene, lights flashing and a siren wailing.

Alex wasted no time. "What did you see?" he asked Matt.

"Red laser sight on Caleb and a second one on Bethany." It hurt to say it aloud. "You?"

"There was a red dot on your chest," Caleb's voice shook.

He glanced at Alex, caught the nod. He'd had no idea he too had been a target. He pulled his son close, looked over the boy's head to Bethany. She nodded, started to speak, and then pressed her lips together as if the outcome would be different if she gave her fears a voice.

Matt had known Alex for most of his career and he'd never seen his friend quite this rattled. Both men understood the complexity of painting all three of them at once in a public park. It hardly mattered that no shots had been fired. The implications had been loud and clear. They were alive, only because someone had allowed them to get away.

The terror of it had been too real and Matt was sure that had been the point. After this, he had to wonder if getting nicked by the bullet at Bethany's house had been an accident, a mistake on the shooter's part.

"Goes without saying that whoever started this has my full attention," Matt said. "And I'm done with being half a step behind."

"Amen," Alex muttered.

"First we need a safe place," Matt said, thinking out loud. "I won't have them in harm's way again."

"Caleb and I could go—"

Matt nipped that suggestion with an oath. "I will not allow the person responsible for this sick stunt to divide and conquer this family."

Over Caleb's head, her rounded eyes and mouth were almost comical. Better if she'd just accept he was staking his claim. Caleb burrowed closer, shamelessly seeking comfort from Matt while still holding his mom's hand.

"Your condo building is ideal," Alex said, getting back to the most critical issue of safety. "Controlled access, good observation locations and emergency egress options."

"Works for me." Matt wondered if a surveillance team would find evidence that he'd been watched by others who'd been involved with this attack on his way of life.

"I still don't understand *why* we've been targeted," Bethany murmured.

"Every action is a clue," Matt said. "Safe location decided. What's next?"

Alex's gray eyes glowed with anticipation. "Once we're set up in the condo, we get to work."

He disconnected the update call and downloaded the video that had come through via an email.

Oh, the spotters had done an excellent job documenting the entire attack. The man running this crew had chosen well and proven himself worth every penny. The most impressive point logistically was how swiftly the marksmen had found positions to tag all three of the eventual victims. The woman was less important to him, but seeing how much she mattered to Major Riley, it could be worth it to adjust the initial plan.

The more torture he could inflict on anyone named Riley, the better.

He flipped a switch, and a painting on the interior wall of his office slid aside to reveal his full timeline. There were notes, paths based on expected results, options and contingencies. Did he have the time to make Matt suffer, and thereby cause General Riley to suffer?

He came around the desk, teeth gritted against the pain that speared from hip to shoulder with every step. Worth it. The reminder of what was at stake kept him focused on the ultimate prize.

He stared at the picture of General Riley, top center of the board. As nice as it would be to torture Riley's oldest child, he couldn't see that it would cause the general enough pain to alter the timeline. He made a note, just in case that scenario changed. The woman was the mother of Riley's only grandchild.

Returning to his desk, he let the video play again. Oh, this was almost as good as being there. This video marked the best minutes of his life since the disaster. He let it run, hit Replay again and again.

The panic, the unadulterated helplessness on Major Riley's face filled him with a bittersweet joy.

"Yes, look all you want, Major. Use your training and your tools. You won't find me." He was protected behind layers not even the Military's top experts knew to look for. Yet. His anonymity wouldn't last. Wasn't designed to.

He would pull back the veil himself soon enough. Because when General Riley's world was in shambles and everyone he loved destroyed, he wanted to look the general in the eye and make sure he understood just who had inflicted so much misery.

Then he would end it. For both of them.

He made a few minor edits to the video and then uploaded it to the cloud storage he'd set for the team. Picking up his desk phone, he punched two numbers and waited.

"Sir?"

"The new video is ready for distribution."

"Yes, sir."

"Move toward the next stage at will."

"Yes, sir."

The line went dead and he dropped the receiver back into the cradle. That was the loyalty, the willing obedience men like General Riley wished for.

And yet, he was the one who had the devoted followers, not the general. He alone commanded the enthusiastic men and women eager to carry out whatever order he uttered. Leaning back in his chair, he closed his eyes, imagining the final moments ahead for Major Riley and his holier-than-thou father.

Chapter 7

Bethany didn't breathe easy again until they reached Matt's condo without further incident. Although the drive had taken only a few minutes, to her panicked mother's heart, it had felt like hours. Matt and Alex made phone calls to their superiors and she didn't pretend to understand all of the information exchanged. It seemed she walked a tightrope between useless tears and blind rage.

They were safe now, just as Matt had promised. While she and Caleb changed into casual clothes, Matt and Alex had hauled a poker table out of a closet and set it up at the far corner of the living area, near the balcony doors. Relieved and delighted to be safe, her emotions kept circling back around to vengeance. She wanted a clear target and a chance to reclaim control over this spiraling situation.

She let Caleb settle with Matt's video game system. Still shaking, she didn't put any restrictions on his choices, but she was secretly pleased when he chose the animated racing game they'd played last night rather than one of the first-person shooters she'd noticed in Matt's collection.

It took all of her willpower not to hover over him, to keep her hands to herself when all she wanted was to touch him, to reassure herself they were safe and whole. Due to the angles in the park, she hadn't seen any laser sights on her baby, only Matt's reactions. Inexplicably, that made it worse. When she closed her eyes, she saw the fleeting shock on his face, giving way in a blink to flat-out protective determination. She'd heard him shouting orders, watched him leap into action to shield Caleb.

Then, before she'd been able to process the crisis, the red laser sight had settled on Matt and she'd waited, a scream of denial lodged in her throat, a prayer for his survival beating wildly in her heart. In those interminable moments, she was sure he'd be killed in front of Caleb. In front of her.

The rest was a blur with Alex bodily moving her behind some semblance of shelter and being escorted to the escape vehicle. *What had happened to the MPs?* she wondered belatedly. How had a leisurely walk in the park turned into such a nightmare? She swiped at the stinging sensation in her nose. The danger had passed and this wasn't the time for tears.

From the kitchen, she watched Caleb game, the color coming back into his face slowly as the wholesome distraction took the hard edge off their ordeal. Seeking her own distraction and some proactive way to push aside the lingering fear that followed her like a cloud, she took a full inventory of Matt's pantry and assembled a grocery list.

As promised, chicken parmesan would headline the

menu tonight, along with salad and the requested garlic bread. The items needed for dinner topped her list. Greek chicken wasn't her only culinary accomplishment, contrary to her son's teasing.

Still, she wanted to do something special, a personal way to express her gratitude to both Alex and Matt for saving them all.

Matt's kitchen was stocked well enough that she knew he cooked frequently, though he was missing a few key ingredients for what she had in mind tonight. Two bottles of wine, Matt's favorite beer and Caleb's favorite soft drink rounded out the list. She passed through the living room, paused to kiss Caleb on the top of the head despite her best intentions to let him be and cautiously interrupted Matt as he worked with Alex to connect computers and monitors Alex had brought in with him.

"The grocery list is ready," she said.

Matt looked up and in his eyes she saw a reflection of her own tightly leashed worry. He might have only been a hands-on father for a few days, but there was no longer any doubt in her mind about his commitment or dedication to the role.

Alex nipped the list from her hand. "I'll make sure this gets handled right away." He read over it and looked up again, smiling. "Garlic bread. You remembered."

It was the lighthearted break she needed. "Thanks."

Alex reviewed the rest of the list and gave Matt a little shove. "She's a keeper, man."

Matt, his eyes locked with hers, nodded. "I've always thought so."

His molten gaze sent a bolt of need through her

system. Residual adrenaline, she told herself before she crawled into his lap. Memories of their brief, hot encounters in college, of his ropy muscles and sexy smirk as he teased her flashed through her mind. With that look in his eyes, she was sure being in his arms again would be exponentially better now that they'd both matured.

She licked her lips and his eyes tracked the movement. If she didn't find some self-control soon, she'd be kissing him again, heedless of Caleb and Alex.

"Let me know if either of us can help you," she said, eager to withdraw to a safe distance again.

"Hold on a second." Matt snapped his fingers and Alex gave him the grocery list. Watching her, he tipped his head toward Caleb, a query in his dark eyes.

She nodded, though she wasn't precisely sure what he was asking this time. It didn't matter. She owed him the benefit of the doubt, not just as the first step in making up for her earlier outburst, but because he was Matt. He'd never push or prod Caleb, never ask him to cope with a situation he couldn't handle.

The realization felt incredible. It was the first time in her life she felt as if she had a true partner in this parenting adventure.

"Hey, Caleb?" He walked over to the couch. "I need a hand."

Caleb paused the game immediately and set the controller aside to give Matt his full attention. Bethany felt a twinge of envy over the instant obedience.

"We need someone to send in this grocery order so we can eat tonight. You text faster than the rest of us combined."

"Probably." Caleb replied with a smirk, though it hadn't been a question.

Matt chuckled as he did something with his cell phone. "Here, use my phone." He handed it over. "The app is easy to navigate and my credit card is preloaded for checkout. If you have any issues, just ask."

"It won't be any problem," Caleb promised.

"Appreciate it." Matt walked back over to join Alex at the computers.

Bethany could see the difference the request made already. Matt was including him and empowering him. The small task meant he was part of the team, contributing in a way that mattered. Whether or not he saw through the effort, the concept of teamwork would be familiar to Caleb and restore his sense of control, despite the chaos at the park.

As Matt passed by, she caught his hand, gave it a little squeeze of gratitude. She was starting to see what her choices had denied all three of them. Could she ever make it up to the two of them?

"Make sure that garlic bread is in the cart before you place the order," Alex said.

"You got it, Uncle Alex." Caleb glanced up and she saw the happiness edging out the fear and stress in his gaze. Her heart swelled with still more gratitude to the man who'd put it there.

While they waited for the grocery delivery, she let Caleb school her on a few of the more challenging tracks with the promise that, once the supplies arrived, he'd take on the role of sous chef for the evening.

To her son's great delight, she let him have a soda as they started by making dessert. "Cookies again?"

His enthusiasm lifted her spirits immensely. "Your

dad's favorite, in fact." She used the *dad* word deliberately, planting that permanence into Caleb's head, in addition to affirming the relationship Matt deserved to have with his son.

"Chocolate chip?" Caleb asked.

"That's his second favorite." Chocolate chip had been bumped to second place when she'd shared the snickerdoodles her mother sent in a care package. "He might have a new favorite by now. Regardless, we're making a batch of both."

"Why?"

"We have plenty of time." And it would keep her busy. Much like Caleb and his games, she needed a happy distraction. "And we don't know what Alex prefers."

"You should've asked."

"You're right," she agreed. "Next time I will." Working from the recipe she'd pulled up on her phone, Caleb mixed the cinnamon and sugar in a bowl and then helped her by adding and clearing away ingredients for the snickerdoodle dough.

Together they shaped the cookies and rolled them through the cinnamon sugar. Matt only had two cookie sheets and one cooling rack, but they managed.

When the last of the snickerdoodles were in the oven, she washed the mixing bowls and utensils so they could start on the chocolate chip cookies.

"Will you tell me how you and Matt met?" Caleb said as the mixer blended the butter and sugars.

"You just heard that story the other day."

He hitched a shoulder and a frown tugged at his mouth. "I know. I thought maybe I'm just remembering it as lamer than it really was." Though he gave it a valiant effort, the grin broke through.

"Brat."

"I get it from you."

"Hmm." With the dough blended, she had him stir in the chocolate chips, purposely ignoring how many of the chips wound up in his mouth.

"Why didn't you ever tell me you went to West Point?" he asked.

Taking the finished snickerdoodles out of the oven, Bethany placed them on the rack while he picked more leftover chocolate chips from the bag. "Because I didn't finish. It's about honor," she said. "They take the honor code very seriously at West Point."

Getting pregnant wasn't exactly in line with the honor code and expected behavior. Cadets were taught to demonstrate single-minded focus and commitment to the academy system. If she'd taken the offered leave of absence in order to return, she risked someone finding out the baby was Matt's. Not to mention missing out on most of Caleb's first three years. Changing schools was the best of her options, and she didn't harbor regrets over taking that road.

"You can get in trouble if you fail to report another cadet violating the honor code," she added.

"That's intense. Quit stalling and tell me the story again."

If he needed the story again, it was the least she could do. "We were in the same class block," she began. "I appreciated his contributions in class and agreed to form a study group with him and a few other cadets later that first week."

"A weekly group date," he said thoughtfully. "Smart move."

She chuckled. She hadn't looked at it as a move back then, but she supposed it could have been. "Move or not, it was practical. The classes were demanding."

"It was a move." He pointed at her. "You knew it. You've got the mushy face." Caleb made a horrible, exaggerated moonstruck face.

"Well, it's a good memory," she said defensively.

"Uh-huh." Caleb pounced on the beater she'd set aside while she dropped cookie dough onto the baking sheets.

"You did ask."

He rolled his eyes, though he didn't backpedal. "How could you even tell each other apart in the uniforms?" At her look, he tilted his head toward the living room. "I saw the pictures. Everyone looks the same."

He couldn't be more wrong. Matt's smile, the stern, square jaw and ever-ready glint of humor lurking in his brown eyes stood out. His confidence radiated like a beacon, whether he was at parade rest or striding down a hallway. "You just learn, I guess," she evaded.

Caleb snorted and reached to grab a snickerdoodle from the cooling rack. She nudged him back with her hip. "You've had enough cookies and cookie dough before dinner."

"Not me." Alex had come into the kitchen for water, completely unnoticed. With an unrepentant grin, he swiped two cookies from the rack, popping one into his mouth. "Mm. Appetizer," he mumbled, walking out.

"Real appetizers will be ready in just a few minutes," she called after him. "Time to pick up the pace," she said to Caleb. "Call it—cookies or appetizers."

"Cookies!"

"No sneaking the dough."

He laughed as he took over dropping cookie dough onto the baking sheet. "When did he ask you out?" Caleb queried. "On a real date, I mean."

Bethany gave him a quick glance as she washed pears and sliced them into thin wedges for the antipasti platter. This too had been asked and answered over that first dinner as a family. Maybe the shock of the drive-by had blurred the details. Or maybe, she wondered with a fresh concern, he had a different reason.

With her maternal intuition in high gear, she proceeded to wrap paper-thin prosciutto around cheese and the pear slices and told him again how Matt had arranged everything so it felt like they were on a private date, even though they'd been surrounded by all their friends.

She knew Caleb was listening intently, taking it all in as he dealt with the cookies going in and out of the oven. Who did he have his eye on? Maybe Andrea or Tina would have an idea, or know who to ask. Better not to intrude on his privacy just yet, she decided. At not-quite-fifteen, he couldn't get into too much trouble between his school load and soccer practice.

What was she thinking? This was the boy who'd tracked down his dad with only a few clues and the help of the internet. Bethany made a mental note to listen more closely the next time Caleb chatted about his friends.

With the antipasti platter ready, she carried it out to Matt and Alex. They'd transformed the poker table and computers into an impromptu command center. Tempted to ask about their progress on a surveillance or security plan, she kept her queries to herself when she noticed the way they both scowled at whatever was on the computer screen.

She left the tray within easy reach. "To tide you over," she said.

Neither man did more than grunt an acknowledgement. What sort of threat had them looking so grim? Hurrying back to the kitchen, she put all her attention to the task of the meal. Too bad her brain wasn't ready to give up on the puzzle of who was terrorizing them. Although speculating only made her nervous and didn't accomplish anything, she couldn't seem to shut down her mind.

Matt's side burned where the bullet grazed him. It was the power of suggestion more than anything else. He and Alex had been reviewing all the footage available, from the drive-by witness video to the street cameras they'd accessed around the park. They'd skimmed through his service record, unable to come up with anyone with a grudge against him to support such aggressive measures.

Who could gain from these stunts?

"This is a big old box of nothing helpful." He pushed back from the table and stalked to the sliding glass door. Mad, frustrated and plagued by the savory scents from the kitchen, he walked out onto the balcony that spanned the full length of condo. He had a table and chairs out here, along with a big grill and a lounge. Beyond the railing, the city sparkled and boats rested gently in the marina below. To the north and east were places a sniper might hide. Someone might even have a decent shot from out in the channel.

Take a shot, he thought, mentally inviting the bastard who'd tagged Bethany and Caleb with laser sights to try it. *Quit messing with my family and take the shot.* He felt Alex behind him, heard the whisper of the glass door closing.

"You know, I forgot about this monster." Alex petted the stainless steel cover of the grill. We should teach my new nephew how to grill a steak." He leaned his forearms on the rail next to Matt. "You're an idiot to stand out here for target practice."

"If you're afraid, leave," Matt grumbled.

"Me, I'd want a clean shot at you and the grill." He angled his head, his gaze following the march of balconies on the nearest building to the most likely floor. "It'd be awesome to blow the propane tank and call your murder an accident."

"You call this helping?" Matt demanded.

"Something else you'd rather talk about?"

Matt pushed his hands over his hair, linked them behind his head. "A couple of things, actually."

"Would those things be named Bethany and Caleb?"

"No." Matt dropped his hands back to his sides. With his family, the answers should be obvious and weren't. He couldn't get anywhere with Bethany until he could convince her that he didn't pose a risk to them. "I'm stuck on who and why."

Alex gave an exasperated sigh. "We aren't the only team looking for a lead. Something will break open."

"She baked my favorite cookies." His mind muddled, Matt changed the subject as though Alex hadn't spoken. He needed a sounding board. "Made appetizers and is working on chicken parm for dinner. She does thoughtful things one minute and then pulls back the next. What is so wrong with me?" He couldn't accept that his first chance with Bethany was the last.

"Did you want that in a standard essay or a series of GIFs?"

"Shut up."

"Don't forget the beer," Alex said, needling him.

"Shut up," Matt repeated. He hadn't forgotten she'd stocked up on his favorite beer. "She ties me up."

"Now you're just bragging."

"Alex, be serious." His frustration ebbing on a gritty laugh, he understood why his dad asked Alex to be here. The man was an elite warrior with an irreverent sense of humor. If anyone could bring Matt balance and perspective in addition to security, it was Alex.

"You're serious enough for a battalion." His best friend gave him a shove. "It's screwed up, I'll give you that. Hiding a kid from you all this time is wrong. But the way she looks at you? That's right. That's something special."

He wanted to believe that it was a glimmer of promise and hope he saw when he looked into Bethany's gorgeous eyes. He wanted to believe he could break down the walls she'd built to keep him out. Every nerve in his body urged him to hold her, to lay siege and never let her surrender. "I've known about Caleb from the start," Matt told him.

"Get out. How…when…?" Alex closed his mouth against the sputtering questions.

"She insisted on raising him alone. I met him for the first time on Tuesday. He's fourteen!" Matt shouted the number, giving free rein to the bubble of anger that rose up, popped and dissipated instantly. "I have every right to be furious," he said, his control back.

"You aren't." Alex turned his back on the view to study Matt. "Not really."

"I am," Matt insisted, though he wasn't convincing either one of them. "She gave up her Military career for me, to raise Caleb. She left West Point to protect my career."

"Impressive."

Matt closed his eyes, rocking back on his heels. It had been more than impressive. He continued to be proud of all she'd done on her own and equally frustrated by the limits she'd placed on him.

"What's the target?" Alex asked. "The kid?"

"Family," Matt replied.

"Well, sure. It's how you're built."

"Right." Matt couldn't argue, but he was driven by more than expectation and duty. Not that he'd ever convinced Bethany of his intentions and sincere affection for *her*. He inhaled deeply, dragging in clean river air that mixed with the pungent scents of industry around them. Gripping the balcony rail, he squeezed hard. "I've wanted to know Caleb from the start." Expressing that willingness had never been enough for Bethany to allow it. She'd been so sure that a meeting would cause too much confusion for their son. He'd felt that a legal battle for visitation would be worse for everyone, so he toed the line she'd drawn. "I could have exercised my rights."

"Once you graduated, anyway." Alex waited another beat. "You still have rights."

"True." Discussing paternal rights with her when his anger was this close to the surface would backfire. "He asked me if I wanted him." His heart still stung, just thinking his kid had to wonder over such a question.

"You were cut from the finest fatherhood cloth, man."

Matt nodded. "We were young and stupid," he said, knowing that much was obvious to Alex already. "But it wasn't wimpy puppy love."

"You still love her," Alex stated.

"I do," he replied, though it wasn't a question. "Caleb asked me the same thing last night."

"In a 'what are your intentions with my mother' way?"

That made Matt pause and think. He grinned. "Yeah, I think so."

"Nature over nurture," Alex said. "My nephew is definitely a Riley."

Matt's momentary good mood slipped away. "You should have heard the lecture Mom gave me. Like it had been my choice to keep him a secret from her all this time."

Alex gave a low whistle, having come to know Patricia well through the years. "So, no one beyond the JAG office and the clearance investigators knew about Caleb or the child support you paid Bethany?"

"No." He thought back to the comment Bethany made as they'd left the Pentagon conference room. "She thinks whoever contacted Caleb wanted to draw me out, maybe even put the two of us in the same place on purpose."

"When you're not in the Pentagon, you're pretty accessible, right?"

"I think so. It's not as if I live behind a gate and guard tower." Matt planted his hands on his hips. He'd worn his uniform to the Pentagon meeting, as he did every day. After the stunt in the park, both he and

Alex had ditched their coats as soon as they were inside the condo. Matt had rolled back his sleeves to the elbow, tossing aside dress code within his home. "I would have sworn we were followed from Union Station on Tuesday."

Alex, ever-ready with a joke, immediately shifted to his focused, serious-warrior mode. "You didn't think to mention that to anyone?"

"I have." He'd shared it during this morning's meeting. "Nothing solid to point to and it's hard to get a lead from a hunch."

"We need to review the security feed at the station."

"They said the same thing." Matt didn't see the point. "Who has time to watch thousands of passersby for someone eyeing Caleb and me? I was in uniform, you know that draws more attention."

Alex swore. "The point is, if someone wanted to take a shot at you, there have been plenty of opportunities."

"Makes me wonder why there haven't been more bullets." In a subtle move, he eased the tugging of the bandage at his ribcage. "Without a motive, I don't know where to look or what to do next, and I won't take a chance with the two of them."

"You could keep them under house arrest here."

Matt shot him a glare. "You've met Bethany. She isn't going to put up with this chaos for long." It was a pipe dream at best, thinking he could convince her to move in, play house and test-drive the family deal. Even if the recent attacks didn't screw up that dynamic, he wanted more than a few weeks of playing. He wanted the real deal. For life.

He cleared his throat, pulled his thoughts back to

the immediate concerns. "Besides that, Caleb has to go back to school, his soccer team and his normal routine soon."

"Say she's right and someone wanted to put you and Caleb on the same street to wreak havoc. Who are the likely suspects?"

"That's the million-dollar question." Matt glanced down, almost wishing to see the red dot of a laser sight on his chest. Once they'd set up the computers, they'd contacted the investigations team and given full reports on the incident in the park. He and Alex had scoured the camera feeds, looking for questionable dark sedans, familiar faces and anyone who'd been aiming a cell phone or anything that might be a laser pointer in their general direction. They kept coming up empty.

Turning away from the view, he watched Bethany and Caleb through the glass door. She moved with the confidence he remembered, but there was another layer to it now, both softer and stronger. She wore motherhood well. Something in his chest clicked as he took in the homey scene. Why couldn't she admit how well they fit with him, here or anywhere, as long as they were together?

If only he trusted those flashes of desire that heated her beautiful eyes and colored her cheeks. He wanted her more than ever. All of her, body, heart and soul. He couldn't settle for a fling in the middle of a crisis.

"We need a lead." It seemed whoever was doing this was ghosting through the world, using tools too common to be helpful, untraceable clues, from the choice of vehicles to the social media apps. "Someone filmed that drive-by, sent it to the networks," he said, thinking out loud.

"And sent that snapshot from Philly to your dad," Alex reminded him.

"For me, that puts a wrinkle in the whole thing." Matt caught his frown in the reflection off the glass. He turned away before Bethany caught the expression and assumed the worst. "Why involve him?"

"To put a wrinkle in it and throw you off."

Matt rolled his shoulders, conceding that point. "None of it follows what I know about a standard escalation pattern, yet this doesn't feel disorganized."

"Look, anyone who's this persistent will make a mistake," Alex said. "My guys are out there now, in addition to the team assigned by General Knudson."

"That doesn't feel like enough of a plan." Matt plucked at his shirt. "I won't let someone's particular brand of crazy take shots at them when I'm right here."

"All the more reason to go inside." Alex studied the surrounding area as the last of the daylight faded. "We aren't likely to get anything more tonight. Let my team finish the recon, let the investigators process what they have. It'll look better tomorrow."

"Go on in," Matt said, not quite ready to withdraw the unspoken challenge of standing here unprotected.

"Not without you. If you take another bullet, it will wreck dinner, and it smells phenomenal in there."

"You're not staying for dinner," Matt decided. So what if it was selfish? He wanted Bethany and Caleb all to himself, no joking uncles allowed.

Alex's jaw dropped in mock horror. "I *am*. She made garlic bread for *me*."

"You have an excuse. Go find your team and track down a lead."

Alex clapped a hand to Matt's shoulder, shaking his head. "You're lucky I love you, man."

"You're my best friend," Matt agreed, wondering what he was getting at.

"For that reason alone, I'm staying through dinner. And dessert."

Matt would have protested again, but Alex was inside, tossing out compliments at Bethany like confetti and volunteering to set the table for her. Idiot, Matt thought, uncertain which of them deserved the insult more.

Dinner was fantastic and, thanks to Alex, the conversation never lagged or veered down troubling or awkward territory. He amused Caleb with stories of their triumphs and foibles during Airborne School and out on various shooting ranges. It wasn't lost on anyone at the table when Alex took all the glory and pinned any faults or blame on Matt. Still, the gleam of laughter in Caleb's eyes seemed divided equally between father and honorary uncle.

He doubted Caleb's real aunts and uncles would show the same gracious understanding over his secret as Alex. Thinking about making those calls put a knot between his shoulder blades. He was actually surprised he wasn't already fielding phone calls from his siblings. He'd expected his mother to spread the news through the family tree immediately.

He rubbed at the low-grade throbbing in his temples.

Alex cleared the table and started on cleanup. Caleb, his curiosity insatiable, pitched in just to hear more stories about Matt.

Bethany remained in her seat across from him. Matt balled up his napkin. Her unspoken questions hovered in the air between them. She deserved answers. Unfortunately, he couldn't see a clear path on any front.

"Coffee?" She offered.

He looked up into her concerned gaze and shook his head. "I'll be up all night anyway."

"Caffeine used to help your stress headaches."

When she said things like that, revealing how much she remembered of their brief relationship, hope flared across his senses. "I'm not sure anything but answers or arrests will help this one."

Her gaze dropped, and just like that, he singlehandedly deflated the happy mood Alex had established. "Sorry." He forced himself to stay put when he wanted to stalk off until he had better control of his mouth. Because he was watching her, he saw the internal debate skate over her face rather than any spark of desire.

Deciding something, she swiftly came around the table, taking the chair next to his. "I owe you an apology."

"You don't." The soft floral scent of her shampoo teased his nose and the warm spices from cooking clung to her skin. Though dinner was over, she presented a new kind of feast and he felt like a man starving. He rubbed his forehead, hiding his reaction and raw hunger from her perceptive gaze.

"Matt." She rested her fingertips on his forearm and the touch sizzled like heat lightning under his skin. "Please look at me. Believe me, I trust you with Caleb. I *do*. What I said this morning was out of line, spoken out of fear." He watched her struggle to maintain her composure. What you did for him today and afterward set his world to rights again. Thank you."

He wanted to close his eyes against the compassion

and gratitude in her eyes, but if he did, he'd only see the laser sights targeting them again. "Bethany, when I saw—"

She leaned closer. "Shh. Stop torturing yourself. You were..." Her hand fluttered as she searched for the right word. "Amazing. Heroic. Wonderful." Her smile turned shy. "I can't settle on just one word. You saved him."

Though her compliments flattered him, there was no escaping the truth. "He was out there because of me." All that fear, those minutes ticking as slowly as hours, were his fault. "I told you I wouldn't put him in danger and then there we were." Victims of laser sight target practice apparently, though he wasn't complaining about the lack of injuries.

"That wasn't you." She stroked his arm, rubbed circles over his shoulder. "That was the person who put this game into motion."

"Pretty high stakes," Matt murmured as Alex and Caleb returned with another plate of cookies.

Without a word, she shed the intensity, the intimacy of their conversation and beamed at them. That was a new skill, one she'd likely had to master as a single parent. What had she said? Just because Caleb could handle something didn't mean he should have to.

Once when they'd been out for pizza with the whole group, he'd managed to get her alone for a few minutes. Her hair had been shorter then, thick and silky and definitely mussed from his hands when they'd returned to the table. Their friends had teased them until she'd blushed, completely flustered by the unwanted attention.

How had he fallen for the myth that his feelings for her weren't strong enough, real enough to last?

He studied her surreptitiously while she was distracted with the byplay between Alex and Caleb. Though she'd always been pretty, there was a depth and richness to her features now, as if every life experience only intensified her innate beauty.

The laugh lines bracketing her warm brown eyes and her luscious mouth let him know there had been plenty of joys through the years they'd been apart. He'd followed her career, careful not to get too close, and he knew she was respected and valued in her department. She'd carved out a good life despite the unexpected detour. More than that, she'd created the stability to allow both her and their son to thrive. He wanted in on that.

He couldn't rewind the clock or make up for lost time, but he could definitely make a positive difference from this point forward. Matt didn't want to miss any more precious time with Caleb or Bethany. All too soon, Caleb would be headed to college and then out on his own.

He'd told Matt he loved history and science. He was a talented athlete and Matt expected colleges to start scouting him soon. Had Caleb given any thought to West Point or a Military career? Matt's chest ached that he didn't know the answer.

Yet.

It didn't matter anymore if being shut out of his son's life was wisdom or folly. Now was the time to carefully consider how they would move forward. This time around, all three of them would be in on the decision.

Although he'd never told Bethany, he'd started a college fund in addition to the monthly child support.

Other than his cars and the occasional vacation, there wasn't much else tying up his money. He'd bought and sold houses at various duty stations, but he'd never really established what felt like a home. For the most part, he lived modestly and invested his income for the future.

While he expected Caleb to get scholarships, especially after meeting him, Matt wanted his son to have options. By the time he was Caleb's age, Matt had decided on West Point, determined to walk in his father's shoes. His parents fostered his interest, though they made it clear his choice mattered more than their opinion. His dad had insisted that the challenges of being a cadet were magnified if Matt wasn't fully invested.

He could see Bethany had instilled that same sense of responsibility and independence in Caleb. Yes, he was still a kid, but the man he would become was peeking through already.

Maybe the two of them didn't need him interfering and upsetting the status quo. If he barged in, forcing his role as a father simply for the sake of his own needs, he'd only inject more strife and stress than they were presently dealing with.

"Hey, you in there?" Alex snapped his fingers in front of Matt's face. "I'm heading out."

Matt scrambled to recover from his daydreams, startled to see Alex buttoning his uniform coat. "I'll walk down with you." He rolled down his sleeves and buttoned his shirt cuffs, grabbed his own coat.

"You didn't have to come along," Alex said as they walked down the hall.

"Do you think they're better off without me?" Matt blurted when they were alone in the elevator car.

Alex gaped at him. "You are *not* thinking right," he said. At the lobby, he stepped out, holding out his arm to stop Matt when he tried to follow. "Go upstairs. Enjoy what being a family feels like and forget the rest of this mess. We've got your back."

"Okay. Thanks."

"I do not want to hear from you until tomorrow unless your condo is invaded. Call or text me at your peril."

Matt held up his hands in surrender. "Duly noted."

"You told me your target is a family." Alex reached in and punched the button for Matt's floor. "No detours, Major Riley."

Matt was almost laughing when he got back to the condo. Almost.

Chapter 8

After Alex left, the evening had taken a decidedly domestic turn. Matt had walked back in, excused himself to his bedroom, and returned in jeans and another long-sleeved T-shirt. This one was a camouflage pattern with a Rangers logo on it, and the cuffs had started to fray. Bethany was sure this wasn't the type of shirt just anyone could pick up in an on-base gift shop.

He'd challenged Caleb to more video game racing and although she wanted to remind them Caleb was grounded, she let it go. Forcing him to sulk wouldn't solve anything and she'd kept the two of them apart long enough. She sat where she could keep an eye on the game and read a novel on her phone while the two of them flung trash talk back and forth.

It was past ten when she finally called an end to the fun and sent Caleb to bed. He argued, begging for more time, and she was forced to remind him he was supposedly grounded. Matt backed her up, which she appreciated, but the verbal scuffle only proved her point that Caleb was still a kid and it had been a long, trying day.

So why did she have this urge beating inside her to make it longer still? She wanted—needed—some pure, uninterrupted adult time with Matt. There were more than a few logistics to iron out, yet none of those topics ranked at the top of her agenda.

Every time his gaze had stroked over her throughout the evening, it put a kick in her pulse. Probably had a heart murmur by now, she thought, rubbing her fist to her chest while he flipped through the selections for his game system.

Sharing a meal and easy conversation had felt so natural and right. It had taken her back to those early days of their relationship and the way he made her feel as if she was the only person who mattered. Watching Caleb light up over the outrageous stories Alex shared about Matt had her feeling more content than she'd been in a long time.

Well, that was selling herself short. She'd been quite happy, thriving really, as a single mother with a bright, well-adjusted son. Year after year, she'd proven to herself that she didn't need Matt to ride in and rescue her.

Great. Three cheers for Bethany. None of her independent accomplishments changed how much she missed his friendship or the delicious thrill of having him within view. She wanted him with a white-hot yearning, which was as intense now as it had been the first time around.

Older, wiser and established, she expected that if they hooked up now, the experience would be infinitely more satisfying. Physically and emotionally. Now they could close a door and not worry about who might walk in on them. How much fun could they create in a bed designed for more than one person? Her skin warmed at the thought. As adults, they were mature enough to share a bed and not feel any unjustified pressure to share a life.

Sex. That's what she wanted from him. All she needed was a healthy outlet, a way to release the pent-up tension humming through her system. She poured herself a glass of wine and turned out the kitchen lights, leaving a lamp on low near the couch. Debating how to start a conversation that she wanted to end with what amounted to a one-night stand, she sipped her wine and watched him for any signal.

Her attention divided, she gave a start when her cell phone rang. Her dad's cell number filled the display. She groaned. If anything could douse her anticipatory mood, it was a call from her dad. She tapped the green icon and answered with a bright hello.

"Are you and Caleb all right?" he asked. "I came by to check on you and a police officer is at the curb. He got in my way when I tried to knock."

"Sorry about that." She hadn't thought the protective detail would stay once they left.

She'd called him Wednesday morning to make sure the national news hadn't sent her parents into a tizzy too, but they'd apparently missed the initial reports. Now, more than twenty-four hours after the fact, she had yet to muster the courage to tell him they'd come to Washington with Matt.

"We're fine, Dad. Just got a jump on Caleb's fall break." She glanced at the time on her phone. "You're out late."

"We were out of milk," he said with a raspy chuckle.

Her father drank a glass of milk with breakfast every day. The habit, the steadiness of it, had her smiling.

Matt looked up, and when his gaze caught hers, he smiled back. Her heart did a slow spin in her chest and tripped over itself again.

"So, this cop out here?" Her dad asked. "How long is he staying?"

Her mind muddled with visions of Matt, it took her a moment to follow the conversation. "I don't know. It's just a precaution, Dad."

Hearing that, Matt's lips tipped up at one corner before he turned for his bedroom. She hoped he planned to come back out. With all this need and desire in her veins, she would likely knock on his door if he didn't.

"After the incident last night, they want to be sure no one else tries to tear up the block again. Caleb and I are in Washington through his fall break."

A brief, tense silence followed. "Your mother and I thought you might spend some time with us next week."

"We can do that. I'll let you know as soon as we're back in town. Remember, Caleb has a big tournament in a couple of weeks. He'd love for you both to come out."

"Right, right. We're looking forward to that."

"Us too," she replied.

Matt's bedroom door opened and he emerged. She watched him pass through the kitchen, picking up the bottle of wine and another glass. Bringing both with him, he sat on the opposite end of the couch. While she chatted with her dad, he poured wine into the glass and sat back. The way his hands moved, the way he filled and possessed each simple gesture made her belly quiver. Maybe she couldn't handle a one-night stand after all.

"He's having a great season," she said, rambling now. Her father had superior recall of his grandson's stats, all the way back to his first season as a four-year-old.

"Washington the city or the state?" her dad asked abruptly.

"City," she replied cautiously. Was he using a video app she didn't know about?

"Bethany. You're with *Riley*?"

"After the, ah, incident, we had to come down here to meet with investigators," she explained in a rush.

"If I ever get within arm's reach of that man." She curled away from Matt to contain her father's booming voice as he worked up to the familiar rant. "You'll hug him, I'm sure. Might even say thanks since he saved Caleb's life." Twice, in two days, but she wasn't going to worry him with all of the details.

"I won't," he barked. "Not after he ruined yours."

That was a blow to her pride. No, she hadn't gone on to a Military career as she'd once planned. She hadn't walked down the aisle in a romantic, white wedding to live happily-ever-after like her parents either. Life came in a wide variety of flavors and circumstances.

"Thanks for calling, Dad. I'll keep you posted on the situation."

"Now, honey. I didn't mean—"

"I know what you meant." She tilted her wine glass, playing with the reflected light in the deep red surface. Feeling Matt watching her made the typically annoying topic of conversation nearly unbearable. "It's okay. We're okay."

"He hurt you. A father doesn't forget those things easily."

"No, probably not." She peeked at Matt. How many hurts was he remembering?

She'd made her choices, both in the moment and after the fact, to protect herself and her baby. If she labeled those choices as hurts or mistakes, it devalued the gift of Caleb. Whatever sacrifice of dreams or personal happiness she'd made for the benefit of their son had been worth it. And she couldn't remind her father of any of that while Matt lounged a few feet away.

She glanced toward the balcony doors and thought better of it. That would only make her conversation easier for Caleb to overhear. "Dad, we're okay." She sounded like a broken record. "I'll call you when we're back in town."

"You could have come here," her father said, stubbornly.

Had he missed her mention of investigators? "Dad, I can't get into all of it right now. I don't even know all of it, really." That was a tough pill to swallow. "But we're safe and protected and we'll be home as soon as possible."

"We love you, honey."

"Love you too, Dad. Give Mom a hug from us."

Ending the call, she set aside her cell phone, flipping it over so she couldn't see the display.

"Trouble?" Matt asked.

She sat forward and twirled the wine glass slowly between her palms, still not ready to look at him. "Dad went by the house and a policeman in a patrol car wouldn't let him near the door. He was concerned."

"Naturally."

"I assumed the police car would leave when we did." She sat back again and took a hearty gulp, let it gently warm a path down her throat. "Did you request that detail stay on?"

"Not specifically, though it's a logical step," he replied carefully. "The investigation is ongoing."

True. "Even though the house is empty?" What more did he think would happen? Caleb had handed over the only hard evidence on the messages he'd received. Her neighbors, as a matter of course, would keep an eye on things. She considered her conscientious and thoughtful neighbors one of the biggest assets of living in her community.

"Caleb was the first to be contacted in this mess. You were the first to be threatened."

She shrugged. In her mind, the order of events was irrelevant. Maybe her intuition was blurred by attraction and affection, past and present, but she was certain Matt was the target. Finally, she dared to peek at him.

His gaze intent, mouth soft, one hand stretched along the back of the couch, he posed an appealing temptation. Without saying a single word, he urged her closer, inviting her to touch and explore. Asking if she'd let him touch her, too.

Wanting the feel of him under her hands, she would. They were no longer subject to the school's expectations and rules. They understood the limits were different than they had been fifteen years ago.

Tonight, mutual pleasure and comfort was the end goal, maybe even closure of sorts. Impatient with her hesitation, she summed it up in her mind as a temporary satisfaction of desire between consenting adults. She and Matt weren't destined to be a normal family, not even within the Military definition of the word. Family was quickly sinking to the last thing on her mind.

"Should we put a bell on the guest room door?" Matt's eyes darkened as they continued to watch each other.

He hadn't moved a muscle, yet she felt caught, as if he was pulling her closer. "Do you have a bell?"

"It's doubtful." One dark eyebrow dipped down. "I should have sent him for a sleepover with Uncle Alex." There was no respect for the honorary title in his voice.

She chuckled. "He did a good job roasting you with some of those stories at dinner."

"Do you remember our first kiss?" His gaze dropped to her mouth.

Her lips tingled under his gaze. "I was thinking of it earlier today, in fact."

The sensual heat in his eyes blazed. An answering heat slid through her veins. "While you baked cookies?" he asked.

His hand curled into the leather upholstery, the only clue that her answer was important to him. Oh, how she wished he'd make the first move here and yet she knew why he didn't. She'd been the one to walk away, to refuse any extraneous discussion, cutting him out of her life cold turkey. It was the only way she could get over him without breaking down in a swamp of "what ifs" and "maybe somedays."

"Yes, actually. Caleb was asking for more details about you and me at West Point. I got the impression he's thinking about asking someone out."

"Good for him," Matt said, his lips tilting into a sexy smirk.

She experienced a bolt of protectiveness, thinking about her little boy diving into the dating pool. And here she thought she was a progressive kind of mother.

"What was that?" Matt wagged a finger in the direction of her face.

"Nothing." She hid behind her wine glass.

"Bethany," he coaxed, laughter in his eyes. "Talk to me."

He'd always been such an attentive listener. She'd done this parenting thing alone for so long that breaking the old habits and patterns was harder than she expected. "You have no reason to believe me, but Caleb was probably three or four before I got over the urge to call you about every little thing."

Based on the way he suddenly froze in place, that wasn't the response he'd expected. "I would have answered," he said, catching up with the topic change quickly. "You can talk to me now," he prompted. "About anything."

"It's not a big deal, really. Thinking about him going out with a girl has revealed a previously undiscovered layer of maternal protectiveness." She dismissed her silly overreaction with a careless wave of her hand.

"No such thing as a girl good enough for your son?"

"Apparently part of me subscribes to that theory." She pressed a hand to her heart and shot a guilty glance toward the guest room. She inched closer, whispering. "I don't know who it could be, or how seriously he might be hung up on her."

Matt scooted toward her, a grin teasing his lips as he whispered back. "Serious enough to ask you about dating."

"I guess that was the trigger," she realized. His

quick grin stole her breath. Suddenly it was too easy to envision more nights like this one, having someone to confide in, sharing quiet conversations and hopes on the journey of raising Caleb. She eased her mind away from that dangerous territory.

He was involved now, sure, and that was a good thing. Caleb needed him. But she couldn't afford to get used to this. One-night stand, she reminded herself. He couldn't possibly want to sign on for family life, not with her. He wasn't yet halfway through his career as an officer. So many adventures awaited him, and seeing him in uniform, in action, today reminded her they were on different tracks with good reason.

"Where'd you go?" His fingertips traced the veins in the back of her hand, where it rested on her knee.

She reached for her wine and tried to smile. "I'm here."

"Caleb's caught in between being a kid and an adult," Matt said. "You remember how it was."

She did.

"It won't last too long," he continued, "but it's awkward for the duration."

For everyone apparently. "You've missed so much." She set the wine glass aside, met his gaze. "Whatever you need from this point on, you can have it, Matt. I promise."

"Whatever I need?"

She'd barely given him the affirmative when he simply flowed across the couch, over her. Arms braced, he held his body up so he wouldn't crush her, while his lips softly claimed hers.

She curled a hand around his nape and shifted to give more to the kiss, to him. That softness spiraled into rough demands on both sides. Countless needs pulsed through her, vying for his attention, seeking release.

Seeking him.

With a low rumble, Matt eased his body down, gently pressing her into the cushions. Propped on his elbows, he lifted his head to stare at her. His fingertips sifted through her hair. "You, Bethany. You're—"

This wasn't the time for discussion. She cut him off with a nip to his jaw, ducking away from all that intensity. Something in his eyes, an emotion she didn't want to analyze, nearly sent her scrambling away. Except, this was Matt. The best friend and lover she'd ever had. She blazed a trail of kisses along his throat, up over his jaw and back to his mouth.

He moaned and his arousal prodded her belly when he slid a hand under her back to bring her closer. She stroked a hand up and down his back, rediscovering the hard slabs of muscle along the way. His mouth made her frantic as he sucked lightly on her tongue, delicately tugged her lower lip, all the while subtly rocking his hips to hers.

She wanted fast and rough, mindless sensation to blur out the past and present. He gave her gentle, thorough attention that brought every magnificent detail and connection between them into sharp focus.

The calluses on his palms, those were the hands of a man who worked hard outside of the Pentagon office. She reveled in his unique masculine scent under the fresh green of his shower soap. His hair, thick and soft under her fingers, the prickle of whiskers along his jaw.

He cupped her breast through her shirt and teased

her nipples into tight pebbles that were straining for his next touch, the next enticing sensation.

He sat up, pulling her along with him. In one fluid motion, he pulled her shirt up and over her raised arms. His hands caressed her bared skin, from her palms all the way down to her ribs, coming around to her breasts once more. Laying her back again, he nibbled a path along the lace cups of her bra, tormenting her until at last his mouth closed over her with more of that gentle, thorough attention.

She was perilously close to a climax already, afraid to let go, almost more afraid not to. She murmured his name, shamelessly grinding her hips against the muscled thigh wedged between her legs. She gave a little cry as he bared her nipple and swirled the tender peak with his tongue.

She felt his smile against her skin as he nibbled his way back to her lips and muted her soft, needy gasps with his kisses. "Shh. Not yet, love. Not yet."

Love.

Her heart did a kick-step and her breath fluttered. The girl she'd been wanted him to mean it, wanted that love to be the true, lasting variety. It was a wayward wish at best. They were all grown up now and everything was different. Too much time had passed and their window for that kind of love had closed.

He was feathering kisses over her ribs, across her midriff, lower still until his breath fanned the sensitive skin between her navel and her jeans. He flicked the button open, slid down the zipper and she clapped a hand over his.

There were stretch marks now. She was in good enough shape, if a bit fuller than she'd been. Why couldn't she have filled out the way he had? He was lean, honed and sexy. Her face flushing with embarrassment, she squirmed backward, stretching for the light.

His hands gripped her hips, holding her. "Bethany?"

She scolded herself that she'd been so caught in the fantasy of him that the ways she'd changed never occurred to her. Covering her face with her hands, she struggled against tears and laughter. "Turn out the light."

"I don't think so." Gently, he drew her hands away from her face. "I don't want to miss anything."

He didn't know what he was asking of her. "Please?" She bit her lip. "What if Caleb wanders out here?" There! She leaped on the perfect excuse.

"You weren't thinking about him a few minutes ago." His tone, planted firmly between smug and conversational, got under her skin.

"Should've been," she admitted, her desire fading under the weight of her obligations. "I definitely am now."

This would be the worst example for him. Especially after he'd caught them kissing yesterday. She tried to wriggle out from under Matt again. Again, he made it difficult. "Let me go."

"In a minute." The words brushed across her skin. "I want to understand what's going on."

"This is a mistake." One after another, she never said or did the right things with Matt. She fanned her face, blinking rapidly and wondering if laughter or tears would win the moment.

"Talk to me, Beth."

Matt caught her hands, held them in one of his, right over her heart.

Oh, if only she could. Guilt slammed into desire and both bounced along on waves of fear. She didn't have the first idea how to put the conflicting emotions into words or even the right order. "I'm sorry. I want you," she said in a rush.

He went utterly still, even his face seemed oddly quiet and expressionless. He stared at her mouth as if he was sure any second now it would open again and offer words that made sense. It felt as if the entire world was on pause, waiting for her to clarify that odd statement.

What had she said? All the sensations, regrets and feelings were jumbled in her head, tangling up the words she needed to give him. She wasn't sorry she wanted him, though the pain in his eyes indicated that's what he'd heard. His lips parted, but he didn't make a sound.

"I only meant—"

He sat back so abruptly that goose bumps raced over her bare skin. He stood up and strode away.

Her stomach did a slow, sick roll. *Crap.* "Matt, hang on." She managed not to shout, but it was a close thing. Grabbing her shirt, pulling and tugging it into place, she rushed down the hall after him, catching up just in time for him to shut his bedroom door in her face.

Could she do nothing right with this man? Certainly she hadn't done anything right since she told him she was expecting. She rested her forehead against the door. "Matt?"

"Not now." His voice was thick with emotion.

"Please, Matt."

"We'll talk tomorrow."

It sounded as if he was mirroring her pose on his side of the door. She almost tested the handle and decided that would be too pushy. "Matt," she pleaded.

"Go to bed."

"I'm sorry for screwing this up." There, that came out properly. He could take that apology and apply it to tonight, or more accurately to all the points in the past where her insecurities had messed up the relationship potential for him and his son.

Her eyes and nose burned with tears. This time, she knew the flood couldn't be stopped. Too much had happened in the last few days for her to hold it in anymore.

As the first tears spilled over and rolled down her cheeks, she wandered back to the living room, wondering what to do now. Her son, hopefully asleep, was behind one door and the love of her life was taking shelter from *her* behind the other. She'd never felt more alone.

Hugging her arms around her middle, she went to the balcony doors and stared out at the night. Matt's touch had been so familiar, so full of promises she wanted to believe, and still she'd managed to hurt him again.

Because she couldn't stop being afraid.

Caleb was a blessing for many reasons, not the least of which was that becoming a mom altered her career path. Things had been going well for her at West Point, but clearly she wasn't cut out for a proper Military career. The men and women who served exemplified courage against long odds. All she did was run as fast as possible for the easier road.

Easier to be alone, to feign strength and handle things on her own than open herself to the emotional risk Matt presented. Or any man really, she thought, disgusted with herself.

Feeling wretched and terribly exposed, she pulled the curtains to block out all that night pressing in. Curling into the sleek recliner, she leaned back and inhaled the scent of him. It wrapped her in comfort and memories of easy affection. It hit her hard, everything she'd thrown away when she shut him out of her life so completely.

She was a fool, she thought, tears flowing in earnest now. She didn't blame herself for the decisions she'd made under the stress and uncertainty when she'd found out she was pregnant. She'd eventually come to the pragmatic conclusion about leaving West Point. It was the only way to keep Matt's name out of it and avoid any unnecessary disciplinary action.

If she'd named him as the father, it could have meant his expulsion, as well as her own. His future had been too bright, and one of them deserved the chance to see their original dreams fulfilled. That was one perk of this entire mess, the firsthand look at his success.

He had a stellar career as an Army officer and, from all accounts, he was as popular a leader as his father. It couldn't have been easy for him to separate himself from General Riley's reputation, between the various schools, the deployments, and the alternating favoritism and bias everyone seemed to have for or against General Riley's eldest son.

Those prejudices had shown up as early as their first year, with some instructors riding him harder, some granting him more leeway. Even their classmates had expressed a tendency to judge him as a young version of his dad, giving him hell or trying to ride his coat-tails.

All Matt had ever wanted was a fair shot, to be judged on his merit alone rather than the long-reaching shadow of his father.

She looked back at her choices through his eyes. She'd judged him, too. Not on his specific interactions with her, but on what she knew of his family and his goals. On how she saw herself fitting into his plans or, more accurately, how her attempts to fit her life to his would surely backfire.

She'd never given them a chance. And now…of all the things that changed in a life, it seemed she couldn't overcome the frightened girl determined to hold Matt at a safe distance.

Eventually her tears slowed to a trickle and she went to the bathroom, splashing cool water on her face to relieve the worst of the redness in her cheeks and gritty eyes. Needing sleep didn't mean it would come. Rather than toss and turn and possibly wake Caleb, she went back to the living room.

Practically tiptoeing around, she cleared the wine glasses and capped the bottle. Looking for another distraction, her gaze landed on the box of Caleb's pictures on the coffee table. During college, she'd earned some good cash with calligraphy. Later she'd enjoyed scrapbooking, as well.

As the idea took shape in her mind, her aching heart eased a bit. Here was something nice she could do for Matt and his parents, too. She didn't have all the supplies with her, so it wouldn't be particularly fancy, but maybe they'd appreciate the spirit of the gesture.

And if she was crafting, she couldn't cry. What else could she do to get herself through to the morning?

Hours later, her back aching and her writing hand cramped, she had two small albums ready, one for Matt and one for his mother. Yawning, she put away the supplies, tucked the pictures she hadn't used back in the box and placed the albums on top. Then she curled into the recliner and let the exhaustion take her under.

Chapter 9

Matt heard his phone chiming on the nightstand charger and reached over to hit the snooze option. Ten more minutes, that's all. It would bring the sum total of his sleeping time to approximately an hour and ten minutes. Every time he drifted off, he'd fallen into a nightmare of Bethany walking out of his life and taking Caleb, the two of them forever out of his reach.

Instead of blissful silence, he heard Alex's voice, too faint to make out the words. He grabbed the phone and put it to his ear. "Hold up," he pleaded. His watch showed it wasn't quite six o'clock. Good grief.

"Wake up," Alex replied. "We have a situation."

The stone-cold business tone caught Matt's attention. Instantly awake, he sat up and put his feet on the floor. "Go."

"There was a new development overnight. General Knudson wants to brief us in his office at oh-seven-hundred. I'll pick you up in thirty."

"We'll be ready." He was sure Caleb and Bethany

wouldn't be happy when he woke them with this, but he knew he could count on them to kick it into gear.

"No we. Just you, man."

"Alex." He wasn't leaving Caleb and Bethany alone. Besides, this involved them, too.

"My team is already shifting focus. We have positions on the elevator, the roof, in the stairwells, the building next door. Every access covered. No harm will come to them while you're out."

He wouldn't win an argument on security with an experienced operator like Alex. "Meet you downstairs in thirty. Twenty-eight," he amended, looking at the clock.

"I'll be at your door, Major Riley."

If Matt hadn't been rattled before, the official address did it. Wearing only his boxers, he bolted to the kitchen and started a cup of coffee to brew. In the three minutes the machine required, he brushed his teeth and showered.

In clean boxers this time, he came back out and retrieved his coffee and headed back to his bedroom to shave and finish dressing. When he came out of his bedroom a third time, fully dressed, his coat over his arm and his beret in hand, he noticed Bethany curled up in the recliner.

She looked so fragile, her cheek pale and delicate in the shadows. He adjusted the throw to cover her shoulder and managed to control the urge to kiss her awake. One of them should get some rest.

He moved on to the guest room and knocked lightly before entering. As he suspected, the quiet knock had done nothing to stir his son. Seeing Caleb sprawled across the bed, in a tank top and boxers and the sheets tangled around his lanky legs, Matt was overcome with love.

Swallowing the swell of emotion, he walked over and gently shook Caleb's shoulder. "Hey, wake up."

He rolled over and took the covers with him. "Five minutes," he mumbled.

"If only," Matt muttered. "Caleb." He gave him another shake and put some authority into his voice. "I need you to wake up now. Your mom needs you."

The boy roused a bit at that, as if his sleeping form just realized he shouldn't be in this bedroom alone. "What?" He blinked rapidly. "Matt?" He scrubbed at his face. "What time is it?" He looked to the window, where the first hint of daylight was trying to squeeze through the blinds.

"Early. I have to go to the Pentagon for a meeting. You and your mom are staying here."

"Where is she? What happened?"

Matt smiled a little. "She fell asleep in the recliner last night. Let her sleep, but when she wakes up *on her own*, let her know I'll call as soon as I can."

Yawning, Caleb sat up. "You're leaving us?"

"No. I have a meeting. And you'll be safe. Uncle Alex has a protection team in place."

"All right." The tension faded from his young face. "Cool."

"Let her sleep," Matt repeated, scrubbing a hand over his son's messy locks. "I'm counting on you. If there's any trouble, you follow the orders from Uncle Alex's team."

"Yes, sir."

Matt checked his watch and decided he had just enough time to down a meal bar and a second cup of coffee. He heard Caleb head into the bathroom, and when he came out, he casually grabbed a soda from the refrigerator.

Matt only cocked an eyebrow, not wanting to risk waking Bethany. With a roll of his eyes, Caleb put back the soda in favor of orange juice. Matt handed him a glass.

"Thanks," he mouthed. He took his juice over to the family room and sat on one of the couches, propping his feet on the coffee table, his attention on his phone.

It might have been the most perfect morning in Matt's recent memory. One way or another, he intended to have more mornings with his family around.

At the door, he checked the peephole for Alex. He opened the door before his friend could knock. "Bye," he whispered to Caleb and started out.

"Matt!" Caleb hissed. Scrambling up, he raced over, skidding across the tile in the foyer like a hockey player. He caught Matt at the waist in a hard hug, and then bounced back. "Hi, Uncle Alex."

"Nephew Caleb." Alex smiled, glancing past Matt into the condo behind them. "You're in charge, huh?"

Caleb nodded. "Tell your team thanks for helping us."

Alex's golden eyebrows climbed his forehead, dropped back into place. "I will. We need to get going."

"Here." Caleb shoved a small square packet at Matt. It had his name in intricate lettering on the front. "Mom must have made this last night."

Matt turned over the cover and saw Caleb's first baby picture from the hospital. Alex leaned in. "Afraid he'll forget what you look like? Probably a good idea."

Caleb snorted. "He's never carried my picture to work before," he told Alex. "Now he can."

"Thanks." Moved more than he could say, he tucked the small album into the inner pocket of his coat so Caleb would know it was close to his heart. Giving his son one more hug, he headed out for the meeting.

As soon as they were out of Caleb's sight, Alex snapped back into his stoic, working-warrior mode. Matt was almost disappointed when they took the elevator down, rather than up to the roof to meet a hovering helicopter.

"What happened?"

"The general wants to tell you all at once. Your parents are en route, as well."

Matt swore, knowing he wouldn't get anything more out of Alex now. The streets were as close to empty as they got in DC and the drive to the Pentagon took half the normal time.

Every minute away from Bethany and Caleb, every mile of distance, made him increasingly twitchy. Didn't matter that they were under the watch of the Army's best team—they were out of his sight and they were ultimately his responsibility.

They cleared security and walked swiftly toward General Knudson's office suite.

"You need a live feed?" Alex asked under his breath. "My team can make it happen."

"No," Matt answered in kind. "I need the situation resolved."

"Working on it, brother."

Neither of them spoke again on the long walk through the eerily quiet halls. The only sounds came from their breathing and soft footfalls. It was all Matt could do not to break into a run as nerves clamped his shoulders. Finally, they turned into the corridor and Alex pulled open the door to the general's suite of offices and motioned for Matt to go first.

To Matt's surprise, General Knudson wasn't alone. His parents were already waiting. "How did you get here first?" he asked after greeting his boss.

Ben smiled easily as Patricia wrapped Matt into a warm hug. "It's good to have friends in high places," he said. "Wish the reason for our visit was better."

Matt wasn't fooled. His father could win tournaments with his poker face if he was so inclined. His gaze moved from Alex to Knudson and back. "What's going on?"

Knudson extended a hand to the coffee service just inside the door. "Help yourselves and have a seat. Major Gadsden will have us ready to go in just a minute."

"Caleb and Bethany aren't with you?" Patricia kept one eye on the door even as she hugged Matt again.

"No." Bewildered, he aimed a look at his father. "I promise you'll meet him." It wouldn't be here, on government property, if he could help it. They'd spent enough time here lately.

His mom leaned back and studied him, her shrewd, X-ray gaze going right through him. "Oh, my sweet boy," she murmured. "I was furious with you for holding out on me."

"So you said." Uncomfortable, Matt glanced over her shoulder and saw the others were giving them some time and space. He straightened his shoulders and braced for another lecture on his failings.

"I'm so, so sorry." She hugged him close once more, and then held him at arm's length. "I shouldn't have jumped down your throat when we found out. Once I had some time, it dawned on me. Oh, just look at you."

"Mom?" She didn't get flustered. It was so out of character, it worried him. "Do you need a coffee?"

"In a minute. Matt, you've paid such a steep price all these years." She moved toward the coffee service now, pouring a cup and pressing it gently into his hands. "I can see it now all over your face. You've wanted to be his father all this time."

All Matt could do was nod and wait for the world to right itself.

"Is he wonderful?" she asked. "Do you have a picture?"

"I, um." Matt floundered for the right response. Then he remembered what Caleb had given him only a few minutes ago. "I brought you a set of pictures. Bethany put it together." He still wasn't sure how she'd managed to put together something so nice with the limited supplies in his condo.

Tears welled in Patricia's eyes. "Gimme, gimme," she said on a watery laugh.

Matt reached inside his coat and pulled out the square, accordion-folded album of Caleb's pictures. "A highlight reel," he explained, handing it over reluctantly.

She opened the cover and, seeing the first picture from the hospital, she pressed her fingers to her lips, just staring. In fanciful lettering, Bethany had written all the stats, including his full name: Caleb Matthew Trent.

At her small gasp, Ben was instantly at her side, his arm around her shoulders. "Look, Benny. Our first grandson."

"He's a dead ringer for you, Matt," Ben observed, his voice rough with suppressed emotion.

Patricia turned the page to the next picture and chewed on her lip the way she did when she wanted to prevent a flood of tears. She leaned into her husband while Matt tracked down a tissue. Together they admired each of Caleb's pictures, murmuring when they found something that reminded them of Matt or one of his siblings.

"Pardon me, General, Mrs. Riley," Alex said from the inner office. "We're ready when you are."

Patricia closed the little scrapbook and tucked it over her heart. "Thank you, Matt." Still tucked up close to Ben, they moved to the office to address the real reason they were all here.

Knudson closed the door for privacy and they all sat down in guest chairs, which were arranged so they could see the display screen Alex had set up on the corner of the general's desk.

"I'll let General Riley start us off," Alex said.

Matt's gut churned, but he held his questions.

Ben curled his hand around Patricia's and something deep and serious passed between them. "After your recent rash of trouble and what happened to Grace Ann last night, General Knudson, Major Gadsden and I decided it was time I got involved."

"Grace Ann?" A chill trickled down Matt's spine. The older of his two younger sisters had followed in their mom's footsteps and joined the Army as a nurse. She was currently stationed in Maryland, at Walter Reed Hospital, and had a good reputation helping soldiers recover from serious, often career-ending injuries.

"She received her official notice of the security

breach earlier in the week, just like you did," Ben continued. "Last night her car was vandalized in the parking garage."

"How?" Matt feared he already knew.

"Someone tagged it with the words 'you will pay,'" Patricia said. She nodded toward the display where Alex had brought up the image from the parking garage.

"Currently, we have zero evidence from the security footage," Alex explained. "We're just getting started."

"So this is bigger than Bethany, Caleb and me?" His mind was already ticking through how that altered the situation.

"Seems to be." Ben nodded. "I believe whoever is behind this is trying to get to me, by hurting my children. Whoever it is started with you and is implying Grace Ann will be targeted next."

"That theory supports the witness video and heavy media coverage of the drive-by in New Jersey," Alex said. "Along with the other disconcerting pictures sent to General Riley."

Matt's stomach had settled a fraction when he realized his parents weren't frantic with worry over his sister. Now it felt caught in a vise as his worry shifted to his dad. It made sense, in a sick, vengeful way. "Why?"

Knudson spoke up. "Career officers make hard choices, decisions that other men carry out. Some of those men become enemies."

Matt knew all of that from watching his father, his other superiors and through his own experiences leading soldiers. "Yes, sir." It was all he could do to sit still. "But it has to be a short list of people with a grudge worthy of the resources that have been demonstrated.

Just sending the threat to Bethany on official letterhead took significant planning or bribes."

"Your father and I will be working with investigators throughout the day to compile a suspect pool," Knudson said.

Matt's gaze snapped to Alex. "I need more information."

With a restrained acknowledgement of what Matt wanted to know, Alex took over the briefing. "My team has found evidence that you were tailed," he explained. "In New Jersey and prior to that trip." Various images filled the display. "General Knudson gave us your itinerary for the last two weeks, and we reviewed every accessible security camera system along your normal route."

Matt swallowed an oath, out of respect for his mother's presence, and started to apologize to all of them for being complacent. His lack of vigilance had nearly gotten his son killed. Afraid he might vomit, he fisted his hands and breathed carefully through his nose until the sensation passed.

"Matt," Patricia murmured. "This isn't a war zone and your post here is hardly a combat assignment."

To his surprise, Alex and the general added their voices, backing her up.

"On top of that," Alex continued, "it's a small team. Two, possibly three, men. They're well-trained and epitomize nondescript. Picking them out of the background required experts who knew where to start looking. Two of the men were near the park during the laser sight incident as well, though I can't give you any proof that those particular men were actually behind the sights aimed at you and your family."

"Three lasers," Matt muttered. That meant three nests. Hard enough to get one such spot in a city like Washington. Processing all of this would take time. His priority would be figuring out how to get this threat under wraps so Bethany and Caleb could return to their normal routine.

That routine most likely wouldn't include him, if last night was any indication.

"Yes." Alex continued. "Facial recognition has yet to give us anything. General Riley doesn't recognize our targets, but we remain hopeful."

"How hopeful?" Knudson asked.

"Well, until Grace Ann's car was trashed, very hopeful," Alex said. "The investigative team will be working around the clock to tie any one of the men who trailed Matt to her area."

That caught Matt's attention. "You're suggesting we didn't find them yesterday, didn't have any further trouble because they moved in on Grace Ann?"

"I'm suggesting the possibility," Alex clarified.

Enduring his friend's hard look, Matt knew Alex was thinking about him standing on the balcony last night, daring anyone to light him up.

"It wouldn't take much to know when and where to find her, either," Patricia said. "You're both in quite visible positions right now."

Ben squeezed her hand. "And we're working to shore up any vulnerable spots, sweetheart."

The understated confidence in the exchange, the way his mother visibly relaxed under his dad's touch and words made Matt ache all over. That was what he'd always wanted. Trust, affection, connection and security. It was what he had been willing to work for and build with Bethany when she'd told him she was pregnant.

The shock of her news had been short-lived, suffused so quickly by the sheer wonder and joy of it. And she'd taken that dream right out of his hands, claiming she didn't need him.

Or to be more accurate, claiming he and the Army were the more appropriate team. He'd tried, in every way he knew, to convince her both of them could have it all. Family, love and satisfying careers.

Since Caleb's birth, Matt had found it almost painful to be around his parents, to know he hadn't been enough for Bethany the way his father had always been enough for Patricia. What would it take to show her that relying on him, letting him in, wouldn't impair her precious independence?

"I'm not going to sit around waiting for the next attempt," Matt said. "Let's make a plan."

He had them on the ropes. It was a beautiful thing, watching Major Riley rush to the Pentagon with his friend, worry stamped on the rugged soldier's face. Riley the younger held himself like his father, walked with the same arrogance, a fresher, stronger version of the man who had asked too much of him and tossed him aside.

His spotters had informed him of General Riley's arrival at the Pentagon and, even without any actionable options within the building, he felt giddy as a child on Christmas Eve. Only one reason to bring in the retired general: they were going to investigate the bastard at last, searching for motives and suspects.

Good.

Let them search, he thought gleefully. Pick apart the general as he had picked apart the many good men and women under his command. Dig up all his secrets, pull back the veil on all the risky orders and shine a spotlight of truth into the murky shadows.

They would find his name, eventually. They might even find his compound here in the desert. It changed nothing.

He'd learned a great deal about planning, contingencies and deniability under General Riley's command. The plans were set and every possible iteration of events for the days and weeks ahead had been accounted for. The teams, organized into compartments for everyone's protection, could operate autonomously if needed.

His timeline and his endgame remained intact. Each day gave him more momentum. He estimated that within the next sixty days the plan would be as unstoppable as a runaway train.

"Whatever you do, wherever you go, you're at my mercy now," he said to the darkened window.

The desk phone rang, interrupting his thoughts. Smiling, he picked up the receiver. It could only be good news. "Yes?"

"The location is ready," the man on the other end of the line reported.

He turned to the wall-mounted display and selected the appropriate image from the various options shown. Indeed, the location was ready and the live feed was coming through clearly.

"Well done," he said. "Make sure our guests arrive safely and, by all means, make them comfortable." He replaced the receiver and poured himself a drink.

The real show was about to start.

Bethany had been awakened by the sound of Caleb munching on cereal at the kitchen island. To her great relief, he hadn't asked any difficult questions, merely explained that Uncle Alex had taken Matt out for an early meeting and would call when they were back.

Embarrassed and relieved, she hurried to the bathroom for a shower to clear away the fog in her head. With luck, by the time Matt returned, she'd feel steady enough to look him in the eye. She had no confidence that she would know what to say or how to rectify last night's blunder.

Dressed in jeans and a loose sweater, she paced the condo, unable to settle, her mind wandering through the minefield of possible explanations for the meeting.

At last a phone rang. Caleb's phone.

"It's Matt," he announced, answering the call. "Hey, Matt. You're on speaker."

"Your mom is there?"

"Yes." Caleb turned his face away from her. "She woke up on her own an hour ago."

"Good job."

She could hear a whisper of a smile in Matt's reply.

"Everything okay?" she asked tentatively.

"Getting there," he answered. "Go ahead and pack up," he said. "We're going to the beach for fall break."

Caleb let out an unholy whoop of delight and punched a fist into the air, but Bethany wasn't as excited. He'd called on Caleb's phone. Did he mean to include her or cut her out for some overdue father-son bonding? "Matt?"

"All three of us are going." His exasperation was clear. "Together. I'll be there in an hour or so."

They'd packed their belongings and she puttered and cleaned to keep her hands busy. When Matt walked through the door in his uniform, looking somewhat weary and just a little grim, she felt awful. The beach would do him good.

It wasn't until the Camaro was loaded and he turned south on the interstate that she realized they weren't going to one of the beaches in New Jersey she and Caleb frequented on short school breaks.

At her query, Matt coolly explained they were driving down to North Carolina to see his parents at their new beach house. There was more to it, plenty more, that he was keeping from her. She could see it in the way he gripped the steering wheel, the hard set of his jaw and the consistent way he monitored his mirrors.

Her desire for a full explanation was eclipsed by the sudden flurry of questions from the back seat. Caleb wanted to know everything about the grandparents he was about to meet.

It was almost a relief when they arrived several hours later, though Bethany had no idea how she would survive the Riley family gauntlet that was surely waiting for her at the end of the long driveway.

Caleb leaned forward between the front seats, his eyes as big as saucers as he checked out the house. She felt the same way. When Matt had said his parents retired to a beach house, this wasn't at all what she'd envisioned. She'd pictured a small, quirky cottage or even a high-rise condo. She expected to find herself in tight quarters with Rileys pressing in on her from all sides, judging her and demanding to know why she'd kept Caleb to herself all these years.

This house could never be the setting for that kind of hellish scene. On stilts, the two-story home was stunning and likely boasted all kinds of elbow room. A low, three-car garage faced the road and Matt followed the driveway around it, coming to a stop closer to the house.

Even more impressive than the house was the area around it. The house stood back from its neighbors, perfectly framed by native palms and grasses. She could already hear the ocean and she hadn't even opened her car door.

"Cool!" Caleb launched himself from the car as soon as Matt was out of the driver's seat. He jogged toward the dunes and back again, stretching his legs. "Can we surf here?" he asked Matt.

"He acts like he's never seen the ocean," Bethany said to Matt and then turned to Caleb, "You do realize this is still the Atlantic Ocean?"

"Well, yeah." He came around to help them unload. "But can we go surfing?"

"It's not like surfing the Pacific, though I'm sure Grace Ann has some gear stored here."

"That's your sister?" Caleb asked.

"The older of my two sisters," Matt replied. "She told me she'd try and come down while you're here."

Bethany felt her smile slipping. He was shoving his family at her, or rather at Caleb, on purpose. "I thought it would just be your parents." His jaw clenched. "It's fine," she said quickly, "I only meant—"

"I get it," he said. "Rileys can be an overbearing force even in small doses."

"That wasn't—"

"Welcome, welcome!"

Bethany turned at the interruption to see Matt's parents waving from the first landing on the wide stairs. When she'd met them during her first year at West Point, she was already infatuated with Matt and she'd instantly fallen in love with the frank general and his exuberant wife. They were warm and kind and, above all, friendly to everyone they met.

She wondered if any of those characteristics would still be in play, or if she'd have better luck in front of a firing squad. She caught the subtle movement as Patricia leaned into Ben, squeezing his hand as if she needed support. Bethany felt a whisper of longing move through her over that trusting, unified moment. She'd destroyed her chances of sharing that sort of intimacy with Matt.

"Need any help?" Ben asked, starting down the stairs.

"I think we've got it," Matt replied as he handed their bags out of the trunk. He paused to give his dad a hug and introduce Bethany and Caleb.

"We remember Bethany," Ben said, smiling warmly.

Determined to set the right example for Caleb, she stuck out her hand. "General Riley, it's good to see you again."

He used her hand and pulled her into a hug. "You're pretty as ever." Releasing her, he turned to Caleb. "This handsome boy must be your son."

She appreciated that he didn't just take ownership of Caleb, declaring him part of the Riley family and sending her on her way.

Caleb dropped his backpack and duffel bag and stepped forward. "Pleased to meet you, sir."

General Riley accepted his handshake and clapped him on the shoulder. "Call me Ben. Or Pop if you like. Sir is for strangers, and you're family." Ben steered Caleb up the stairs to meet Patricia.

He might as well have painted an *R* on Caleb's

chest, Bethany thought glumly as she and Matt followed. She'd be lucky if Matt didn't have her in court for a custody hearing by Monday. Not that she had any illusions about the situation. Holidays would now be shared, and rightly so. Along with two weekends a month and half of his summer vacation time.

Yes, she owed his parents an explanation, along with loads of time to make up for. Still, her heart ached at what they would take from her in the long run.

"They'll give him back," Matt murmured at her ear, low enough that he wouldn't be overheard.

She must be thinking too loudly. "Of course they will."

"If you're polite, they probably won't even make you walk across hot coals after dinner."

She stubbed her toe on the next step and when she caught her balance, she glared at him over her shoulder. "Ha, ha." She kept moving, knowing she'd soon face Patricia, mother-to-mother.

"Do you think if I ask nicely," Matt continued, "they'll babysit so you and I can have a date?"

A date?

The situation would have been challenging enough if, as she suspected, they were only here to test the reach of whoever was targeting them. On the drive, Matt had told them that Uncle Alex was dealing with the threats and needed them safely out of the way and his parents had insisted they all come down so they could finally meet Caleb.

Two birds, one grandson, she thought darkly.

In her mind, she spun around and drilled a finger into his chest and demanded that he stop messing with her. This wasn't a typical family vacation! In reality, she pretended Matt didn't exist and greeted Patricia with as much grace and dignity as possible under the circumstances.

Patricia startled her, pulling her into a hug that felt remarkably warm and comforting. "We're happy you're here. *Both* of you." She glanced past Bethany to Matt. "All three of you, I should say."

"Gee, thanks for remembering me, Mom."

She gave him a mom look that Bethany understood completely. Somehow it smoothed away the worst of the strain she felt about this visit.

Inside the house, a wide, airy foyer gave way to a space perfect for entertaining, with expansive views of the ocean through the windows all along the far wall. Ben and Caleb were already out on the deck overlooking the beach. Patricia instructed her to leave the bags to Matt and told her son to take everything upstairs.

"She's the real commanding officer around here," he teased.

"We'll give you the full tour in a bit," Patricia said. "Would you like a glass of wine or something else?"

"Water, please," Bethany replied. Warm welcome or not, with her recent lousy conversational track record, she didn't want to risk getting too relaxed too soon.

Patricia poured cold water from a ceramic pitcher for both of them. "How did you like the Camaro?"

Bethany grinned. "It's loud and wonderful," she said. "Caleb was over the moon. I think it might be the best incentive to make sure he studies for his learner's permit test."

Patricia aimed an irritated glance toward Ben. "That one managed to be deployed while the twins were at that age. I'm still not sure I've forgiven him for putting the bulk of their driving lessons on me."

Bethany was secretly dreading teaching Caleb to drive. She couldn't imagine trying to teach two boys at the same time. "I hope you found a way to get even."

"Naturally."

Patricia's eyes sparkled the same way Matt's did when he was in an ornery mood. It made Bethany's chest ache with guilt. This family was so close and she'd robbed them of Caleb's first fourteen years. Suddenly her reasons didn't seem so valid anymore.

She stepped around the broad kitchen island that angled outward to give cooks ample room in the kitchen, while guests had plenty of space to watch and chat, and sipped her water. "You have a lovely home."

"Thank you." Patricia beamed. "We're delighted to share it. Ben wanted to live on the boat when he retired, but I wasn't about to retire from the Army just to become a Navy wife." She laughed. "Besides I wanted a place where the kids could relax and visit and eventually bring their own families."

With every word, Bethany felt the walls around her heart crumbling. She'd built up her defenses as a means of protection and shelter for Matt, as well as for her and Caleb. Barely an adult, she hadn't believed that raising a child together would lead to anything other than resentment. Better to have fond memories of tender affection and young love than to destroy it completely.

Now? Well, now she didn't have any idea how to piece this situation back together. "Patricia, I'm sorry. It was never my intention to, to..." To what? None of the ways to finish that sentence would make either one of them feel better. She started over, leaning on the point she thought would matter most to Patricia. "I wanted Matt to have the career he dreamed of."

Patricia studied her. There was kindness in her assessment and, thankfully, not an ounce of pity. "Matt gave me the little photo album you made."

"He did?"

"Before our briefing this morning." She tucked a wayward strand of hair behind her ear. "It's wonderful. He tells us Caleb is an excellent soccer player, and history and science are his favorite subjects."

"Yes, to all of that," Bethany replied, trying to keep up. "A college scholarship for soccer is likely if he sticks with it." As she answered more of Patricia's questions, she realized Ben was keeping Caleb outside according to a well-orchestrated plan. Just when she was sure Matt was in on it too, he came down the stairs and went straight to the refrigerator, pulling out a beer.

"Do we have a dinner plan?" He stopped in the process of twisting off the top, his gaze taking in everyone's place and coming to the correct conclusion. "Mom. You're grilling her?"

"I'm not," Patricia defended.

Matt snorted, and tipped the bottle to his lips. "Caleb was talking nonstop about surfing. Does Grace Ann keep any gear here?" he asked, blatantly putting an end to the conversation.

"She does. Still, I'd rather he waited for Grace Ann to teach him."

"Why?" Matt cocked an eyebrow. "I know my way around a surfboard."

Patricia shook her head. "Mark can teach him. He hopes to be here by Monday or Tuesday."

Bethany was still processing the fact that more Rileys

were on the way and that she and Caleb were expected to be here when Matt swore.

"Mark might be a SEAL, but I'm his dad. I'll teach him."

"Calling dibs?" Patricia teased.

"He's had a little experience," Bethany said. "We spend time at the beach most summers."

"That sounds lovely," Patricia said. "Still, we don't want him to pick up bad habits. Both Grace Ann and Mark are better than Matt."

"At *nothing*," Matt sputtered, indignant and yet clearly amused. "I'm your firstborn, your favorite and better than all the others combined. You always said so."

"You *were* my favorite," she countered, though her eyes danced with laughter as she teased her eldest. "You might be again if you can convince this wonderful woman and her son to spend more time with this side of his family."

Bethany wanted to melt into the woodwork. Unfortunately, Patricia noticed. "Only so we can get to know both of you better."

"Mom, stop pushing." Matt's voice had turned as stern as his gaze. "If Bethany agrees, I was hoping you and dad would let our son entertain you while we go out for a while."

"On a date?" Patricia's expression brightened. "Tonight?"

Matt turned so only Bethany could see him rolling his eyes. "If putting it that way means you agree, then yes, call it a date."

Bethany smothered a chuckle behind her water

glass. She'd never expected General and Mrs. Riley to give her such a relaxed or tolerant reception.

"Fine." Patricia glanced toward the deck, where her husband and grandson were talking. "Go on. Have fun." She shooed them toward the door. "Be careful," she murmured.

"You too," Matt said.

"No worries." Patricia waved that off as if anonymous strangers threatened her family every day. "We'll load him up with energy drinks and show him the puppy we bought for him."

Bethany skidded to a stop at the front door. "Puppy?"

"She's kidding," Matt pulled her outside and closed the door behind them.

"What if I don't want to go out with you?"

He stopped. His grip tightened on her wrist for a brief moment before he shoved his hands into his pockets. "You'd rather stay here and chat it up with my mom?"

Well, no. "Maybe," she hedged. "I didn't expect her to be so nice. I like it," she admitted.

Matt pressed the heel of his hand to his forehead. "Are you worried more about Caleb or me?"

Him, definitely him. Her son had Ben and Patricia as protection. Matt only had her, and she'd only proven herself capable of hurting him. "Since I don't have all the facts, I'll assume this entire situation has enough worry to go around." She started down the stairs.

He caught up with her before she reached the car and opened the door for her. His manners had always charmed her. He couldn't really have meant that he wanted to take her on a date. Surely he'd rather keep his distance after last night's fiasco.

"Fair point," he said as she slid into the seat. "I thought you'd appreciate my choosing not to discuss the particulars of the morning briefing in front of Caleb."

That was a far more believable explanation for him wanting to take her on a date. "Thank you." His slow smile moved across his face and stirred her desire as he gently closed the door. She gathered her composure as he settled in behind the wheel. "Were you expecting any of your siblings to come out?"

"No," he admitted. "Well, Grace Ann, maybe. She lives close enough. Not the others." The engine started with a low growl and he put the car in reverse, backing neatly out of the driveway.

As he drove toward the sleepy little beach town a few miles up the coast, he shared the current theories on the case, along with recent developments and the current plan. It was hard to believe all of the threats and trouble they'd been navigating were most likely an effort to cause General Riley pain.

"I suppose it makes sense," she mused. "Though whoever it is has a long reach."

"Agreed," Matt said. "He's made a few enemies along the way, but the tactics used so far should work in our favor by thinning the suspect list."

It finally dawned on her that this "date" might well be another way to test the enemy's reach. Not that spending time with Matt was any hardship. "I really missed you when I left West Point," she said, the smooth ride and the salty ocean relaxing her.

"I missed you, too," he said with such tenderness, her heart ached. He reached over and took her hand in his.

The touch reminded her that they really needed to

set some clear boundaries. The last thing she wanted to do was drag Matt with her down memory lane. What they'd had was youthful and foolish, and though she would never regret becoming Caleb's mom, she had to accept that she and Matt couldn't be together. Not like Ben and Patricia.

"Hey." He smiled. "Where'd you drift off to?"

She glanced around as he parked the car and cut the engine. "Nowhere in particular." She smiled, a little lost in his warm brown eyes. If she wasn't careful, she'd be right back in love with him. Who was she kidding? She'd never really stopped loving him.

She should tell him. He deserved that honesty from her. So why did it feel as if saying the words would put her heart in more danger than ever before?

Chapter 10

Matt had never seen Bethany so distracted. Granted, her life had been turned upside down by someone bent on revenge against his father and the people she'd kept out of her son's life would now be fixtures in his world. He supposed, in her mind, the risks were only adding up and the odds of him getting what he wanted were probably dwindling exponentially.

Still, Alex would be furious if he gave up on the plan now. One of them had to be willing to make the first move, to take a decisive, clear step toward a positive change. Every recent moment with Bethany had played through his mind overnight and during the drive as he'd fielded Caleb's endless questions.

Despite the words that cut so sharply, the spark between them was still there, along with the respect and affection. He just had to encourage her to help him fan that spark into a steady flame. He wouldn't let her down. She had to know that by now. In fact, he had a suspicion that that was part of her problem.

At last he found himself with an advantage. While his career was centered on building teams and fostering cooperation, she'd been facing life's challenges on her own. He just had to show her he wasn't trying to take over or nudge her aside. He had to prove he could be there for her, ready and willing.

He gave her hand another quick squeeze. "Let's go inside and get a drink and pretend we're hot for each other," he teased.

She gave him a quelling glance, but didn't move.

He came around and opened her car door, leaning in. "You can't possibly want to go back. My parents aren't going to do anything stupid or hurtful. Mom was kidding about the puppy."

"I know." A wistful smile flitted over her lips, gone far too quickly. "They raised you, and four other kids who probably believe they're the real favorite."

He laughed, offering her his hand.

She put her hand in his and let him help her out of the low-slung Camaro. He held on all the way to the door of the scruffy little dive bar that was a few blocks removed from the action at the renovated pier. He didn't think Bethany would appreciate the loud crush of people tonight.

Stopping at the bar, he ordered wine for her and a beer for himself and picked up a basket of the hand-cut potato and sweet-potato chips the place was known for.

Bethany seemed as if she was sliding behind a shell since he'd given her the brief update on the case and he'd refused to let her withdraw from him again without a fight. This was their first outing as a couple, since he'd managed to surprise her on Valentine's Day of their second year. The day they'd apparently conceived. He discarded the notion that he'd miscalculated this move. They needed to find a way to reset their relationship and he wasn't about to settle for a platonic arrangement.

"Care to fill me in?" he asked after the waitress delivered their drinks. "Your mind is wandering."

"I'm just nervous about hanging out here like bait," she said with a shy smile.

"And," he prompted. "You know we wouldn't be here if I thought you were in danger."

Her smile wobbled. "Danger or not, it still feels like we're treading water, waiting for this guy to drop another bomb into our lives."

"I promise you, there are plenty of people working behind the scenes to cut him off before he causes any more trouble." He nudged the basket of chips closer to her. "Is it so awful spending time with me?" Though he said it as a joke, his breath backed up in his chest while he waited for her response. This trek might officially be a test of the enemy's reach, but Matt was determined to make it a success on the personal front.

"No." She shook her head, her gaze firmly on the glass of white wine in front of her. She peered at him from under her thick lashes. "Spending time with you is always easy."

A flood of happiness washed over him while questions chased through his mind. Would she let him kiss her, in front of Caleb or anyone else? Would she let him come up on the weekends and stay at her house? In her bed? Would she bring Caleb to Washington so they could talk guy stuff? Somehow he managed to keep that all inside rather than bombard her with his rash of insecurities.

"Until I screw it up," she said into the silence. "Can you ever forgive me, Matt?"

He didn't see what there was to forgive. Sure, she'd tossed some hard words at him. Looking back at those moments, she'd been frightened. And with good reason.

"Bethany," he began.

"I mean it," she said. "I thought I was doing the right thing, but now, seeing you with Caleb, seeing him with your parents, I know I screwed up."

What was the best way to convince her to let him be part of her world day in and day out? He gave himself a mental shake. Overthinking it wasn't working for either one of them. He had to be candid, give her no room to doubt. "Would it put your mind at ease to know none of us plan on pushing for custody?"

Her head snapped up, eyes wide with panic. "You discussed custody this morning?"

He touched her hand. "I made it clear that the previous arrangement was a mutual decision."

She snorted.

"This morning we discussed the investigation first. Afterward we talked about how important it was to *not* upset Caleb's life. Or yours. You've done a great job without any of us in the mix. Yes, we want to get to know him, to be sure he understands he has family that loves him. No one wants that to create a problem for you."

She shifted in her seat, avoiding his gaze. "How long do you plan on staying here?"

"At the bar or at the beach?" He was rewarded with an unamused glare. "Maybe a few days. It depends on the investigation and the attempt to draw out the ringleader."

"Okay."

He hadn't intended to dwell on custody arrangements or other practical matters tonight, but there wasn't a good way to separate Bethany from Caleb. Not in his heart and apparently not even in conversation. "You won't get any grief from the office about your absence?"

"I've banked plenty of leave and vacation time," she said, her eyes still on her wine. "My supervisor won't complain."

"You like your work?" he asked, carefully. A contracts officer wasn't the type of career she'd once planned on.

A reluctant smile played with her lips. "I really do. Admittedly, the career track didn't go according to my plans." There was no hostility or regret in her voice or her gaze. "I wouldn't trade a single day with Caleb to go back and do things differently at West Point."

Was that a signal to back off? Matt floundered for a more neutral topic. "You mentioned beach trips," he prompted. "Is there a specific area the two of you enjoy?"

She sat back and glared at him again. "Are you conducting an interview?"

"Maybe," he said, exasperated. "Aren't first dates a type of interview?"

"First dates?" Incredulous, she leaned forward. "You might be pretending a little too much."

He suppressed the frustration that wanted to just drag her into his lap and prove his true intentions here. "We were friends, and more, once." With his end game in mind, he blurted out his first thought, his only thought, every time he looked at her. He would tell her, over and over, until she finally believed him, believed *in* him. "I've missed you. When you told me you were pregnant, I knew things would change. I never thought I'd lose my best friend."

She stared at him, clearly stunned. "I send you updates several times a year."

He shook his head. She wasn't getting it. "That hasn't been enough to satisfy me about Caleb, and none of those updates included anything about *you*." He managed to stop himself just short of telling her he loved her still. He could see she wasn't ready to hear that yet. Well, he wasn't ready to retreat or surrender. They could have everything, be everything, as a family.

He knew it. He'd felt the hot desire in her touch and the sweet tremble under her skin last night. "Are you seeing someone?" he demanded, more roughly than he intended.

"I didn't lie to the investigators," she said, her mouth tense. "You know I'm not."

"Do you have any interest in reclaiming our friendship?"

In the process of bringing her wine glass to her mouth, she paused and returned it to the table as if any sudden movement would transform the glass into a snake that might bite her at the last second. "We definitely need to find a way to be friendly. For Caleb."

Friendly? Some deep and primal instinct protested at that limitation. "That's one factor." He thought his composure under the circumstances warranted an award for meritorious service. "What about for you?"

"Being friendly and establishing clear communication is essential," she said in a prim tone.

How was it everything he did to bring them closer seemed to have her moving in reverse and throwing up more roadblocks? He leaned forward. "Bethany, I don't care who or what put this in motion. The truth is out now and things will change."

"I'm aware."

She didn't sound too pleased about it. "I want what's best for all of us," he said. "You and Caleb. Me and Caleb. Caleb and my parents. You and me." There was some essential, clear communication for her to chew on.

She took a deep breath, her soft gaze tangled with his. "Your definition of 'us' seems to have several facets and a few moving parts."

"Together we will find the balance," he promised. "You'll find I'm pretty damn steady." Impatience to have everything in place, to have her willingly beside him, where she belonged, threatened to unravel his composure. Hadn't he demonstrated his reliability with the child support, the accommodation of her needs all this time?

She laid her hand over the back of his. "I know that, Matt, and I appreciate it."

He should appreciate that she'd never bad-mouthed him to their son. Single-parenting couldn't have been a picnic. Recalling his own teens, he suspected the next few years would be harder still. One of the many reasons she needed him.

"What was the last movie you saw?" he asked.

She blinked a few times at the abrupt return to first-date territory. "Caleb and I went to the latest superhero release. My girlfriends and I typically catch foreign films at this artsy little place down the street from our favorite wine bar."

"Foreign films?" That was new.

One blond eyebrow arched in challenge. "And that tone right there is why it's a girlfriend thing."

He wasn't the least bit ashamed by the relief he felt on that score. "I'd rather read a book than see a movie most of the time," he admitted.

"Caleb will cure you," she said. "What's the last book you read?"

He grinned, happy to be cured if it meant time with his son. "I'm in the middle of a detective thriller set in the early 1900s," he replied.

She named the author, beaming when he confirmed she'd guessed correctly. "I love his books, too."

"Really?"

She launched into her favorite parts of the previous book in the series, and the easy conversation carried them through a second round of drinks. On this topic, her face became a beacon of happiness. They enjoyed a lively analysis of the stories currently out and those the author might address in the future. Matt thought he could bask in the common ground and her enthusiasm all night long.

Riding that newfound connection, he paid the tab and invited her to walk on the beach, under the stars. He wasn't about to waste the romantic potential of a clear, warm night.

She accepted his hand when he offered it to steady her as she slipped out of her shoes. He kept her hand in his while they crossed over the loose sand near the dunes.

When they reached the packed sand near the tide line, he didn't want to let go. Fortunately, she didn't pull away.

The ocean rolled in, lapping at the shore, the sound a steady backdrop to their conversation. It was the first time in days he didn't feel the crawling sensation of being watched. It was just the two of them and it gave him a taste of what they could have. He wondered if her chattiness was because she too felt safe out here with him.

She seemed to read more than he did, across a wide variety of genres. An image flashed to the front of his mind, the two of them on opposite ends of a couch, comfortably engrossed with their books. And then he would set his novel aside and seduce her away from her story and into his arms with irresistible kisses and touches. *Please*, he thought, give him a chance to show her how sweet life could be if she let him in.

It wasn't a completely new vision, he realized, just a fresh rendition of the days they'd studied together in the lounge. Before she'd left West Point to protect his career. The thought sobered him momentarily. No matter what he did tonight or in the future, he could never repay her sacrifice. His sincere gratitude had fallen on deaf ears every time.

As the talk of books waned into a comfortable silence, he stopped and dug his toes into the sand. "If I could go back to our days at school, there's only one thing I would do differently."

"Use two condoms?" she quipped, proving just how relaxed she was.

"No." He smiled. "As you've said, everything about Caleb is a gift, not a regret." He smoothed her hair behind her ear as she gawked at him. "No," he repeated. "I would have given you a better reason to trust in me."

She frowned. "What are you talking about? I trusted you with everything."

The cool foam of the rising tide swept over his feet and he traced the soft glow of moonlight on her cheek. "Not everything. You didn't trust me to provide for you."

"Matt. Don't do this." She jerked back, out of his reach. "We were having such a good time."

"What did I do?"

"We can't keep poking at the old wounds." Her voice cracked. "I could have dropped out of West Point, out of your life without a word, but I told you what was going on. I trusted you with the truth. Why wasn't that enough?"

"You wouldn't let me step up and take responsibility."

She pushed at her hair and the sound she made sounded like a growl. "Because you had other commitments and so many expectations." She wrapped her arms around her middle now. "Better if only one of us gave up the dreams and goals we'd brought with us to school."

"I stand by my answer," he insisted. "I respected your decisions every step of the way. And every day, for the past fifteen years, I've wanted to give you and Caleb more than money."

"You're angry," she murmured.

"Not with you," he said.

On an oath, she stalked off, the breeze from the ocean lifting her hair like a cape behind her.

"Well, not entirely with you," he admitted. She shivered and he slid his arms around her waist, drawing her back into the warmth of his body. "Bethany, you're one of the strongest, most stubborn people I know. What good would arguing have done? All this time, I've kept out of the way, giving you space and privacy at every turn. Everything you said would make you happy, I agreed to. Now I want more."

"More?" Her voice cracked. "Why are you doing this?"

"Last night you said you'd give me whatever I wanted," he reminded her.

"And look how that ended," she muttered. "I keep hurting you, Matt."

"Not intentionally," he said. He kissed the soft, delicate skin where her neck and shoulder merged. Her body seemed to sigh in response. "I want you. Trust that." He turned her slowly within the circle of his arms. Her gaze was fixed on his chest and he tipped up her chin, the moonlight painting her face in a lovely glow. "Trust me."

As soon as his lips touched hers, he knew. Nothing had changed. Hurtful words aside, his heart was still hers. Would always be. What they'd shared years ago hadn't been a fluke. This heat and need were as current and tangible and constant as the tide.

Matt wanted her as a woman, as mother to their son, as his family. He wanted his best friend back in his life. She and Caleb had been the family of his heart all this time and he refused to neglect that need any longer.

He slid a hand into her hair, taking the kiss into that wild territory known only to the two of them. Her hands gripped his shoulders and she pressed those soft curves flush against him. It was a wonder his shirt didn't flare and ignite from the need rising to a demanding blaze between them.

He felt light-headed and completely grounded at the same time. He didn't know how it was possible, except for her. No other woman did this to him. Never would. She was everything. Moonlight and sunshine. In her, he felt both a sweet freedom and a stable foundation.

He brushed a kiss over the shell of her ear, nipped her earlobe lightly, drawing out a shivery gasp. She didn't retreat now, only tilted her head to grant him better access to that slim column of her throat.

Painfully hard, he pulled her hips to his so she could feel what she did to him. "More?"

"Oh, yes, Matt. Please."

He cupped her breast in one hand, thumbing the nipple through the fabric of her sweater. She arched into his touch with a moan that made him want to lay her down right here on the sand.

Her fingers tugged his shirt free of his jeans, and when he felt her skin on his, he growled with pleasure. Those clever fingers slipped under his waistband and gripped hard.

He wanted more, far more, than sex. He wanted her as addicted to him, to them, as he was. But not here on the sand, on a public beach. Although an arrest for public indecency might make for a humorous story, it wouldn't do anything to prove she could trust him with her every need and desire.

With his lips fused to hers, he pulled her hands back and threaded his fingers through hers. "Let's go back," he said. "Soft sheets are better than sand."

"In a minute." She linked her hands behind his neck and gently pulled his mouth down to hers. Her velvet tongue tangled with his and he suddenly wasn't sure it was safe for him to drive.

Was she testing him or was she as overwhelmed as he was? They should probably stay here until he could see clearly again. He nudged her further up the beach, away from the chill water of the incoming tide, his hands cruising up and down her mouthwatering curves.

If he wanted to get out of here, he should make more of an effort to slow things down. He'd remember how to do that any minute now.

In the dwindling part of her brain that was thinking logically, Bethany agreed that sheets and a soft mattress would be better than sand, yet she wasn't ready to put these incomparable feelings on the back burner for the drive back.

Back to a guest room in his parents' house.

Just anticipating the awkwardness of that scene made her blush. They had to go back, and better to go back earlier rather than later. She hadn't even thought of Caleb in close to an hour. What if he needed her?

Right. She nearly laughed aloud. Caleb hadn't exhibited any reservations about meeting Matt's family. She knew her son was polite, confident and adaptable.

And she'd denied him his rightful place with the Rileys because of her fears. Fear, specifically and singular, of the man kissing her now.

She eased back, her mind reeling and her heart aching with what couldn't be. Even if he really had forgiven her for denying him his son all these years, how would he ever trust that she wanted him on his own merits and not just as a protector from a persistent enemy?

"Hey." Matt smoothed her windblown hair back from her face. "You disappeared on me again. What are you thinking about?"

"I had an image of facing your parents and Caleb after making out with you."

"So what?" He grinned. "Caleb is solid evidence we've done more than make out in the past?" He nibbled at her lips again. "My parents know where babies come from."

"Stop." She gave him a nudge back, but she couldn't stop the giggling that bubbled up.

He'd always known what to say to draw her out of herself, until she'd taken herself too far out of his reach.

"You're overthinking it," he murmured.

And that quickly she bristled, once more on the defensive. "Which part?" She folded her arms over her chest, if only to keep her hands off him.

"We're not kids anymore," he said. "There's no curfew. If we both want to spend time here on the sand or sleep in the same bed, that's up to us."

"And what example would that set for Caleb?" she challenged his logic with the only argument she had left: parenting.

"How would it be anything other than good news that his parents want to be together."

Exasperated, she stalked away from him. The space and cool breeze off the water helped her regain her composure.

"What's the real issue?" Matt asked, trailing her. "I can't help if you don't open up."

She couldn't tell him she loved him. She should, she just couldn't seem to bring those words up out of her frightened heart. "Why didn't you ever marry?" She'd asked him before, but over the last few days, she realized he hadn't given her the full truth.

He scowled and turned that dark gaze out to the water. "If I tell you, will you answer the same question?"

"Yes." Once she heard his answer, she'd know how to couch her own reply.

He shrugged out of his jacket and laid it out like a blanket on the sand for her, another example of his chivalrous manners. She'd done her best to instill those same values in Caleb, if for no other reason than so he would make his father proud if they ever met.

And they had. She realized she was more than glad; she was truly relieved that they would have a relationship from this point forward.

"Come here." Matt drew her down to sit next to him, sliding his hand down her arm to clasp her hand.

She stared at their joined hands, balanced on his knee. How many times had she had dreams of stolen moments like this one? "Plan to keep me waiting much longer?"

He rubbed his shoulder to hers. "I never married because no one else was you."

Her heart did a happy pirouette in her chest and she resisted the urge to lean into him.

"Don't get me wrong—I dated."

"Me too," she said. "I wouldn't have expected anything else."

"Whenever things started getting serious, I imagined what would happen if you ever relented and gave me a chance to know Caleb," he added.

Me too, she repeated in her mind. "You must blame me for so much."

"We're both responsible, Bethany. I'm sure it hasn't felt that way, when you've been in the thick of it day in and day out on your own, but I don't blame you for anything."

"There are times when you are too good to be true," she said.

"What a crock," he said. "You're just trying to get me into bed."

She laughed, snuggling into his warmth as a breeze raised goose bumps along her arms. Matt wrapped his arm around her shoulders, sheltering her with his bigger body.

"You're my best friend, love," he said. "You know my flaws, as well as my strengths."

The endearment left her dizzy. "I'm not so sure."

Matt gave her a squeeze. "It's your turn. Why didn't you marry?"

She stared out at the blackness of the ocean. Lights sparkled from the pier in one direction. Homes dotted the shoreline in the other direction. Somewhere out there Matt's parents were getting to know their grandson.

"I came close once." She felt Matt's body tense. She hadn't meant to lead with that. It seemed rude when a few minutes ago they'd nearly had sex right here on the beach, heedless of their surroundings. "My reason isn't much different than yours. When it came time to explain why Caleb's father wasn't around, I couldn't do it."

"Why not?"

Where to start? She'd discovered in the nick of time that to settle would have been a disservice to both of them. All three of them. Her heart had fallen into

Matt's care when she was nineteen. Every day as Caleb's mother had only intensified that one-way bond. Her son resembled his father in some obvious ways: the dimple in his cheek, the shape and color of his eyes, and the hair. It didn't stop there. Athletic and bright, she saw her son growing into more of Matt every year. If she'd remarried, she opened Caleb up to influences she didn't know or understand as well as she'd once understood Matt. She told herself that if she truly loved the man it wouldn't have bothered her.

"You did it again." Matt spoked quietly near her ear, and then kissed her cheek.

"What?"

"Drifted off."

She shook her head. "He was a good man and I'm sure in general he would have been a good stepfather to Caleb."

"But?"

"But he wasn't the *right* man and it wasn't the right time." Only Matt had been the right man, and unfortunately, they'd crossed paths at the wrong time.

"Do you think there's a right man for you?"

Recognizing the opening, she dodged it. She stroked his arm, enjoying that she had the chance to touch him again. "I think I was very fortunate that my son's father is an amazing and honorable person. Beyond that, if my Mr. Right is out there, he'll show up when I need him."

There, she'd been honest without pasting her heart on her sleeve. At least the conversation had muted the blinding heat that had nearly overtaken them earlier. Maybe she wouldn't feel so much like an errant teenager when they returned to the Rileys' house.

"I want to be your Mr. Right," he said.

She turned, gawking at his bald admission, and found him watching her intently.

"Was that communicating too clearly?"

Suddenly the full force of the changes time had wrought on him crashed over her. Even at twenty, the angles of his face hadn't been so hard and unyielding. Experience and commitment had refined his handsome features. A sense of him in a command role filled her with pride and a purely feminine flutter.

"You have been," she answered at last. "All this time, you've supported my needs and Caleb's, too." Shutting him out had been the only way she knew to survive, to give all three of them the best chance at happiness. It would have been too easy to simply let him take over and lead their lives, to lose her identity in the shadow of his career and charisma. That would have ended badly for both of them. She didn't know how to explain all of that without hurting him again.

"You have been," she repeated. "You've helped financially and abided by my terms when you could've been a jerk about everything."

"I wanted to be a jerk more than once."

She smiled. "I know. You've shown admirable restraint."

He kissed her again. "No truer words," he whispered.

It took a few seconds to catch her breath. "Come on, your parents are probably ready for a break."

"Not a chance." Still, he rolled to his feet and reached back to assist her. "You'll be lucky if you get an hour alone with Caleb while we're here." He carefully shook the sand from his jacket and folded it over his arm. "Fair warning, your suitcase is in my room."

She'd assumed she was bunking in a separate spare room with Caleb. "That was presumptuous." But her pulse leaped at the idea of sharing his bed.

He leaned in and brushed his lips over hers. The kiss sizzled through her, from her lips to her toes. "That right there," he stroked his thumb over her inner wrist. "Tells me it wasn't."

"Matt."

"I suppose I'm a fool for hoping you're about to thank me."

"Why would I thank you for that?" she demanded.

"Not for presuming, for saving you." With his hand at the small of her back, they walked back to the car.

She never could resist that teasing charm. "Is the house haunted?"

He shook his head.

"Monsters?"

"Worse," he said. "There are too many people. I've saved you from getting caught sneaking to or from my room."

"You thought that would be a problem?" she asked, incredulous and more amused than she should be.

"I am irresistible," he said with false modesty.

She certainly thought so. While she searched for the strength to say no, to tell him this wasn't the right time to make this kind of move, he kissed her again.

He pulled back, breathing hard as he touched his forehead to hers. "I've never felt that with anyone else, Bethany." He guided her over the dunes. "You make me weak."

"Same goes," she admitted.

He paused when they reached the car, caging her between his body and the door. "You really shouldn't give me that kind of ammunition." He brought her close to his body to open the car door and then eased her down into the passenger seat. He'd upped his game significantly since their days at West Point.

They were both aware how much she wanted him, but she couldn't quite forget where they were and what had propelled them to this point. "I want you," she confessed a few minutes later when he turned off the road toward the house. "I just don't want to offend your parents."

He parked the car and leaned in. "That might be better remedied if you worried about it less and just kissed me more."

"That sounds like self-serving advice."

"Stay in my room tonight. I need you close." He traced each of her fingers in turn. "I'll sleep on the floor until you invite me to the bed."

Though she rolled her eyes, she let him hold her hand as they walked up the stairs and inside. Instead of a greeting of censure and judgment, the house appeared to be empty. "Where is everyone?" Fear that they'd been followed and the culprit had struck again made it impossible for her to do anything other than cling to Matt.

"Easy." Matt squeezed her hand. "Listen." He tugged her toward the glass slider leading out to the deck. Down on the beach, four people sat around a little fire. In the light of the flames, she could see happy faces all around.

"Grace Ann arrived," Matt said. "Doesn't look like we're needed out there. Unless you'd rather go shoot the breeze over s'mores than dive into all of this." He spread his arms wide.

Smothering a laugh, she turned away from the scene on the beach. "I might have had enough of both for tonight," she teased. Can you show me to the room? If that won't be perceived as rude."

He gestured for her to start up the steps. "You can relax around my parents," he commented from behind her. "They think the world of you."

She didn't understand his confidence under the circumstances. "How do you know?"

"I can tell." At the landing, he stepped around her to lead the way to the bedroom they were apparently sharing. "I'm the favorite, remember?"

At the far end of the hallway, he opened the door and flipped on the light. The surprises kept coming. A queen-size bed was centered on the far wall, under a row of transom windows. At this end of the room, a loveseat and easy chair were anchored by what appeared to be a set of antique nesting tables. The view of the beach would be stunning in daylight, though the curtains were drawn at the moment.

"The en suite bath is through there." Matt tipped his head. "This is a pullout." He patted the back of the loveseat. So we can share the room."

She managed to turn away from the lovely bathroom. "And your crack about sleeping on the floor?"

"A misguided attempt for sympathy." He grinned, the dimple creasing his cheek.

And it had nearly worked, she thought, feeling an answering grin tugging at her lips. "You're shameless."

"Yes." He tucked his hands into his pockets.

She glanced to her suitcase, which was tucked beside his at the closet door. After all this time, he was still the man she wanted. Caleb was outside, safe and happy, getting to know this new branch of his family tree. He was with people as committed to his safety as she was, regardless that they'd just recently learned of his existence.

This was a moment out of time and she decided to seize it. Closure or a new beginning, she wasn't yet sure. It didn't matter. She crossed the room, reached past Matt and closed the door. She turned the lock, simply to make her point. And then she walked over to the foot of the bed.

He'd given her so much more than good conversation and a couple of glasses of wine. He'd restored her confidence in them, whatever relationship they established in the hours, days or months ahead. Her heart yearned for him. Rather than risk further conversation, she decided to let her actions do the talking for her. She tugged off her sweater and unbuttoned her jeans, pushing the denim over her hips and down her legs.

If the stretchmarks were a problem, best to find out now.

His gaze was hot, focused, as she stepped away from her discarded clothing and approached him in only her black lace bra and panties. There were other colors that were better on her skin, but when she'd dressed this morning, she hadn't anticipated making love to Matt tonight.

Boldly, she unbuttoned his shirt and smoothed the panels apart. His chest swelled as he dragged in a deep breath under her touch. He'd left the wound uncovered, and it seemed to be healing well.

Her hands skated lower, down his rippling abs to

his trim hips and then back up, until she gripped his shoulders.

On a low groan, he boosted her up, her legs coming around his waist as he carried her to the bed. She expected him to toss her down and cover her, but he was gentle, treating her as if she was a special treasure to savor and explore.

His lips met hers and then cruised leisurely down her throat to her breasts. He teased and tantalized, working her aching flesh with his tongue and teeth through the fabric of her bra. When he flicked the clasp and removed the barrier, she bit back a cry at the heat of his mouth as he suckled each throbbing nipple before moving lower.

He murmured words she couldn't decipher against her skin. Whatever he said, she felt adored and precious. Loved. Love was there in his hands, in his breath, in the way he brought her to a hard, fast climax that left her gasping and reaching for him.

Ditching his jeans and stretching out beside her, she felt his heart hammering in his chest, a deeper, heavier echo of her own. It seemed the more some things changed, the more they stayed the same. Matt Riley was an unassailable constant in her life.

A small voice in her head scolded her for doubting her love for him, for resisting the facts that had been so evident from the start. Her passion expanded, exploded with that realization. She rolled him onto his back and straddled him, filling her hands with the heat and shape of his muscles. She taught herself the planes and hollows of his body once more, wringing out the pleasure for both of them as she explored what she remembered, and what was new.

A scar here and there, combat or training, she didn't know. Her fault for pushing him away. No longer. She took him deep inside her body, rocked slowly as his hands gripped her hips. On a sigh, she savored what was so familiar and what was equally new and fresh.

The sheer power of him, of *them* together, overwhelmed her senses. She surrendered control, simply holding him close with body, heart and soul before he shifted her underneath him and drove them both to a shuddering climax. Thoroughly satisfied and spent, she relished the heavy weight of him covering her.

When he rolled off her at last, he tucked her close to his side, his hand moved up and down her spine in lazy, soothing strokes. The best feeling in the world and one she'd only ever shared with Matt.

I love you. The words were right there, three words she'd wanted to give him for almost half her life. She kept them to herself. Again.

He'd told her he wanted to earn her trust, but that was never the problem. She'd always trusted him. She hadn't trusted herself enough to stand strong and independent of his name and career. If she'd accepted his first proposal before Caleb was born, or even the two that had come later, she might never have finished school or found her way into a job that challenged her.

Fantastic sex aside, once the current threat was removed, they would most likely go back to a modified version of the way things were. Oh, sure, Caleb would see the Rileys more often, and she'd have to share holidays. That didn't change that deep down she'd still be a single mom who'd tossed aside her chance at true love.

She watched the rise and fall of Matt's chest as his breathing evened out. When she was sure he was asleep, she whispered the three words she'd needed to say for so long.

"I love you."

Chapter 11

"*I love you.*" Those three words followed Matt all morning, distracting him when he tried to keep up with appearances and conversations around his family, his son.

Bethany had thought he'd been asleep when she'd whispered those words against his chest. It had taken every ounce of willpower to hold back his response. He'd wanted to share the moment, to give her those same words back, over and over, until she believed it, accepted it, and him. Until he'd smothered all of those fears she wouldn't share and they could be a complete family.

His mother had raised a knowing eyebrow when he'd come down early for coffee, but otherwise nothing was said about the two of them sharing a room. When Bethany had made her way downstairs sometime later, her long hair pulled back from her face, damp and fragrant from a shower, he was swamped with contentment.

"Tea?" He tipped his head toward the carousel of options next to the machine. Her shy smile as she tried to avoid his gaze left him grinning.

"Good morning," she said as she waited for the machine to fill her mug with black tea. "Where is everyone?"

"Outside on the deck," he replied.

"Mom!" Caleb barreled in from outside, swim trunks and T-shirt plastered to his skin, along with a fine layer of sand. "Aunt Gracie is teaching me to surf. Come watch."

"On my way," she said. When he bolted back outside, she turned to Matt. "He's been surfing before."

"Not with Aunt Gracie," Matt said with a shrug. The kid was happy. He was more startled by her easy acceptance of an Aunt Gracie in Caleb's life. Was it too soon to hope they were gaining ground as a family?

He escorted Bethany out to the deck, where they joined his parents, both of whom were engrossed with the action on the beach.

"He has excellent balance," Ben was saying, leaning forward in his chair.

"Better than Grace at the same age," Patricia noted.

"Weren't we in Germany when Grace was that age?" Matt asked, subtly calling out his mom's favoritism for her grandson.

"We vacationed in Hawaii that Christmas," she said, not missing a beat.

"And there's no difference at all between the Pacific and Atlantic surf."

She pointedly ignored him.

"I can't wait to tell Grace Ann her star's been replaced."

Ben patted the chair next to him. "Come on over here, Bethany."

Matt wondered what his dad was about, but his mother gave him a "let it go" look. He supposed it was a need-to-know type of conversation. He sipped his coffee, pretending not to listen.

"Caleb chattered for quite some time last night about Matt's Camaro," Ben said. "Have you given any thought to what kind of car you want for him?"

Getting an idea of where this conversation was headed, Matt wanted to intervene. He should have expected his parents to make grand gestures to compensate for what they saw as lost time. At the very least, he should have mentioned the possibility to Bethany.

"General, s-sir, Ben," Bethany stammered. "He has another year or two before he's ready to drive and care for a car."

"On the contrary," Ben said with a smile. "I think he's just the right age to appreciate what it takes to keep a car in working order. If you think he has the interest and the time."

"What are you suggesting?" Bethany asked, her gaze moving swiftly past Matt and on to where Caleb was sitting on a surfboard out in the water, dialed in to whatever instruction Grace Ann was offering.

"Caleb didn't give me the impression that your dad worked on cars," Ben said.

"Well, no. They usually go fishing or hiking," she replied. "Caleb hasn't had much exposure to basic mechanics."

Matt stiffened at the apologetic note in her voice. No one had the right to make her doubt her parenting. He'd only met her parents once. It had been their freshman year at West Point, on the same family weekend when she'd met his parents.

In his vague recollection, he thought they'd been nice, decent people, full of love and pride for Bethany. She'd always claimed they were supportive of her choices as a mom, a student and a professional.

"I didn't want to bring it up until I knew we wouldn't be stepping on any toes," his dad was saying. "Yours or your dad's." Ben's enthusiasm was clearly building.

"What is he up to?" Matt whispered to his mom. She ignored him, pointing to the water, where Caleb was watching rollers push to shore. Matt wasn't so easily distracted.

"I'm not sure if you're stepping on toes or not," Bethany said. "What do you have in mind, sir?"

"Ben," he reminded her. "We're family now, honey."

Bethany nodded, her lips pinched between her teeth and her hands clinging to her mug of tea. This really wasn't the right time. She'd barely had a chance to wake up.

"I was thinking we might take Caleb out to find a car this afternoon."

"What?" Her mouth dropped open in shock. She leveled an accusing glare at Matt. "What?" she repeated.

He opened his mouth, to explain he'd had nothing to do with this, but his dad drew her attention. Good. Matt didn't want all the progress they'd made to get undone because his dad saw a chance to raise another grease monkey.

"I haven't mentioned it to Caleb yet," Ben said. "In case you didn't approve."

"No." Bethany's shoulders rolled back. "I do not approve of you buying a fourteen-year-old a car."

"To be fair, calling it a car might be overstating it," Ben said. "I'd like to buy something he and Matt can work on, take their time with."

Bethany had opened her mouth to argue and snapped it shut again when the words sunk in. Her lips slowly formed a small circle that dumped Matt's mind right back to last night and scenes he'd rather not dwell on while sitting next to his mother.

"How about Dad and I take him out this afternoon and gauge his interest?" Matt suggested. "We won't push him into anything."

"That's a great plan," his mother said, chiming in. "That leaves the three of us time for a girls' day. I'm overdue and I bet you are, as well."

Bethany smiled and murmured a gracious agreement and let the ensuing conversation swirl around her. Clearly they'd overwhelmed her. Damn. That would probably backfire on him.

Matt was sure he was the only one who caught the flicker of sadness in her pretty brown eyes. He wanted to know what she was thinking, though he wouldn't press her in front of his parents.

At the sound of a sharp whistle, Matt's attention snapped to the beach. "Check him out!" He stood up and pointed to the beach, where Caleb came in on a low wave, executing a cut back to ride the wave right into shore as if he'd been born to it.

His parents and Bethany stood as well, applauding and cheering. Caleb hopped off his board as the wave fell apart on the beach, and he punched a fist into the air and then took a deep bow.

The kid was fitting right in as a Riley. Matt wished he could feel simple pride about that. Instead, his mind kept drifting back to whatever was haunting the woman he loved. Setting aside his coffee mug, he headed down to the beach, pleased to hear Bethany excusing herself to join him.

Caleb, surfboard under his arm, came loping up to them. With a flick of his head, he shook the water from his hair and pushed it off his face. Laughing a little. Matt gave him a high five.

"You did a great job," Bethany told him.

"Aunt Gracie's awesome," Caleb launched into the key things he'd already learned while the three of them waited for Grace Ann to ride in to the shore near them.

"Hey, squirt," Matt said as his sister joined them after a few minutes. He slipped his arm around Bethany's shoulders and made the introductions.

Grace Ann's dark eyebrows twitched just a fraction as she correctly interpreted his possessive gesture. "Pleased to meet you," she said. "Your son is a quick learner."

"I think he comes by it naturally from the Riley side of the family," Bethany said.

"Mom has decided you're having girl time while Dad and I take Caleb out this afternoon."

"Where are we going?" Caleb asked.

Matt shook his head. "Pop wants it to be a surprise. You'll find out soon enough." He wasn't about to steal his dad's thunder. "Tell them we'll be back in a bit."

For several minutes, they walked along in silence, not touching. Finally Matt couldn't take it anymore. "You okay?"

"Sure," she said. Her lips twitched with the fib.

"Is that code for you're feeling blindsided and don't

want to talk about it?" He caught her hand and swung it a little as they walked on.

"Sure," she repeated, laughing a little. She tipped her head back to study the clear sky above. "The idea of a car bugged me, but thinking of it as a project you can share, it makes more sense."

"Good." He tried to wrap his head around what he wanted to say. It was important to state things in a way that she wouldn't argue with him.

"Have you heard anything more on the investigation?"

"Eager to get out of Riley territory?"

"No." Her smile was sincere, calm. She pressed up on her toes and kissed him lightly. "It's peaceful here, which is a nice feeling."

Agreeing with her, he kept the lack of any developments to himself, and just let them enjoy these moments, not sure what to expect when this interlude ended. Eventually, they turned back and watched Grace Ann and Caleb bodysurfing.

"He's a Riley to the bone," she said, leaning into his arm. "I've always seen you in him, but he moves like Grace Ann."

Matt knew what she meant. "You know what I see when I look at him?" He waited until she dragged her gaze away from their delighted son. "I see you. In every school and team picture, I see your fire and grit."

He'd never held his son as a baby, never played catch out in the yard or taught him to swing a bat. And with every hour, he discovered how little those missed moments mattered. None of what they hadn't done lessened his love for Caleb or Bethany.

They'd reached the house and his mother was calling all of them up for breakfast. He kissed her fast before anyone had a chance to notice.

"When you're out today, try to relax and have fun," he said. "I know it's not a foreign film, but there will probably be mimosas or margaritas."

He stole another kiss. If he could keep her dazzled, he might have a better chance making this permanent. "They like you already," he promised. His hands on her hips, he urged her up the stairs. "And take notes," he whispered at her ear, pleased when she shivered.

"Notes?" She cocked an eyebrow. "On a girl day?"

"Yes. Then we can compare tonight," he wiggled his eyebrows, "in bed."

It made her laugh, which is exactly the Bethany Trent he wanted his family to see.

They ate breakfast amid a great deal of happy chatter before the three women dashed off to do their thing. From Matt's perspective, life didn't get much better than three generations of Riley men on the hunt for the right project car. Caleb had been a bit wary about the search when they set out, but once Ben, aka Pop, shared a few stories about the potential, he got into it.

Now with the sun going down, Matt stood under the bright lights of his dad's garage, shaking his head at the little rust bucket his son had chosen as a first car. It was going to take a solid year of weekends to get it in working shape.

And when it was done, Caleb would be careful with it on the street, making him a more conscientious driver, which was the real point of this endeavor. His parents had handled each of their new-driver children in a similar fashion. Matt smiled to himself, looking forward to every greasy, frustrating hour in store with his son.

He had so much to be thankful for and yet he couldn't drag his mind from all he would lose if the persistent predator had his way. There hadn't been any real trouble for either the men or women this afternoon, and so far nothing new had happened to his siblings, but Alex's team wasn't any closer to identifying the opposition that had been working them over. He'd squeezed out a few minutes alone with his dad, talking over various missions and problematic soldiers. He'd passed along another few names, though it would be some time before they knew if the names panned out.

Matt wanted to insist that Caleb and Bethany stay here with his parents, out of harm's way. They would happily stock the boat and head out to sea for a few days while Matt flushed out the troublemaker. He could go back to Washington and draw out this vengeful jerk.

Of course, he already knew Bethany would never go for it.

The garage door opened and Bethany walked in as if his thoughts summoned her. If only life was so easy. "I came to tell you to stop thinking about it," she said, planting her hands on her hips.

"You're back." He started to move to her and then stopped, a little dazed. Her hair was voluminous, artless waves cascading all over. Her fingertips were painted with a shell pink. He glanced down, and found a brighter hue on her toes. He nearly scooped her up, intent on taking her to the nearest flat surface. Girl day had been good to her.

"Stop looking at me that way. I'm serious, Matt."

"About what?" he asked, in case they weren't on the same page.

She pinned him with a sharp look. "Your mother and Grace Ann were hinting all afternoon about taking a cruise on the boat. If we do that, you'll stay behind and try something stupid."

He was insulted by that. "We'd make a smart plan."

She flicked that away. "We're better off sticking together."

"Beth, come on."

"No, Matt. A divided front never wins." She came over and leaned against the workbench with him. "You may have the West Point diploma and ring, but I got you through that first year of Military history."

"You're delusional," he shot back, laughing now. Ben Riley's children knew their history, Military and otherwise, backward and forward. "And it's clearly hereditary." He lifted his chin toward the sad little car. "Our son thinks that's a car."

"Hmm." She tilted her head, as if a fresh angle might make it look better. "I could make a similar argument, if you believe I'll go sailing off and let you handle this alone."

He reached for her. The knot in his stomach loosened as she slid her arms around his waist. "You do understand I'm trying to protect both of you."

Her mouth curved. "Of course I do. The same way you understand I won't let you go into this alone. He fired bullets at my son."

And him too, Matt thought, keeping it to himself. "Feeling bloodthirsty?"

"More than a little," she admitted. Her hands smoothed up and down his back. "I know you're the real target, that Caleb is a bonus or something, but I won't let you just handle this *for* me." She stepped back.

He immediately closed the distance again. "Beth, you've done *everything* for me," he countered. "I respected all of your choices and boundaries. Can't you give on this one thing?"

Her lovely eyes went wide and then she laughed, dropping her head to his chest. "Is that how you saw it?"

"Saw it?" He frowned, tipping up her chin so he could look into her face. "That's what you did," he said. "You left West Point and your ideal career plan. You flat-out told me to go have a career and leave you and the baby alone."

"I should've known you'd see my selfishness as an honorable sacrifice." She hugged him hard.

"Bethany Trent, you've never been selfish a day in your life."

"Self-preserving then," she said. "Matt, I refused to marry you because I wanted to say yes. Desperately."

"That makes no sense." He'd loved her, never actually gotten over her. She'd just told him last night she loved him too, though he wasn't supposed to know that. Starting a career with a young family wasn't an insurmountable challenge. People did it every day. "You told me a child needed stability." And in those words, she'd flat-out condemned the way he'd been raised. It had taken a long time for him to get over that.

"Matt." She reached up and stroked his jaw, her fingers toying with the scruff since he hadn't shaved since their arrival. "I'm sorry for hurting you in my effort to…to survive us."

"Us?" He felt about as intelligent as a brick wall in this conversation, but she was finally opening up and he was determined to understand what went wrong then so he could fix it now. "Can you spell that out for me? Please?"

"I loved you more than any of my plans. It scared me, Matt. I would've done anything to stay with you. Neither one of us could have grown into who we needed to be under that kind of pressure."

He shook his head as if he'd just come up for air after a deep dive. His chest constricted and his heart raced. "You thought it was better going alone as a single mom rather than trying a family with me?" he asked through clenched teeth. It was water under the bridge, nothing to be gained by rehashing it, and still his temper had him by the throat.

Her gaze lifted to his. "Yes. I was barely twenty, and you?" She stepped back and flung an arm at him. "Well, you were General Riley's legacy."

He blew out a long slow breath. "You were the only person I knew who didn't hold that against me."

"*I* held it against me," she said. "I didn't want you feeling trapped or limited by obligations I thrust on you." She bit her lip and pushed at her freshly styled hair. "Caleb and I watched your graduation."

"What?" She had to be lying. He would have seen her.

"We were there," she said. "I asked another friend in your class for tickets. I was so proud of you. The ceremony made me more determined than ever to keep going on my own. When you reached out and proposed again that next week, I wanted to say yes, but—"

"You said no."

She shrugged. "Caleb and I were making things work."

"And you decided I didn't need a wife and kid tagging along," he said before she could. He'd heard her say it too often through the years.

"I had goals, too," she said, bristling. "Goals and plans for myself that were a little bigger than being your wife."

"Stop. Please." He stalked away from her. Time and again they came back to this point where her goals and his "couldn't possibly" line up.

No matter what had brought them together, he'd been thankful for another chance, another opportunity to look her in the eye and ask to start over. From this point forward. Right now.

"I love you." There. He saw her eyes go wide with shock. Everything he wanted to say, every thought in his head and heart stemmed from those three words. If she could tell him, but not accept him, there wasn't any sense in spitting out the rest of the plans he wanted to make.

"Oh, Matt."

She didn't sound like a woman about to leap into his arms with joy.

"A part of my heart will always love you, too, as Caleb's father," she added after a lengthy hesitation. Her mouth didn't twitch. "Caleb loves you already, too. He's looking forward to spending time with you—with his dad."

Matt's ears were ringing. She was pushing him away. Like every other time. What was it his mom had said this morning? That he should count his blessings Bethany hadn't married anyone else. Maybe he would have gotten over her if she had.

No. Not a chance. She'd been it for him from the beginning. And though he'd tried, he couldn't make her see him as her Mr. Right.

He reminded himself he'd lived with the disappointment and no son for fourteen years. He had more to love about life than Bethany. Now he could build memories and create a real bond with his son.

"I'll arrange to ship the car to a garage near your place," Matt said, his voice echoing in his ears. "We'll rent out a work bay and tools by the hour as needed. I'll be up there as often as possible."

"Caleb will be thrilled."

Matt nodded. "Me too."

"I've made you angry. I wish I could give you what you want."

Harsh laughter burst out of him, backing her up. "No. I'm not angry." There were too many other emotions for anger to play into it yet. Sad? Yes. Miserable? Definitely. And he was sure as hell confused. "How can I be angry with you?" he asked. "You were clear about your needs and intentions from the start." He backed away, toward the door, any escape.

Color stained her cheeks and he was reminded of her in his arms, her supple body twined with his. Hope had taken root inside him last night. Holding her was something he'd felt he was meant to do. Would he never stop being a fool around her?

He blew past her and walked straight out to the beach, his heart in pieces again.

Bethany wanted to kick herself. She lingered in the dark privacy of the garage, wishing for the courage to give Matt what he needed.

He deserved more from her than she'd ever been comfortable giving. Even after last night, after all the talking, she still wasn't *sure*. Holding back might have protected her once, shoring her up to face the challenges ahead. Although locking her feelings away from everyone other than Caleb might have turned into a habit, it brought her no comfort now. She'd tried to be honest—she did love Matt—and managed only to hurt him. When he walked away, it felt as if a priceless treasure had slipped through her grasp and crashed into pieces on the floor.

Again.

She'd entered West Point so sure of herself, her goals and her courage. It wasn't easy to accept she was a coward at heart, too afraid of love to take the chance.

Being afraid of her reactions to Matt was senseless and maybe more of a habit than she'd thought. He'd shown her nothing but support and loyalty in the strict, limited ways she allowed.

Caleb had made it clear how he felt about having a father and being welcomed by the Riley family. They'd given her a warmer welcome than she expected, more than she deserved in light of all her mistakes.

After all of that, how could Matt send her on a cruise while he faced the risks alone?

Because he loved her.

Everything he did was for love. She could see it now, in the small moments and the big ones. He would stand and shield her and Caleb for as long as necessary. She might not be brave enough to let herself love him outright with a day-to-day relationship, but she could be brave enough to watch his back.

Chapter 12

They left as early on Sunday as Matt could reasonably get away. He'd used the investigation as an excuse to distance himself from Bethany and the rest of his family. His mother had nearly cornered him a time or two, but he'd managed to get away with the help of Grace Ann. Though he'd tried to hide it, his family knew something was wrong.

Caleb had rambled about cars in every shape and size, practically without taking a breath, for the first half of the drive back to DC. It was an enjoyable distraction for Matt, who savored his son's enthusiasm as he wondered what was going through Bethany's mind. It shouldn't matter. Once the threat was removed, the three of them would establish a new normal. Whether or not he could have a relationship with her, he'd made it clear he wouldn't walk out of Caleb's life.

"How long will we stay with Matt, Mom?"

"Through your fall break," she replied. "I booked a

hotel near the Mall so we can walk to the monuments and museums."

This was the first Matt heard about a hotel. With Caleb listening, he pretended this wasn't news. They all knew he had plenty of room at the condo, but he supposed that had been wishful thinking. He'd have to tell Alex about this shift at the first opportunity. Thanks to two generals tugging on strings, two dedicated security teams were being briefed. One to protect Bethany and Caleb, and one to back him up.

"We're not staying with Matt?"

"Matt has to work," Bethany supplied smoothly enough to make Matt's teeth ache. "This way we can all come and go as we please."

Yeah, his key assignment this week was to draw out the man threatening them. As of the last report that came in before they left, Matt was still the primary target. Good news, as far as he was concerned.

"Your history teacher is looking forward to pictures and a brief report when you get back," Bethany said.

Caleb groaned and flopped backward. "You had to tell her where we were going?"

"She's my friend, as well as your teacher." Bethany swiveled around. "What's the big deal? You can do reports like that in your sleep."

"Can we go to the National Air and Space Museum?"

"Sure." Bethany's voice carried a wealth of maternal patience.

"What's your favorite place in Washington, Matt?"

"It's been a long time since I've done the tourist thing," he admitted. "I remember the view from the top of the Washington memorial as a kid."

"That would be awesome. It's always been closed when we've been before." Caleb yawned.

Matt slid a glance to Bethany. "What about a tour of the Pentagon? You've only seen a few corridors and missed all the good stuff."

"Seriously?" Caleb sat up again. "Please?"

"Do you like photography?"

In the rearview mirror, he caught Caleb's half-hearted shrug. "I guess. Why?"

"Just thinking out loud," Matt said. "General Knudson's daughter is a freshman. She knows DC inside and out and she's already on her school yearbook staff. If she has time, she might help with the photography part of your report."

"Huh."

Bethany pressed her lips together and turned her head toward the passing view, clearly not buying into the ultra-casual reply. The easy conversation continued off and on during the rest of the route. Matt's vigilance ratcheted with each mile that brought them closer to DC.

A weekend of peace wasn't exactly a statement of the enemy's limitations, but it had been a welcome respite, regardless. Traffic increased as they passed through Richmond and they unanimously agreed to stop for a treat when it was time to fill up with gas. It wasn't as if they were on a clock. Matt finished filling the tank and called Alex to check in.

"How are things looking?" Matt asked as soon as his friend answered.

"Looks to me like you lost sight of the target," Alex said. "We just got an update this morning that she booked a hotel room. Why aren't she and the kid staying at your place?"

"Her choice." Matt couldn't hide his aggravation from one of his best friends. "I tried to get her to stay back with my parents."

Alex snorted. "Even I know she's not the sort to go for that. Tell me, did you give her any kind of good reason to stay *with* you?"

Clearly not. His gaze drifted to Bethany and Caleb at the booth inside the restaurant. "Drop it," Matt warned. Alex could hassle him later. On their next fishing trip, maybe. "What am I driving us into?"

"Nothing worse than typical traffic," Alex reported. "The first walk through shows all quiet and calm at her hotel. The team on your place has two possible suspects, but still no definitive IDs at this point. Gotta say, as temporary duty goes, this is as cushy as it gets. Thanks, man."

Matt laughed a little. "Let's hope it stays that way." For everyone involved. "Intel isn't any closer to getting a name for this jerk?"

"Not so far. We won't let anything happen," Alex promised. "Will I get another chance to hang out with my nephew?"

"I'll talk with Bethany. I can't see it being a problem."

"Uh-huh. Is fatherhood still working out?"

Matt thought about the car project and the conversations. "Incredible," he admitted. And nearly everything he'd hoped for. "He surfs as well as Grace Ann." Alex whistled. "Dad and I discovered he's interested in cars and we found one to fix up together."

"Sounds like a good start."

"I think so," Matt said, turning away from the window. "Assuming we get through whatever is going on with the jerk who put a target on my back."

"No worries. You've got the best team available on your six. Just do your usual Riley tough-guy strut and let us take care of the dirty work."

"You're a riot."

"That's why I'm so popular, man."

Matt ended the call and walked back inside to join Bethany and Caleb. But they weren't in the booth. His stomach dropped and he sidestepped around customers and staff to reach the table where they'd been moments before. A plate of french fries sat in the middle of the table, barely touched. Bethany's purse was in the corner, her cell phone on the bench, screen shattered.

The sound of squealing tires brought Matt's head around in time to catch a glimpse of a silver four-door sedan tearing out of the parking lot. Delaware license plate, he noted before registering that it was Caleb's face pressed to the back window.

The world seemed to grind to a halt and roll slowly off its axis.

"No." Matt would never know if the desperate denial had been a shout or a whisper. The next words out of his mouth were orders, barked with authority and efficiency. He grabbed Bethany's purse and demanded someone notify the authorities as he ran out of the diner to his Camaro.

The engine roared to life and he used the redial option on his cell phone to get Alex back on the line.

"Matt?"

"Ambushed," he reported. "Caleb and Beth were kidnapped. In pursuit, northbound." He gave the details of his location and the car he was chasing. "I'm closing in now."

He swerved around an eighteen-wheeler and stomped on the gas pedal. The speedometer edged past eighty, past eighty-five. Grateful for every investment in this rebuild, from the oversize engine to the superior tires and upgraded suspension, he pressed on.

No one was going to take away his family.

"Hang back. Don't engage," Alex ordered. "Wait for backup."

"Can't let them disappear," Matt muttered. He needed that license plate.

"Matt, listen! Listen to me."

"Caleb is in that car."

Alex was relaying details to another party. "Do you have a visual on Bethany?"

"Negative. I have her purse. They broke her phone," Matt said.

"Where is Caleb's phone?"

The question threw him. "Unknown."

"Hold on." Alex's voice was low and rough as he spoke to someone else. "Matt. We have a location on Caleb's phone, consistent with your report."

"Good." Matt slithered around slower vehicles.

"State troopers are en route."

"Good," Matt repeated. He was right on the bumper of the silver sedan now and he read off the license plate number, along with the definitive make and model of the car.

"Let the authorities handle it, Matt. We can track them by Caleb's phone."

No way was he letting his kid think he'd given up. "Only until they realize that's what you're doing."

"Matt—"

Sirens blocked out whatever Alex was saying. No one could say anything that would pull Matt off this chase. Not until he had his family back safely. When he did, the bastard driving the car, endangering his family, would pay.

Bethany struggled to haul herself up into the back seat, beside Caleb. She feared the man who'd caught her trying to call Matt had broken her hand, as well as her device.

"Mom?" Caleb reached down to help her.

"Shut up, kid," the driver ordered.

Bethany was tossed into the back of the passenger seat as the driver swerved and accelerated again. She tasted blood and realized her lip or nose had taken a hit somewhere along the way.

"Are you okay?" she mouthed the words to Caleb.

Wisely, he nodded. His eyes were huge and his face pale as he helped her fasten the seat belt.

She could see him fighting back tears and she covered his balled up fist with her good hand. "I'm fine. We'll be okay."

Pointing to the empty front passenger seat, she raised an eyebrow in question. They'd been hauled out of the diner by two men. One had held a gun to Caleb's back, while the other had muscled her into the car.

Caleb shrugged.

Well, she wouldn't complain about the advantage. The two of them could overpower the driver with the right opportunity. They just had to wait until he slowed down a bit.

"Dad's right behind us," he said, too low to be heard over the sounds of the engine and tires.

She smiled, though it aggravated her split lip. She wondered if he realized he'd called Matt Dad. In her heart, she vowed Matt would hear Caleb call him Dad soon.

Up front, a radio crackled. "Take the next exit and turn west."

The driver swore at the traffic blocking his path.

Bethany turned just enough to see Matt's prized Camaro keeping pace with them in her peripheral vision. The driver couldn't slow down or Matt would overtake him. "He won't quit," she told the driver. "You might have a chance if you surrender."

"Shut up!" His eyes were cold when they met hers in the rearview mirror.

It was enough of a distraction to have him miss the exit he'd been instructed to take. The radio erupted with a furious voice and new directions.

"Don't blow it again," the man on the other end of the radio barked.

"Get him off of me and it won't be an issue." There was no response.

Fear spiking through her veins, Bethany twisted in her seat in an effort to warn Matt. "Oh, no." A motorcycle surged up the interstate, weaving in and out of traffic. The rider was only two car-lengths back from Matt.

She shouted despite the futility as the rider raised a gun. The muzzle flared—once, twice, three times—and she blinked back tears as Matt's car jerked and shimmied, the back end skidding wide toward the shoulder. At the speeds they were traveling, she knew he could only hang on as the car became unmanageable.

Caleb shouted, his hand reaching toward the rear window as the driver distanced himself from Matt's problems, pulled around another big truck and skidded into the off-ramp, leaving the interstate behind.

A cheer came over the radio and Bethany pulled her son into a hug, praying fervently for a way to escape, for Matt's survival. "Your dad is as tough as they come," she murmured into Caleb's hair. "He loves you. Don't give up on him."

Matt had to be alive; she wouldn't accept anything less.

Since he'd met Caleb, he'd demonstrated a tenacity and dedication that he wouldn't be denied his place as father any longer. A few bullets hadn't stopped him before; she doubted he'd stand for a kidnapping.

"He loves us," she said. "We'll hang on until he can get here."

And if he didn't get there? a little voice in her head dared to ask. If he didn't get there, he would never know that she loved him, truly loved him. She'd simply been afraid of needing him too much and driving him away. Keeping him at bay had been safer, had left the control in her hands.

"Mom?"

"We'll make it," she repeated it.

Though tears threatened as temper, frustration and confusion battered her mind and heart, she fought back against the urge to cry. This driver would not get any satisfaction from her. It was time to step up. She would not let Matt Riley's son be used as a weapon or pawn in someone's sick game of revenge against Ben.

The driver slowed for a curve as he drove along a winding road, deeper into the Virginia forests, and she sat forward. "Get back." He shot her another glance through the rearview mirror.

A calm certainty washed over her. "You will die," she told him. "If Major Riley doesn't kill you, I will."

The driver only laughed.

Matt's ears were ringing. It was all he could hear. The traffic and sirens were a distant memory. Smoke and dirt choked the air, making it hard to breathe. His vision was blurry. He kept blinking, but he couldn't be sure if the problem was weather, haze or something worse.

He tasted blood in his mouth and felt the stickiness of it on his shirt and hands. Voices started to cut through the incessant clanging in his head. Familiar voices mixed with those of strangers. Some called his name, and others called him by rank.

As Matt struggled to get his bearings, he started to recall what had happened and what he'd been trying to do. "Sh-shot," he stammered in the direction of the nearest voice. "Tire was shot."

"Yes, sir. Stay with me, Major Riley."

As if he had a choice. "Motorcycle." He pushed the word out through a throat full of gravel. "Silver s-sedan."

"We know, sir. Stay still for me now."

"Uh-huh." Feeling was coming back into his legs and arms, along with the chaotic, fractured images from that last second before he lost control of the car and the sedan sped away.

"My f-family." He coughed, wheezed.

"Notifications in process, sir. Hold on."

A loud and mechanical ratcheting sound jarred him.

Someone had covered his face with a blanket or coat to shield his face. Though he tried, he couldn't move his arms to push it out of the way. He had to move, had to get back on the trail of that sedan. "Kidnapped my family."

At last the pressure on his chest released. His arms were free and he could pull air deep into his chest. First responders helped him from the car and helped him stand. With every inhale of the cool, clear air, his mind and vision cleared a little more.

"My family was kidnapped," he said, his voice firmer, more familiar in his ears.

The paramedic pushing an oxygen mask to his face murmured some comforting nonsense. Matt resisted, looking around for a state trooper or someone who might listen. "I'm fine. My family's in danger."

Slowly, he started registering the scene. He was in the center median, surrounded by emergency vehicles. His car wasn't visible from his position near the ambulance. He wasn't sure he wanted to see it anyway.

"Any other cars involved?"

"No, sir. Not sure how you managed it, but good job."

Well, he'd done something right. Still, it stung that the sedan and the attacker on the motorcycle got away. "Any witnesses to the motorcycle that attacked me?"

"Sir, my job is you." The paramedic cut away his shirt sleeve, tracking the origin of the bleeding.

"Where's my phone?"

"No idea, sir." The paramedic found the wound and plucked out a shard of glass and started cleaning the wound.

"I'm fine." Matt squirmed away, wincing at the

aches and weak spots. He'd taken fire on deployments, been in the thick of it when a convoy had been attacked. Though he was scraped up, nothing was broken. Adrenaline could mask serious symptoms, sure. He didn't care. Right now only Caleb and Bethany mattered.

He grabbed the first state trooper he saw. "Matt Riley. My family was taken against their will from—"

"Yes, sir. I've been briefed. We have units in pursuit."

Matt almost took comfort in that. "I need to be in pursuit, as well."

The trooper's jaw worked in thought. "Do you know where they were taken?"

Matt shook his head.

"Then I say you've pursued enough, sir. My orders are to get you to a hospital."

"Do you have a wife?" Matt demanded. "Kids?"

"Yes. Both," the trooper replied.

"In my shoes, would you let someone else handle it while you were still alive and fit?"

The trooper sighed. "No. But Major Riley, you're not fit."

"A security team was tracking my son's cell phone signal."

"I've been told to reassure you that they are still tracking that signal. I've also been asked to keep you right here if you refused transport to a hospital."

"Beg your pardon?"

The trooper pointed to the sky. A helicopter rotor sounded overhead. Belatedly, Matt realized the traffic on the interstate had been cleared away to make room for the helicopter to land.

A lanky man hopped out and jogged over, bent at the waist until he was clear of the rotor wash. He stood upright and Matt felt a spark of hope. "Alex."

"They tell me you're being a pain in the ass after heroically throwing your car into the median to prevent a pileup."

"There was a motorcycle." Matt didn't find that a good enough excuse for allowing an enemy to surprise him.

Alex listened to him explain the ambush as he checked over Matt as much as the paramedics had done. "All right," he decided. "You have backup now. Ready to get this done?"

Matt nodded and turned to thank the trooper before heading to the helicopter with Alex.

As the pilot lifted them up and away from the highway, Matt studied the scene below. Angry black lines marred the pavement and carved ruts through the median, ending at his car. The Camaro looked as if a giant had smashed it. It really was a miracle he'd managed to prevent any other personal or property damage.

"Awful courteous of you," Alex said, his gaze on the scene below. "Avoiding collateral damage."

"Someone must have seen the biker who shot out my tire."

"The troopers will deal with that. You and I have bigger fish to fry."

"Caleb's phone is still showing up?" Matt asked.

"Yes. I'm guessing they haven't taken time to search him. The team will continue to narrow down possible routes and destinations while you and I prepare for the rescue."

Matt wanted to argue, to insist they use the helicopter to get a visual on Caleb and Bethany, but he'd tried it his way.

"She was in the car. The silver sedan," he said. "I saw her just before..." He wanted to believe he'd see them both again. Then something worse occurred to him. "What if she thinks I'm dead?"

"That can only work in our favor," Alex replied.

"Why?"

"Because that will just make her angrier, and she has a spine of steel. She'll keep them both alive."

The helicopter set down again, this time at a small airfield. Matt had no real idea where they were as he followed Alex and two other men from the security force toward the fabricated building that served as the airfield office.

"Between Knudson and your dad," Alex began, "we can access whatever we need with little more than a phone call."

What he needed was a plan to successfully rescue Bethany and Caleb. "Does anyone have any hard intel to work with?"

"According to the radio chatter we picked up, you are still the desired target." Alex scrubbed a hand over his face, his expression grim. "Your dad already received a video of your crash."

Matt swore.

"Agreed. Caleb's phone is still moving too fast for him to be on foot."

"Which means whoever is behind this won't stop, even if it looks like I died," Matt said.

"Correct."

Losing Bethany and Caleb would destroy him. His parents, too. They were already locked in and delighted to be grandparents.

"The phone is still, sir," A technician reported to Alex.

Matt turned toward the uniformed woman sitting in front of a laptop. "Show me."

She pointed to a secondary monitor, pulling up an aerial image of the location on the internet. A few seconds later, she had the location pin overlaid on the image. "Less than thirty miles off the interstate," she reported. "By accident or design, this is a remote corner of a national park."

Alex whistled. "Score one for the home team."

Matt agreed. The charges would mount if crimes were committed on federal property. He just wanted to make sure the crimes didn't involve any injury. He made a mental note of the location, his mind swiftly transitioning to weapons and communications options. "How soon can we get there?"

"Park rangers and state troopers can be diverted immediately," Alex began. At Matt's glare, he reconsidered. "Fine. I'll direct them to set up roadblocks well back from the phone's location. You can ride along with my rescue team."

"Better." As a father, Matt resisted the implications that he could pose a threat to the rescue. As a soldier, he understood he was a risk.

Alex pulled Matt aside as the team moved to gear up. "If we only find the phone, can you keep it together?"

"I'm a rock," Matt lied.

Alex rolled his eyes. "I'll shoot you in the leg before I let you do something stupid. Hear me?"

"You've been watching too many movies," Matt said. "Save your bullets for the kidnappers."

Chapter 13

Bethany and Caleb had been hauled out of the car and shoved into a drafty little cabin in what appeared to be the middle of nowhere. Two folding chairs, a card table and an empty fireplace were the sum total of the amenities in the single room. Other than the door, there was one narrow window in the bathroom, too small for even Caleb to crawl through. Over the door was a surveillance camera, the red power light glowing. Someone was watching.

She had a general idea of where they were, based on where they'd been taken, the eventual exit from the interstate and the backroads to this location. The driver stood as a guard outside, occasionally giving a status report to someone on the other end of the radio. He'd patted them down and found and destroyed Caleb's phone, but he hadn't seemed worried about it and he hadn't done anything else to restrain them.

The man clearly saw a weak woman and a cowed boy. She was happy to be underestimated.

Caleb hadn't spoken more than a few words since Matt's car had gone off the road. As much as she wanted to give him more comfort, she knew everything she said might be overheard.

Twice she'd shouted through the door for water or food and been denied.

"Try to sleep," she murmured to Caleb as they sat side by side, huddled up for warmth. They'd tucked themselves into the corner under the camera to limit the access of whoever watched them.

"Are they gonna kill us?" he asked, sounding defeated.

"No," she said fiercely. "We'll get out of here alive."

"They killed Dad."

"They did not." If she let her mind slip down a path into a world where Matt was dead, she'd be paralyzed. "Your father is a soldier. A highly trained warrior. He's been through every survival school and skill training available. He's been deployed multiple times and overcome all sorts of trouble on dangerous missions. Bullets haven't stopped him yet," she reminded him. She could go on and on about his intelligence, bravery and perseverance, but she summed it up with, "He's alive."

"'Kay." Caleb dropped his head to her shoulder.

She'd been biding her time, trying to get a feel for the cadence and frequency of the guard's check-ins. Not knowing the reasons behind this entire mess made it difficult to predict anything their captor might do next. Didn't matter. She'd decided they would not be moved from this location against their will.

She judged their guard as being low in the pecking order, based solely on the radio interactions. As the hours ticked by, she started to wonder if all three of them were meant to be abandoned out here.

It didn't much matter what anyone else had in mind. She'd put her trust in Matt's determination and resiliency, along with her own capabilities. At the first opportunity, she and Caleb would overpower the guard and steal the car. It was their best option.

"You asleep?" she asked.

"Nah."

"Good. Here's what we're going to do." In a whisper, she outlined her plans allowing for every contingency she could think of.

Caleb quietly repeated the plans back to her, promising to head toward the interstate or follow the river south if he came across that first.

"Whatever happens, your only goal is escape." She squeezed his hand. "Clear?"

He nodded.

"We'll move right after the next radio check-in."

They were closing in on two hours with no movement on Caleb's phone. Matt started wondering if it had been found by the kidnappers and discarded. They could be anywhere by now. No. He had to shove his mind away from that abyss, close out any stray thought that someone had stolen his family.

While strapping into his tactical gear and checking his weapons and ammunition load, he imagined eviscerating the person behind this. It seemed a fair price to exact on whoever had been keeping his stomach in knots all this time.

"Think she'll marry you when this is done?" Alex asked.

He had no idea. Dialed into the rescue, he couldn't even tap into the normal level of pre-mission bravado and camaraderie with the small, lethal team.

They were probably breaking laws on several levels. Not his problem. Alex had coordinated those details and all Matt could do was give thanks. Over and over. He put his mind on how good it would feel to have Bethany and Caleb in sight, to hug them close.

Whether or not she ever agreed to marry him, his heart was hers. If they survived this, he would probably be foolish enough to propose again. If she said yes, he'd be the happiest man alive. If she turned him down, he resigned himself to the fact that he'd try again.

The team fanned out, picking their way in relative silence through the forest to the remote cabin. The tools they had in play had shown one cooling vehicle and three heat signatures. Two in the cabin, one loitering outside.

Although the scout reported no sign of traps, the team continued to move with caution.

What was the goal of the person pulling this stunt? Matt wondered as inch by inch they closed in. All three of them had been threatened indirectly and directly, plus the vandalism of his sister's car. The bland warning his father had received still carried the most weight with the investigators, so why were the people who meant the most to *Matt* out here in the woods?

Alex gave the signal to halt.

"New contact," came a voice over his headset. "Broadcast signal in play. Tracing transmission."

Matt crept up beside Alex. "What's that mean?" He knew what it meant in combat, but couldn't put it into context out here.

His friend shifted, silent as a shadow. "Whatever is going on in that cabin is being broadcast out." Alex confirmed his worst fears. "Wi-Fi relay, most likely."

Matt peered up into the trees, but there were simply too many layers of dark on more darkness to pinpoint a small piece of tech.

"Torture," Matt murmured.

"No signs of that," Alex warned. "Easy."

"Not here," Matt said. "The broadcast. He's going to use it to torture Dad. Or me."

Alex's features turned stony under the camouflage paint he'd applied to his face for the mission. "Not happening." His grip on Matt's shoulder was firm and steady.

Matt nodded once in agreement. Words were beyond him now. He needed action. Swift, decisive and preferably deadly.

They'd just started to move on the cabin and lone guard when a quiet engine rumbled up the road. Matt's heart pounded against his ribs as they waited for the vehicle to pass. It didn't. Instead, headlights sliced through the night and it rolled to a stop at the bottom of the slope, not far from the sedan. As close to the cabin as a vehicle could get.

One man got out and hiked the rather steep hill with ease. He greeted the man at the cabin door. Their voices were too low to be overheard and they seemed in no rush to move. It seemed like an eternity before the scout reported the cars were unguarded.

Knowing the numbers, Alex signaled the team to move. Matt stayed in position at his friend's shoulder as the others subdued and cuffed the guards. It was over without a single bullet fired or punch thrown.

Matt would appreciate that more later, if the investigators could get them to talk. Right now he wanted to be sure the two people *inside* the cabin were his.

"Go, go, go." Alex said.

Matt didn't need any further encouragement. He surged into the cabin, his gaze landing on Bethany and Caleb as he shouted their names.

They scrambled to their feet and rushed him. Relief coursed through his system as the three of them embraced. He kissed Caleb's hair, heedless of the tears tracking down his face.

"You're all right?" He stepped back, pushing them to arm's length for a good, long look.

"We're fine." Bethany slid back, her arms holding him in a long hug. "We were about to escape—"

Suddenly the cabin door slammed shut and the light overhead popped with a sizzle. In the darkness, Matt and Caleb lunged for the door, but it was locked.

"Welcome to the party," a silky male voice filtered through a speaker.

Bethany gave a startled scream and Matt shoved her and Caleb behind him.

The voice laughed. "There's nowhere to run, Major Riley. The cabin is rigged to blow." A flame sparked in the fireplace, following a trail of accelerant around the opening, snaking out along the edges of the room. Smoke started to build, curling toward the ceiling. "You can die slowly, or show some compassion and take the lives of your son and his mother. Personally, I'm hoping for some brave heroics to share with your father."

"What do you want?" Matt demanded, his face tipped up toward the speaker. "Who are you?"

"I have all I want. Dinner and a show. Now, don't disappoint, Daddy."

Matt swore as he looked around the tiny cabin. He called to Alex, heard only static in return. Something jammed the communications. He pulled Bethany and Caleb down low, under the building smoke. "We're getting out of here," he promised. He pulled the pistol from his holster.

"What are you doing?" Bethany gaped at him.

"Creating a vent." The smoke would kill them if he didn't. He raised the gun to the ceiling and pulled the trigger several times. It wasn't perfect, but it seemed to help alleviate the worst of the choking smoke.

Pounding sounded at the door and Alex called out to them. Matt rushed forward. "He says the door is wired to blow."

Alex swore. "Next option?"

Matt pulled the collar of his T-shirt up over his nose, encouraged his son and Bethany to do the same. The temperature was rising as the flames had caught all along the walls. He had to hope this bastard had overlooked something.

"Any windows or a back door?" Matt asked, the smoke making his voice harsh.

Caleb shook his head. "Just a vent in the bathroom."

A bathroom gave him hope for running water, until the three of them were crammed into a space barely big enough for one and he realized the well must have been disabled.

This time Bethany was the one cursing.

He used the butt of his pistol to break out the small vent window. Alex joined him on the other side, with more bad news.

"This was the only trap. Explosives are wired all the way through. If we breach, the place goes up faster."

"And if we don't?"

"The fire will do it for us. Eventually. Fire department might get here in time to save a big forest burn. I've got a guy working on the well."

Matt looked around the bathroom, swiping away the tears tracking down his face. Smoke and desperation had reduced him to this. Well, smoke and desperation and a madman. "Either guy outside have a helpful suggestion?"

"No. Grunts," Alex said. "They did flip on the man who hired them."

With that kind of good news, Matt wasn't going to give in. He wanted to see the man's eyes when all three of them walked out of here alive. "We're coming out through this window," he decided. "We'll open up the wall, mindful of the explosives."

A slow grin crossed Alex's lean face. "I'm in."

"Don't let the muscle know what we're up to," Matt said. "They might be wired."

Alex jogged off to look for something to cut away the exterior wall, while Matt ripped out the window frame with his bare hands, and then dug into the thin layer of drywall, revealing the frame construction.

He kicked at the framing under the window. There was hardly enough room to maneuver, but he couldn't bear to send Caleb or Bethany out into the main room in the middle of that fire, in view of that camera.

The two of them huddled in the shower stall while he alternated between heavy kicks and throwing his shoulder into the framing. The wall started to give and a spark in the corner told him the fire had reached the next fuse in the chain.

On a roar of frustration, Matt kicked out again and a center section of framing cracked and gave way.

"Out." He grabbed Bethany, kissed her forehead and helped her through the opening. Then she was outside, coughing and sputtering, beckoning to Caleb.

A sickening sizzle and crack drew Matt's gaze upward. He'd tripped another string of explosives. The ceiling over the bathroom caught fire and flaming debris rained down on his head.

Matt covered Caleb with his body and shoved him toward the narrow opening. The kid was through, his hoodie torn by the broken framing before he was caught up in Bethany's embrace.

Now he could rest easy. He would've taken a deep breath if it had been possible.

The fire beat at his back and he knew the odds were slim that he could break through the wall without tripping another explosive wire.

"Come on," Bethany shouted. "Now, Matt!"

"Get them clear," he said, although Alex was already moving her back, understanding. His friend had been in enough tight spots to recognize the risks here. Alex gave him a thumbs-up and Matt charged through just as an explosion popped what remained of the cabin right off its footings.

Matt, already airborne, was propelled further still by the blast. Landing hard, the wind knocked out of him, he slipped and rolled until a tree in the back halted his momentum. Bethany reached him first, her hands fluttering over his face, brushing dust and who knew what away from his face.

"Matt? Matt!"

"I'm fine," he rasped. He reached up to reassure Caleb, but his arm fell back weakly. "Just give me a minute." Alex stepped into his line of sight and Matt knew his family was safe at last. He let the blackness take him.

"Matt!" Bethany wailed when Matt's eyelids drifted closed. Her hand throbbed and her soul felt completely wrecked. "Wake up, Matt. We need you." Beside her, Caleb sobbed, clutching his father's hand.

"Easy, now," Alex said. "He's not dead."

Bethany saw him press his fingers to Matt's neck to be sure. "Pulse is strong," he said. "He's just worn out. It happens." He smiled, and the flash of white teeth in his camouflaged face had a gruesome effect. "Let them get him moved. It's all good now."

She turned to see an ambulance had made it out here, and between the paramedics and Alex, they eventually convinced her he would live.

She clung to Caleb, unable to let him wander more than a few feet from her side while Alex arranged for them to get out of the forest.

They were met at the hospital by more uniformed Military and the investigators, too. She and Caleb gave their statements, a doctor treated her hand, along with their scrapes and burns, and through it all they waited for good news on Matt's condition.

General and Mrs. Riley had been flown in and the four of them sat together, helpless, in the charged silence.

"Hey, General?" Caleb began. "Pop," he corrected himself at the raised eyebrow. "The guy on the speaker said you would get a show. Did you see anything from the cabin?"

Ben nodded, his face pale and grim. "It showed up on my cell phone as a link from the moment you two were tossed inside."

Caleb swallowed. "I shoulda done something."

"Come here." Ben raised his arm and Caleb changed seats to sit by him, letting himself be comforted. "You did all you could," he said. "You kept your cool with the cell phone. Huge help there." He rubbed Caleb's shoulders. "Everyone gets into a jam now and then and has to rely on someone else. You listened to your mom, helped your dad when it mattered most. Be proud of that."

"Same goes," Patricia said, joining Bethany at the bank of windows. "You're a remarkable, strong woman and you've raised a fine young man."

Bethany felt weak as a kitten right now. "Thank you." At Patricia's touch, she turned and let the older woman hold her. "I wanted to marry your son," she confessed. "I've wasted so much time, convinced he'd come to resent me."

"Marriage is scary, sweetheart," Patricia said, smoothing her hair. "It takes a strong woman to nurture love in a child, to grow in love with a husband. There are no guarantees, no matter what we choose in life." She cupped Bethany's cheeks, love shining in eyes so like Matt's. "When you find someone who makes you stronger still, stronger than you are alone, that's a man who is worth taking the chance on."

Bethany nodded, understanding. "I'd say yes. Assuming he asks again."

"We should ask him, Mom," Caleb said, stretching his arms around them and making it a group hug.

The idea sounded absurd. Then Patricia beamed and Ben laughed and Bethany knew it would be absurdly perfect.

If he looked at the recording of the scene at the cabin, he would lose his temper. He filed it away for evaluation at a later date.

There was a more pressing decision to make. He studied the arrest record and weighed his options. His personal recruits understood the price of failure and the penalty for getting caught. According to his sources, the men who'd been arrested at the cabin didn't have names or information that could give the authorities any valid leads, but it was too early in the game to take any unnecessary chances.

Picking up the phone, he gave the execution order. Everyone was expendable, a simple truth of war. In his place, General Riley would have made the same decision. They were more alike than anyone would ever suspect.

Although he wasn't happy to lose this first skirmish, he'd allowed for setbacks in his overall plan. Matt might be the prized heir apparent, but he was hardly the only person General Riley cared for.

Killing the firstborn, even the first grandchild, would have sent a clear and profound message. He regretted that it hadn't worked out. The plans had been so perfect. There were definitely positive takeaways from this first exercise that would improve their next attempt. He had a better idea of how the family would rally and the long-reaching favors they could call in.

Moving from his desk to the window, he stroked his beard, thinking and anticipating, heedless of the puffy clouds moving across the clear blue expanse of the sky. The chess-match challenge was a key part of the appeal of this payback.

Yes, there would be another opportunity, another opening. Already he had scouts in place, gathering intel so he could make his next plan.

Everything he was now, he could trace back to the tutelage of his superior officers, those who'd been good and those who'd been dreadful.

If his brief tenure under Riley's command taught him anything, it was tenacity and how to look beyond the obvious for a workable solution.

This dance was far from over.

Chapter 14

In his uniform, Matt looked around, studying DC like a tourist rather than a current resident. It wasn't New Jersey, nothing familiar here for his son. He could commute, at least through the current school year, if not longer. Once his post at the Pentagon wrapped up next year, he'd be tapped to command a battalion in another location. In that post, he'd be stationed long enough to get Caleb through high school. Assuming this went as he hoped. Life with a career Army officer wasn't the typical family stability Bethany had always insisted on for their son.

Then again, they weren't the typical family unit.

This was a fool's errand, he thought, his hand closing around the small velvet box in his pocket. He'd circled around it all night long and couldn't give her any logical reason to tie her life to his.

He loved her. He believed her when she'd said she loved him too, though she'd only offered those words when she thought he'd been sleeping. Love hadn't been enough when they'd been young and overwhelmed by the surprise pregnancy. Now, he wouldn't live without them. If it came down to it, he'd resign his commission and find another career. If she could take that kind of chance, so could he.

"One way to find out," he muttered to himself. Digging deep for courage, he walked into her hotel. He hadn't seen her since they'd discharged him from the hospital. He'd wanted to give her some distance, a few normal days, while he dealt with the multiple debriefings and the ongoing hunt for the true mastermind behind their ordeal. Although the two men they'd taken into custody had been killed in jail, the methods used at the cabin gave them significant intel and they were winnowing the suspect list. Investigators were confident they would soon have a name.

Matt had spoken with Bethany and Caleb every day, chatting about adventures, discussing the case and precautions, and how to start blending together as a family. Last night they agreed to meet for breakfast at the hotel before she and Caleb headed home later today.

Home. He wanted that to mean something other than him in one place and his heart in another.

He spotted them at a corner table, light spilling in from the windows, turning Bethany's hair to spun gold. She had it pulled back in a sleek, simple ponytail, but he remembered the silk of it against his chest, the citrus fragrance lingering in the air. Caleb waved and Bethany turned, her smile not quite reaching her eyes.

Good sign or bad? For a man who'd been good at reading both allies and enemies through the years, Matt was at a loss to pin down that particular expression.

The waiter brought him coffee and the three of them

made the most of the buffet. Twice, while Caleb was up getting more pancakes, Matt started to propose. Twice he chickened out. This was all wrong, as far from romantic as possible, and yet his question would affect them both. If he'd learned anything in the recent chaos, it was that Bethany and Caleb were a team. He loved that about them and hoped they'd let him join.

The waiter cleared Bethany's plate and refilled Matt's coffee. Bethany glanced toward Caleb at the buffet and with a resigned look asked for more hot water for another cup of tea.

"I'm glad—" He stopped short since Bethany had also spoken. "Go ahead."

Her smile wobbled. "I just wanted to say I'm glad your family knows about…us."

Matt felt a pinch behind his sternum, knowing that "us" didn't include him. Yet.

"Mom reached out again already?"

Bethany fiddled with her hot water and tea, her fingers trembling. "She invited us to Christmas," she said as Caleb returned to the table.

"We're going, right?" His eyes danced with anticipation. "They said they'd teach me everything about the boat."

Bethany gave Matt a helpless glance. "I know you have a life," she began.

He cut her off this time. "I have a career. You and Caleb are my life."

Caleb's jaw sagged and the huge chunk of pancake headed toward his mouth returned to the plate with a clatter. He shot a look at his mom.

"Just because I couldn't be around didn't mean you weren't on my mind every day," he assured his son. He set the velvet box in front of Bethany. "I'm going to ask you a question and you can take all the time you need before you answer. I'll even let you discuss it privately."

As he opened the box, he noticed matching shocked expressions as mother and son stared at the square-cut diamond surrounded by smaller citrine stones in a platinum setting.

"Matt..."

"Let me ask first." He wouldn't let her turn him down before he'd even voiced the question. "I love you both so much. Always have. Bethany, will you marry me? Will you let me be your husband and," he turned to Caleb, "let me become your dad, day by day?"

When she started to answer, he pushed back his chair from the table. "Talk it out. Whatever you decide, I'll never stop loving either of you."

"Matt, you don't have to leave." Bethany stopped him with a feathery touch of her fingers to his forearm. Her gaze caught Caleb's. "We already know our answer, right?"

Caleb swallowed hard, but he nodded. When he met Matt's gaze, his eyes were bright. "When you were in the hospital, I told her we should ask you."

Hope flared, wild and raw, in his chest. "Is that right?"

Bethany reached into her purse and pulled out a small box. "The concierge helped me out. And your mom."

Though Matt wasn't sure of anything after that comment, he opened the box. Inside were two rings. Both simple circlets, one black silicone, the other polished titanium.

"Caleb thought you'd appreciate having something

to wear during field exercises. I wanted you to have something more elegant or, ah, striking for formal occasions."

"Formal like a wedding?" he asked.

"To start," she agreed with a smile. "Your mom gave me your probable ring size," she said, answering the question he hadn't yet asked.

They read each other so well, as they had from practically their first date.

"We can make exchanges, obviously," she said. "If you want something different."

"This, from the two of you, is exactly what I want." He nudged the box with her ring just a little closer, prompting her. "How about you?"

She held out her left hand and he slipped the ring over her slender finger, where it seemed to be a perfect fit. "It's gorgeous." The ring sent sunlight bouncing around the table as she turned it back and forth. "These yellow stones are your birthstone, Caleb," she said, showing him.

"Really?"

Matt and Bethany nodded in tandem. Happy as he was, there were other details he knew needed to be addressed. "I know we'll all be making adjustments," he said.

"Mom said being your family means we have to move," Caleb said. "I told her it would be worth it."

Just when Matt thought he couldn't get any happier, one of them did something more to prove him wrong. "There's less upheaval lately. At least the Army is trying to minimize it."

"You thought of retiring," Bethany murmured. He nodded. "Neither one of us wants that for you or for us."

He'd walked in here ready and willing to give up his career, to find another option, whatever it would take to make Bethany and Caleb happy.

"Well, I'm here in DC for one more year. Then I'll have my own command for a few years. Not sure where that will be, but we'll have some choice in where we want to go, and what you need. We'll need to keep in mind where your mom wants to work, too."

"Like a family," Caleb said decisively.

No sweeter words had ever landed on Matt's ears until Bethany said the three words he'd been aching for.

"I love you," Bethany said, her voice strong and clear. Helpless against the surge of emotion, he leaned in and kissed her soundly.

"Hey, will I be adopted?" Caleb's bravado faded and his gaze dropped to his half-eaten pancakes.

"No." Matt curled a hand around his shoulder. "No need. You've always been mine, legally." He waited for his son to meet his gaze. "I would like to make it more obvious to the rest of the world, though and change your name, if that's okay with you."

"Yeah. I'd like that, Dad." Caleb grinned when Matt did a double take.

Matt saw hints of his little brothers in the expression. The kid was a Riley to the bone, and his aunts and uncles would do their best to give him roots, as well as ornery ideas.

"Can you come to my next game?"

"Already on my calendar," Matt replied. He covered Bethany's hand with his. "No doubts or lingering fear?"

"None. You're the only man who's ever made me strong enough to face anything," she said. "You've always been there, shoring me up. It just took me a long time to stop running away from the truth and run toward you instead."

Her admission startled him and made him happier still. "Side by side, love. That's all I've ever wanted."

"I know. I love you, Matt, so much." She pressed her lips to his. "Always have." She gave his words back to him, punctuated with sweet kisses. "Always will. It's past time we started living like a real family."

His heart beat with a steady contentment in his chest. "Let's go home." With one hand in hers, his other arm draped over his son's shoulders, the three of them headed out to their first day as a family whole, at last.

* * * * *

Don't miss previous books in Regan Black's Escape Club Heroes series

Braving the Heat
Protecting Her Secret Son
A Stranger She Can Trust
Safe In His Sight

Available now from Harlequin Romantic Suspense!

COMING NEXT MONTH FROM

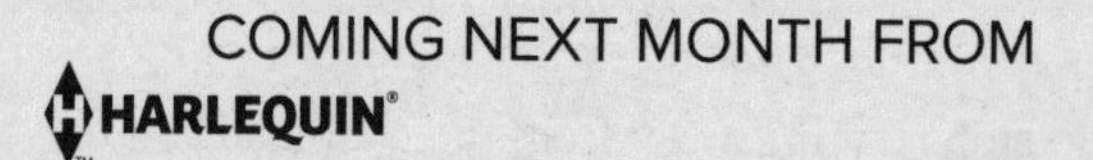

ROMANTIC suspense

Available February 5, 2019

#2027 COLTON UNDER FIRE

The Coltons of Roaring Springs

by Cindy Dees

The signs all point to a serial killer loose in Roaring Springs, and Sloane Colton fits the victim profile much too closely. Detective Liam Kastor is determined to save her, but they'll have to learn to trust each other—and their flaring attraction—if they hope to escape the serial killer's crosshairs.

#2028 NAVY SEAL TO THE RESCUE

Aegis Security • by Tawny Weber

Headhunter Lila Adrian's career is on a roll, until she witnesses the murder of her latest target! Former SEAL Travis Hawkins is the only person who believes she's in danger, and together, they have to find the murderer and get out of Costa Rica alive—no matter what it takes.

#2029 GUARDING HIS WITNESS

Bachelor Bodyguards • by Lisa Childs

Rosie Mendez won't live to testify against her brother's killer unless she allows bodyguard Clint Quarters to protect her, but she holds him as responsible for her brother's death as the man who actually pulled the trigger. Can she allow him close to her long enough to make it to the witness stand alive?

#2030 SHIELDED BY THE LAWMAN

True Blue • by Dana Nussio

Having escaped from the abusive ex-husband whom the police protected, Sarah Cline and her young son, Aiden, find an unlikely safe place with an atoning rookie cop, who helps to shield them from a bigger threat than she ever realized.

Headhunter Lila Adrian's career is on a roll, until she witnesses the murder of her latest target! Former SEAL Travis Hawkins is the only person who believes she's in danger, and together, they have to find the murderer and get out of Costa Rica alive—no matter what it takes.

Read on for a sneak preview of
New York Times *bestselling author Tawny Weber's first book in her new Aegis Security series,*
Navy SEAL to the Rescue.

"I think I might be pretty good at motivating myself," Lila confessed.

"Everybody should know how to motivate themselves," Travis agreed with a wicked smile. "Aren't you going to ask about my stress levels?"

"Are you stressed?" she asked, taking one step backward.

"That depends."

"Depends on what?"

"On if you're interested in doing something about it." His smile sexy enough to make her light-headed, he moved forward one step.

Since his legs were longer than hers, his step brought him close enough to touch. To feel. To taste.

She held her breath when he reached out. He shifted his gaze to his fingers as they combed through her hair, swirling one long strand around and around. His gaze met hers again and he gave a tug.

"So?" he asked quietly. "Interested?"

"I shouldn't be. This would probably be a mistake," she murmured, her eyes locked on his mouth. His lips looked so soft, a contrast against those dark whiskers. Were they soft, too? How would they feel against her skin?

Desire wrapped around her like a silk ribbon, pretty and tight.

"Let's see what it feels like making a mistake together."

With that, his mouth took hers.

The kiss was whisper soft. The lightest teasing touch of his lips to hers. Pressing, sliding, enticing. Then his tongue slid along her bottom lip in a way that made Lila want to purr. She straight up melted, the trembling in her knees spreading through her entire body.

HRSEXP0119